HAVOC
AFTER DARK

HAVOC AFTER DARK

Tales of Terror

ROBERT FLEMING

Dafina
Books

KENSINGTON PUBLISHING CORP.
http://www.kensingtonbooks.com

DAFINA BOOKS are published by

Kensington Publishing Corp.
850 Third Avenue
New York, NY 10022

All Kensington titles, imprints and distributed lines are available at special quantity discounts for bulk purchases for sales promotion, premiums, fund-raising, educational or institutional use.

Special book excerpts or customized printings can also be created to fit specific needs. For details, write or phone the office of the Kensington Special Sales Manager: Kensington Publishing Corp., 850 Third Avenue, New York, NY 10022. Attn. Special Sales Department. Phone: 1-800-221-2647.

Dafina Books and the Dafina logo Reg. U.S. Pat. & TM Off.

ISBN 0-7582-0575-9

First Kensington Trade Paperback Printing: March 2004
10 9 8 7 6 5 4 3 2 1

Printed in the United States of America

ACKNOWLEDGMENTS

First, this book would not exist if it were not for the support and vision of Linda Dominique Grosvenor and her husband, John Riddick Jr., two people who truly care about writers and books. Thanks for the opportunity to grant you this gift.

To my daughter, Ashandra, for her love and words of truth that hold a mirror to my choices so I can see them clearer and truer.

To my soul mate, Donna, for your wisdom, patience, grace, support, and love—all of which make both living and writing a blessing rather than a task.

To "our" children, Nichole, Dawne, and Matthew for proving that blood ties—or a lack of them—have nothing to do with love or family.

To my friends and readers, both new and old, who never fail to keep me honest and ever striving.

And most importantly to God, who sometimes steps away from the phone when I call, but always picks up when I need to hear His voice most. Thank you for your many blessings.

*"Because my breath is getting short
And my heart is beating awfully slow . . ."*

—Sonny Boy Williamson
"Bad Luck Blues"

". . . to carry into the human heart a degree
of appalling horror not to be
tolerated—never to be conceived."

—Edgar Allan Poe
The Narrative of Arthur Gordon Pym of Nantucket

CONTENTS

FOREWORD

What is horror? There is no single definition that makes a story horror. Sometimes these stories are supernatural, sometimes they are psychological, and sometimes they are portraits of nightmarish scenarios similar to those we can relate to our lives: People who are unkind. Circumstances that turn casually horrific. The faceless creatures that children believe are watching them when they sleep. All of it is horror.

Robert Fleming has compiled a collection of short stories that readers will not soon forget. His characters are men, women, and children, black and white. Fleming draws on experiences as different as the Nazi Holocaust to the plight of black children charged as adults in the criminal justice system, subjecting them to curses, rage, and terror, all part of the recipe that makes horror what it is. Fleming's stories amplify the real-life horrors from history and daily headlines. Many of these tales are angry, bearing the wounds of racism. The villains in Fleming's stories are larger-than-life, the stuff of nightmares, depicting a world meaner than our own and yet one that we can clearly recognize.

Why do readers like horror? Maybe, just maybe, it's because these stories demonstrate to us that we would rather live in the world we know than in Fleming's imagination.

But don't worry, it's a nice place to visit. You just wouldn't want to live there.

Tananarive Due
Author of *The Living Blood* and *My Soul to Keep*

INTRODUCTION

What you hold in your hands is *Havoc After Dark*, a collection of horror stories written by a black writer. A first of sorts. Although there have been several such collections written by white writers, mainstream publishers have frowned on African-American writers taking a shot at the genre, ignoring the overwhelming success of black horror novelist Tananarive Due. With short fiction horror collections, publishers reply that there is no demand despite soaring commercial popularity of the Hot Blood series, the Shadow series, and Ellen Datlow's erotic fairy-tale anthologies. Ironically, a little known fact is that African-Americans comprise a sizeable number of the readers supporting the printed works of Stephen King, Dean Koontz, John Saul, Clive Barker, and John Farris. Yet the door for both the short and long forms of horror fiction remains relatively closed to black writers.

Personally, my love for horror fiction can be traced back to my mother, who thrived on a good scare or two and took my brother and me to every fright film released during our youth. According to her, there was something "cleansing" about a real scare. As a teen, I borrowed books by Poe, Lovecraft, Hawthorne, Bierce, and Collier from the library along with my usual favorites by Wright, Baldwin, Himes, Yerby, Petry, West, and Hughes. There was something intriguing about mortals existing in a tenuous world between magic, terror, and reality. The other element that interested me about these horror yarns was that there was no customary fairy-tale ending. They were like real life in that way because there were no guarantees that everything would work out in the end.

Bold, provocative, and disturbing, the stories in *Havoc After Dark* are a mixed lot. Many of them use the conventional other-worldly characters of the genre, but some employ horrific realistic themes such as slavery, the horrors of war, and capital punishment for juveniles to elicit a shudder. I've worked hard to make the stories contemporary, diverse, and striking in both execution and theme. To me, there's so much more to the horror genre than just chills and thrills gained from watching a pair of fangs pierce a neck or a group of ghouls gnaw on human flesh. The idea of mixing modern themes with some screams and a bit of sex is not a new one. Publishers now realize it has been an effective way to lure people to the genre. In recent years, erotic horror has become one of the most powerful means of capturing the attention of millions of readers curious about the macabre.

Sit back and allow your imagination to get the best of you. Open your mind to possibility, chance, and dark fantasy. Here, you will find unusual slants on the old themes of love, jealousy, guilt, shame, revenge, loneliness, obsession, and lust. Embrace the twisted dreams and nightmares of people like you struggling to answer the challenges of personal crisis without any help. This is a murky territory of image, myth, and terror where there are few marked boundaries. This is horror told with soul, heart, insight, and rage. It is sometimes a very forbidding, dark place. It will leave you spooked. It will make you think.

Enjoy!
Robert Fleming

LIFE AFTER BAS

I.

Low Voltage

Marlene Baye insists she has come back from the dead.
She sits in a darkened room, a padded room, a room with wire mesh over the windows. Dressed in a shapeless frock, she resembles the tormented saints of old, strong but silent, bearing her anguish with steely resolve. No one has seen her leave this room in so many years, yet her power is felt throughout the quarter. Some say her gris-gris is throughout New Orleans proper, all the way out to the back roads of the bayou, even out to the rowdy zydeco dance halls in Lafayette, the Cajun capital. The bouncing backbeats of the music of the Neville Brothers, Clifton Chenier, and the Sam Brothers wilt in artistry in comparison to her work with High John De Conqueror root.

Out there, the housewives spill a little Love Oil offering on their wood floors at midday in tribute to this woman who sits stone-still in this airless cell. Among the rigs and derricks in the oil fields near Morgan City, the workers cross themselves at the mere mention of this woman with the anointed name of Madame Baye. Her sister, Elspeth, puts the mojo woman's birthday at forty-six despite claims from some that she has always been here, always existed since the dawn of time. Madness. Evil. The vapors are a key ingredient here. The Baye clan say Marlene's illness has nothing to do with hoodoo, roots, hants, or Doctor John. They link her odd behavior to a head sickness.

At the old hospital on the outskirts of the city, where she is chained to a bed, spread-eagled, doctors marvel at how easily she could free herself from any bonds. Nothing could hold her for long. The nuns, walking in a flurry of white rustling robes past her room, dare not look within for fear of infecting their souls with her curse. Their heads are down, faces tense, as they almost trot in a huddle through the dimlit corridor.

One morning, Madame Baye vanished from her room and reappeared in another ward of the hospital. In her place in the secluded ward was a box full of bleached human skulls, nestled in a bouquet of fresh pink roses, and wrapped in red ribbon.

II.

Dark, Darker, Darkest

From her earliest days, Marlene was not like other women in her family. She seemed distant, odd, eccentric. Both boys and men followed her through the streets of the Crescent City, whistling at her long brown legs, offering themselves for carnal sacrifice. Local wizards wanted to crown her birthday as a new type of All Saints Day, the holiest of days, a trick of the calendar designed to celebrate her arrival into this life with a caul over her face.

Her mother, now a twisted gnome, saved the caul, the thin film from her womb, in an emerald-laden jewel box given her by the Loup Garou, the werewolf who sired the girl. That thing, which she had thought was a large shadowy man with huge hairy arms, the demon who prophesied the magical caul, calling it the gift from the other soul. A blessing of both Light and Darkness, the power of second sight, the wings of travel into the Other World. The child would be able to see things no mere mortal could. She would be able to walk into the chilly embrace of the mirror, talk to the spirits trapped between this world and the next. But the Lupus smiled his grin of amber knives and whispered to the girl's mother one last time that the price for such gifts would be high.

Her mother never warned her of the penalty. The girl was terrified when she started seeing shadows following her, began hearing voices with no physical bodies, and sensing the hues of auras hovering around the fleshy forms of her loved ones. At the age of three, she frightened her family when she told one of her mother's friends that she was being eaten from the inside, that her soul light was pale and weak. The woman died two nights later in her sleep.

Marlene filled out as a beautiful young woman, the finest mix of black, Cajun, and Creole blood. Her mother feared for her every time she ventured out among the men, having noted the glint of lust and raw desire in their faces. However, none of the young bucks tampered with the girl after a would-be suitor who had caressed her with vulgar intentions at a roadhouse near Algiers turned up dead in a swamp, horribly mangled by something in the dark.

Sleep eluded Madame Baye much of the time. In her room, she rarely moved from her spot on the cot, except to occasionally watch the bees flit from flower to flower and to map out cloud patterns in the azure sky above the city. Sometimes a wave of desperation would wash over her and the voices would return, burning her ears, making her cry, making her miserable.

III.

Dead from the Neck Up

When Marlene was at the asylum near New Iberia, everyone was so nice to her, all of the doctors and nurses. For three months, they fed her pills and shots that kept her harmless and tame. Then she had a relapse and allegedly attacked an attendant, gnawing him badly. The attendant said he saw Madame Baye materialize in front of him, enclosed in a silver mist, floating above the floor. She spoke to him but her voice came from a point above his head. Like from the ceiling, he added. He also said he had a feeling that there was something else in the room with the two of them.

Much of that winter, she spent her time in a straitjacket, sitting quietly, waiting. The staff whispered she might hurt herself. Once or twice, just to entertain them, she complained she didn't belong there. "Just examine my head. Then you'll know," she said, smiling strangely at them.

The doctor. He was trying new things out on her. A narrow white man with a bony neck and hands, he watched her in her cage of concrete and wire mesh. "Sit down, Marlene, and tell me what you're thinking and feeling as I came into the room. Maybe I can help you."

"Close your eyes, Marlene. Let me guide your mind."

"Yes, Doctor."

"You're asleep, in deepest sleep. I want you to rest your mind, empty it of all thoughts while I talk to one or two of the voices inside you. This is only hypnosis and will not harm you in any way."

"I understand, Dr. Broussard."

"You have been sick for a long time but you are no longer sick as of this moment. We diagnosed you as having a severe psychotic episode. That's behind us now. You're well, and we're going to talk to the spirit who's there inside you. Can the spirit hear us?"

"Yes, Doctor."

"What is his name? Or is it a her?"

"It is a man. His name is Pere Bas. It is He who guides me to the Other World. It is He who teaches me the secrets of the Spirit Realm. He learned me the medicines, roots, fixes, and gris-gris. The loas. He is the Keeper of the Gate and friend of Dumballah the Bearded Serpent."

"Can you see him?"

"Yes, He is with us now. In this room."

"Describe him to me."

"Would you like him to possess you? He'll come into you, Doctor, and then you would see Him, become a part of Him."

"No, I'd rather you tell me what to look for. That's better. Mr. Du Plux said you did that to him, said a spirit took hold of him, made him dizzy and confused, then the voice of another person came from his mouth. It was the voice of his child, his dead son."

"Where is Mr. Du Plux now?"

"He asked for a transfer to another ward. He said you threatened him, threatened to put his soul in limbo. What foolishness! So where is this Pere Bas?"

"He's right next to you on the cot. He's in a white suit, with a red rose and a top hat. He's smoking a cigar. He wants to ask you what kind of aftershave you use. Don't tell me. Old Spice, right?"

"How did you know that? Never mind. This Bas fellow, correct? Are you still taking the medicine I ordered for you?"

"Sometimes. He wishes to have you see Him. Touch my hand and close your eyes."

The doctor did as she asked. That was when the staff heard the screams, a husky male's voice, and agonizing shrieks. They rushed into the room, only to find Madame Baye cradling the doctor's head in her lap. She was smoking a thick, foul-smelling cigar, which left a blue mist in the room. There was a look of utter terror on the unconscious doctor's gray face and blood coming from his ears. Later, he remembered nothing about the incident.

IV.

Supernatural

You can never tell them the truth. Nothing could be more frightening. You wanted to stop these thoughts for so long. The thoughts that kill, the thoughts that hurt and maim. There is never any let-up, no slacking of their power. They seize you and nothing can loosen their grip.

Years ago, Marlene's mother once brought the parish priest, with his cross, rosary, and holy water to the house to save her. They prepared to do battle for her soul. The old woman confessed her sins, revealed her torrid nights with Loup Garou, and sobbed as she told of his fur against her lips and his claws deep in her flesh. The holy man spoke to her of God's might, Jesus' healing power, and the redeeming gifts of the Holy Ghost, man and sin, the Devil and the forces of the dark.

With the help of two neighborhood boys and three nuns from a nearby convent, they built an altar in the Baye home and surrounded the young girl with white candles and holy water. The group of soldiers in the army of God prayed all day and night during a long weekend before finally leaving the girl in the hands of the Most Righteous.

Nothing could save her now. Such was the power of Pere Bas, or Loup Garou, whichever name you wanted to call Him. Among the candles and crucifixes, He came to her on the Fourth of July in the form of a long black snake. It slithered to her as she lay naked in the vortex of the holy circle. The serpent spoke to her in a rasp of a voice, flicking its tongue near her ear, taunting her with delicious visions of pleasures only known to the soulless. He teased her about her chasteness, her purity, her virginity. This young girl on the verge of womanhood. She held the snake above her head, spun in the center of the circle, while it rubbed its length along the smooth, soft skin of her body and spoke to her in tongues.

The serpent coiled around her long neck and peered into her eyes. "Come and do my bidding," it hissed sweetly to her. "The loas must be pleased. You are the Chosen One." Morning found her fully clothed, refreshed, and the altar destroyed.

You can never tell the truth. No one understands. No one understands what the voices say but you.

V.

Virtue

The room is cool, almost cold, yet you wear nothing. There is only the voice, his voice, Pere Bas' deep, gentle voice. You follow in the dark. Follow its sound. In the distance, there are lights, dots of light, but none here where you are feeling your way in the blackness. Your fingers glide along the wall, over the contoured rock, toward the lights. You stumble but regain your balance. When you reach out your hand once more, you touch the furry snout of the beast, and it brushes against your bare leg. It searches your face, looking up at you, with its searing yellow eyes. Pere Bas. Loup Garou. Werewolf and man and spirit. You feel its long, rough tongue in your warm, sweating palm.

Her protector. Always there. At her school, there was a group of girls in her class who were mature for their age and had women's bodies in their middle teens. She was thinner, coltish, and almost masculine in her movements. But still beautiful. The other girls went around with boys and sometimes older men. She went around with books and her imaginary friends. During breaks between classes, they huddled and whispered about their romantic conquests, the men they had been with, the kisses and caresses they collected.

There was a time when Marlene wanted to be like them.

There was a time when she wondered if she would ever be attractive enough to make a man love her. Or a wolf.

VI.

The Art of Reversing

It was on her bed, waiting for her. Before it came back for her, she could never sleep. Every night, the haunting was the same, full of bad dreams and horrifying visions. He could only come to her like this, black as the night, in the dark. Only its piercing yellow eyes visible or its gleaming smile. Some nights it would fall asleep against her young body, with its long tail sprawled across her bare legs. One night, she awoke, and it was standing over her, its large wolf's head inches from her perfect face, its breath strangely sweet.

Was this how it happened to her mother? The seduction.

"What are you thinking?" Pere Bas asked in an even voice. "Are you thinking that you could run? Are you thinking you could escape me? There is nowhere you could run where I could not find you. We are one."

His metamorphosis was startling and sudden. He transformed himself into the young, virile man who she often saw selling cane juice near the docks. The young man's muscled body, bulging arms, narrow waist, steel thighs. The face of a caramel cherub. Curly black hair. He offered her some Red Devil Juice. When she refused that, he offered her some Eternal Love Drops, which she denied herself as well.

"Let me love you, my sweet," he cooed to her, holding out his massive arms.

"I'm about to go crazy with wanting you but I cannot let you do me like you did my mother," she said. "I cannot let you poison my soul and twist my heart."

He touched her forehead lightly and what happened after that was a fevered dream of passion, lust, and frenzied coupling. She felt one of his hands on the small of her back just where the spine dips into the curved plums of her buttocks, and his abnormally long tongue was suddenly everywhere at once—on the nape of her neck, at her swollen nipples, on her tender flanks and inner thighs, and inside her. She tried to catch her breath but couldn't. His assault was intense, overwhelming, powerful, beyond man. His tongue withdrew, taking the remainder of her wind with it, and then his lips were upon hers, igniting countless sparks within the back of her head as he kissed her in an endless variety of wet, burning kisses. Her hand slid around his hips as her desire became more urgent but he broke free and returned to licking, stroking, and sucking her between her legs, his tongue more agile than a cat's in her folds and contours. Now she understood why her mother smiled so mysteriously, so knowingly at the mere mention of Loup Garou. Her sugar man.

Her body overheated with pleasure, seeming to melt from the flames generated by his electric tongue darting upon the sensitive folds of skin around her clitoris, on the alert bud itself, and deep within her velvet cavern. She bucked and pumped against his face as she screamed in wordless shouts while each mounting wave of ecstasy surged through her. Just as her entire body seemed at the very brink of delirium from an excess of sensation, he placed one of her legs up against his shoulder and lowered himself into her moist tightness. She felt the thickness of his bone inside her, but there was more. It felt strange as he started to move slowly, measuring her width and depth, sensing its texture. It filled her completely, and she had not taken it in fully. This long, fat bone surrounded with coarse hair. He ground and twisted his hips in ways accustomed to man and when she gasped for air and tried to pull away for fear of an exquisite death, the knotted bone held her close. Her inner walls quivered, vibrating with each deep thrust and stroke. Twice she fainted during the night from his loving. She would never forget this, never.

When she revived, Pere Bas was a white woman, cold blue eyes, straight nose, long blond hair, thin lips, very European features with a full bosom and alluring body. Dressed very smartly in a Paris high-fashion style. The white woman sat there on the edge of the bed, stroking Marlene's bare, damp thigh.

"Sore?" the woman asked Marlene, pursing her painted lips.

"Yes, quite a bit," Marlene answered weakly, noting the muted throbbing between her legs. She also noticed the walls of the room became like glass, mirrored. In their reflection, the woman was still Pere Bas, the black man in the white suit but when she looked at him dead-on, he was the white woman inspecting her long, crimson fingernails. She was now wearing the same white suit as the man in the mirror. The top hat was at her side.

"Is this better?" the white woman asked in Pere Bas' voice. "I think the beast in me frightens you. Black women are always less frightened of the Miss Ann of the house."

As Marlene lay on the bed recovering her strength, he talked to her about symbols, omens, and charms. He let her practice the Evil Eye on Him. The jokes about silver bullets and full moons were lost on her. Pere Bas laughed enough for both of them at his own jokes.

"I'm possessed by demons," she told Him.

"No, that's not true," the woman replied, tossing a length of her blond hair over her shoulder, wrinkling her long nose in Marlene's direction. She could smell the fear and confusion on her like a perfumed scent.

"What are you sniffing?" Marlene quizzed her mentor.

"This is tiresome," the white woman said, crossing her legs at the ankles. "Mind if I change into something more comfortable?"

Pere Bas changed back into his manly self. Instantly He plucked a cigar from his pocket, sniffed it, bit off its tip, and lit it. The moon was rising and it was full. They sat quietly at first, watching each other in the mirror. Her mother heard the talking and looked in on her. Satisfied that Marlene was alone and talking to herself again, she closed the door and bolted it from the outside, locking her child in the room.

VII.

Life After Bas

It's Mardi Gras. Shrove Tuesday, the last day of Carnival. The last and wildest day of the fun and frolic. Marlene is alive once more.

Marlene insists she has come back from the dead.

In her new cell at the hospital in New Orleans, she hates the fact she has missed the Krewe of Venus, the only time in Carnival where the women ride the floats instead of men. Everything else the men run, but not this. The other Krewes keep the females away. Once, she had been chosen to be Queen Venus, elegantly gowned, bejeweled amid a mantle of satin and ermine. She waved to her minions while the other women tossed trinkets to the onlookers on Canal Street.

Through her bars, she can see them; nothing is as it seems. Or as it once was. Women dressed as men, men as women. Blacks dressed as Indians, monsters, royalty, devils, apes, Zulu chiefs, gypsies, ghosts, wizards, magicians, gods, sultans, and wolves. The women throw fake doubloons, confetti, and beads down from the grilled balconies as the floats in all of their splendor drive past. A skeleton stops and takes a picture of a group of black nuns staring at three young white girls lifting their blouses to reveal their breasts. Two men dressed as Pan kiss.

Somewhere, a saxophone wails above the mayhem. She feels so low, so desperate, so trapped. She feels as if they watch her all the time. She knows she may never get out. "Your illness," her doctor says, "seems to be worsening. We're going to increase your medication." On one bad day, she held out her wrists and showed her self-inflicted wounds to an attendant. The vertical slashes from the palms down, done with precision and the jagged edge of a soup can lid. He ran off and returned with his supervisor. There were no marks on her arms when they were inspected this time. The supervisor chided the attendant for wasting his time, angry he had been called to such a farce.

Pere Bas comes to her that next night for the last time. Only she can hear his howling. The floor shakes. The room tilts. Her lupine lover stands in the corner of the room, an enormous male covered with thick black fur. Quite silently, He crosses the floor to where she sits on the bed, looking out the window. The dampness of his snout makes her tremble in erotic remembrance.

What was found of her the following morning was her shell of flesh, intact, except for the rivulets of dark blood on her cinnamon-hued legs. She never talked to them again. You can never tell them the truth. No one would understand.

Marlene Baye insists she has come back from the dead.

THE TENDERNESS OF MONSIEUR BLANC

Port-Au-Prince

U nder the cover of night, Roy Capote arrived in Haiti's anguished capital city onboard an American Coast Guard cutter, carrying a large duffel bag and little else. The tall, pale man was dressed in khaki, top and bottom, and wore a pair of battered Air Jordan shoes. It was as if the Plague had arrived, for wherever Roy went, or Monsieur Blanc as he was known in some circles, a pile of corpses would soon follow. Libya, Angola, the Philippines, Thailand, Croatia, Congo, Nicaragua, all over the globe. Deaths that sent a brutal message to the enemies of the State. Imperialism's golden hit man. Democracy's enforcer. And nobody knew which agency in the American alphabet soup employed him or whether he was just a surly freelancer, much like Death itself.

On shore, a group of armed American soldiers watched this gray sliver of a man move silently along the pier. His reputation in the world's intelligence community was a grim one, a cold-hearted lone wolf who prided himself on his professionalism, resourcefulness, and artistry. The soldiers glanced at him as he passed the military checkpoint but didn't stop his exit. This quiet, savage killer. No one said anything but three cars of Macoutes, some of them former crew members of the Docs—Papa and Baby, lounged in their rusty dark sedans, watching the white man through sunglasses, ready for a bit of wickedness.

When the *dechoukaj* or the Turbulence erupted, Roy was called up from a job he was doing for the Company in the Middle East, working with the Saudis and Kuwatis. Something involving subtle pressure on Saddam and the Iraqis. Things had deteriorated quickly in Haiti, going from bad to worse in record time, and he was called in just as Baby Doc was being airlifted to safety with his pretty mulatto wife. That was not his first stint here, before during Reagan's term, and now this was in the time of the Clinton regime. Some of the old guard at Langley wondered if the new policy of intervention was worth it with several pots heated on the stove in other parts of the world: Bosnia, Somalia, Iraq, and now Haiti. To hell with this globalism, they said. Nothing much was said when American blood was shed to protect oil interests in the Persian Gulf but somehow a foreign policy move to defend darkies a hop and skip away from Cuba brought only hesitation and debate. Long gas lines were one thing but what did the Haitians export of note?

Hey, I love this shit, Roy thought, while one of the Haitian military escorts later talked to him about his schedule in perfect French. His stiff, ramrod posture indicated the well-dressed black man was one of the big boys in the Port-au-Prince elite. Monsieur Blanc was there on a job, a nasty purging mission; everybody understood that. The military escort handed him some documents to assist him in moving around the country, with the understanding that the killer would not be hampered by protocol or bureaucracy.

To these blacks, Roy concluded, he was just another *blanc* brought in to keep their repressive government's spiked foot on their collective neck. He smiled at the grim thought. However, he was totally surprised when a few of the local cops presented him with a large bottle of Barbancourt rum to cool his nerves that evening before his taxing tour of the prisons the next day. These black monkeys bowing and scraping before him amused him to no end. He shook each man's hand, mumbled thanks, and then asked for the men's room. *Remember: America first.*

After that bit at the less-than-clean toilet, Roy walked around with the cops and the military escort through the building that was one of several housing the joint covert Haitian-American operations. Etienne, his government contact, and his superior, Mr. Constant, advised Roy to stay off the streets at night. For his own safety. Starving Haitians, many of them peasants from the countryside, were looting whatever warehouses and stores were unguarded.

Complete chaos. People rampaging, being hurt and killed. Soldiers fired on the crowds at one location, striking men and women lugging heavy bags of rice and onlookers watching the mayhem from the steps of a nearby church. When the looters fell and the sacks split open on the ground, the horde descended upon the heaping mounds of rice with eager hands, cups, boxes, buckets, and any container within reach. According to Etienne, the kids and older people got on their knees after the rest left and picked up whatever tiny grains of rice remained. The looters, he added, would sell the pilfered rice to whoever could pay their steep black-market price. Things were out of control throughout the country.

"They're looting over in Cap Haitien, Gonvaives, and near the airport as well," Etienne said solemnly. "Your troops are in place around the Parliament. We got barbed wire, Humvees with machine guns, foot patrols, everything's in place."

"What about this amnesty thing about General Cedras and his sidekicks?" Roy asked, taking an English newspaper from one of the aides, a tall, mango-colored man, sharply dressed in a white suit, with a shiny .45 peeking from his jacket. These men were followers of the Father, Aristede. The Savior.

Once outside, Etienne opened the door to the aging black Cadillac and the roving Yankee troubleshooter got in, tossing his bag onto the backseat. "Our constitution says the Father can only grant amnesty for political matters, not crimes. Still, many of the exiled opposition are flying back from your country and Canada. They are being taken to a private house, which is under guard. Do you want to go there or to the Parliament building first thing in the morning?"

"I don't think so, neither place," Roy said. "I've got to meet someone at the Normandy Bar tomorrow at noon. Business."

"No sir, you don't want to go there," Etienne said, touching the American lightly on the arm. "That place on the Rue Champs-de-Mars is a very bad one. It is the meeting place of the FRAPH, the ruthless supporters of the army, and they are fully armed. They have shot many Aristede people. Very bad place."

Their conversation was interrupted by the sound of gunshots echoing from not far away. The Cadillac pulled off the main road, heading away from the action, and one of the same Macoutes sedans seen at the pier followed at a safe distance. Etienne said they would first get Roy settled in at his hotel. On the way there, Roy noticed the clusters of American troops stationed at key intersections, policing the ever-present crowds, protesting friends and foes of the exiled priest. Their yells filled the smoky air. A rock struck the back window of the Cadillac, denting but not shattering the reinforced glass, and the driver put his foot down on the gas pedal. To make matters worse, the streets were thick with roving bands of angry young boys and men carrying clubs, knives, machetes, and guns. Haiti on the edge.

"Don't go there," Etienne said, looking worried. "You'll get hurt."

Roy smiled coldly and watched the mob around them on the street shower a convoy of speeding ambulances with stones and bottles. He wondered if they were safe in the car. Etienne said proudly that the bullet-proof windows were sturdy and could withstand any shot from an ambitious sniper. That was good to know.

"There's nothing to worry about," Roy said. "I know these people. I don't expect any trouble from them. This mob scares me more than those jokers. Because a mob is all emotion, no brains. There's no reasoning with it."

"So you're going anyway to the bar tomorrow?"

"Yup." Roy did his best John Wayne drawl. "That's my job, what I get paid for. Tell me. Are you a big fan of Aristede?"

Etienne was mute. Haitians knew better than to chat with foreigners or strangers about their political or class preferences. In a country where a person was lucky to live to fifty, where a person was happy to make eighty dollars a year, where only slightly more than thirty percent of the population could read, it was a real asset to know when to keep your mouth shut. Etienne also knew the rumors. And Roy knew the score. The truth was, Washington was uneasy with the Father, especially since the Company released a report saying the priest was possibly psychologically unstable with bad mood swings. The army felt he was planning to cut off their drug cash bonanza, the Company didn't trust him, the Pope was jittery about a tiny black guy with too many rebel ideas. Meanwhile,

American warships were packing up to back a U.N. oil and arms blockade, causing some to wonder who was running the store.

"Whose side are you on?" Etienne asked him in that flawless French again. "The generals or Aristede and the *lavalas?*"

Roy rubbed his temples with both hands. "Listen buddy, I'm on Uncle Sam's side. He pays my salary and whatever the man says I should do, I do. No question. We'll be around no matter who wins this thing."

The Cadillac stopped before a barricade, manned by two Marines carrying weapons. One of them walked stiffly to the car, shining a flashlight into the face of the driver and demanding ID from everyone in the vehicle. Roy took his Company ID from his wallet and handed it to the young soldier, who smiled and returned the laminated card.

"And now the spooks are in it," the sentry said with a smirk. "Oh man, this thing'll really heat up now. You can go on through, sir."

The pair moved the barricade and waved the car to move on. Roy laid his head back on the seat and recalled his first trip to Haiti in the eighties. He did a little black bag work for the Duvaliers. On that trip, he told the military types working with them that their time was running out. However, the secret police kept the show going until Aristede won the 1990 election. But the junta deposed him after only eight months of rule. That aside, the President was more irritated by the thousands of boat people flocking to Florida from the island across 700 miles of rough sea. Send the spooks back in.

"What time do you want to wake tomorrow?" Etienne asked while the driver maneuvered between two cars parked in front of the hotel.

Casually, Roy looked out the rear window at the Macoutes' car, now indiscreetly parked across the street. "Have your man get me up at seven. Breakfast at seven-thirty. Briefing at eight-thirty. We should be on the road by nine. OK?"

Etienne nodded. "Anything else you desire? More spirits? A woman, cigarettes, food, anything? I was told to get you whatever you want. You're a very important person around here."

Roy ignored the courtesies from his Haitian contact and concentrated on his mission. His bag was already in his room on the third floor. The Toussaint, located close to the Parliament in the capital, was formerly a four-star hotel but it had seen finer days and was now used by foreign journalists, gunrunners, and drug smugglers. The rooms were large enough, furnished with run-down imported French furniture, poor phone service, but still known for excellent food. He noticed three men loitering in the lobby, possibly hired gunmen to ensure the safety of the guests.

Once settled in the room, Roy unpacked his clothes, poured himself a shot of the hibiscus-flavored rum and lit a Dunhill cigarette. Shortly, a small boy knocked on the door and handed him his messages. One was from his superiors in Langley, a full report needed by the next day. Another came from Joseph Michel Denis, one of the wealthy heirs of the mulatto elite and influential pal of the FRAPH. Lunch the next day. The rich were aggravated by the turmoil of the revolt crap. They wanted the army to crush the oppression and restore order. Or the death squads to prevail. Unfortunately, the mulattos were forced to carry guns and walkie-talkies or to employ hired bodyguards. Unable to sacrifice, they blamed the coup for the blackouts, shortages, and the unrest that prevented their servants from coming to work. No doubt. Denis wanted to know what was going to be done about the bothersome Father Aristede.

"General Joseph informed the staff that emergency measures have been put into effect," Etienne informed Roy, placing a collection of the day's newspapers on a table. "There's panic in the streets. People are forcing themselves on trucks and buses, anything going to the countryside, to get out of the city. Your president has ordered security increased around your embassy and there's talk of evacuating all American citizens from the island. And there's a message for you from someone in the ambassador's office."

"Alright, I'll call them as soon as I settle in," Roy said, lighting another cigarette. "Maybe I'll take you up on that offer for some female company."

Etienne smiled shyly and gave a mock bow. "I know just what you like. Tonight or tomorrow after we get back from Cap Haitien?"

"Tonight, in a couple hours if that's alright." Roy turned back to his chore of unpacking, never noticing the man's quiet departure.

In the real world, Roy was a killer, a paid killer, a scholar of the art of Death. He trained others in the dark craft, taught them how to torture, how to prolong pain and suffering, how to extract confessions when there was none to get. To friend and foe, he was known as Monsieur Blanc, the Scholar of Death.

For much of his life, he'd wanted a family, something stable and nourishing, but his work denied him that. There was a bitter emptiness in him that his work didn't satisfy, but he had come close to having it, just once. With Claire. In the beginning, they'd been deeply in love, completely entranced by each other, caught up in the reverie of love's bliss. They expressed their closeness by enjoying the pleasures of the flesh, having sex everywhere, every chance they got. One night, they married on a lark, going to a small town outside of New York City, hiring a justice of the peace to do the honors.

Less than three months after the happy day, the problems started. Claire said sex was no longer a high priority for her. That pronouncement had an immediate effect on their marriage, driving a wedge between them, compelling Roy to seek solace in his wet work. He suspected Claire had a lover but lacked the guts to tell him. This was the easy way out, to make his life a living hell in the hope that he'd walk away. He hated coming home. Claire became very critical of him, his every move and word. He could do nothing right. He was never able to please her. Claire never talked about what he did right, only harped on what he did wrong. All she ever talked about was their crumbling marriage, analyzing its shortcomings, taking apart its strengths.

Once things started to go wrong, the disappointments and arguments mushroomed. Everything he formerly liked about her became a liability, something to turn him off to the possibility of an enduring love. Claire the efficient. Claire the planner. Claire the perfectionist. She always found time to hug and kiss him in public but once home, that desire for intimacy withered and died. Night after night, she refused his advances, said she was worn out from the day's activities.

Once after a job in Bonn, Germany, he'd ravished her, threw her on the bed and forcibly took her, with her screaming bloody murder the entire time. He wasn't without a heart. Felt bad for having done that. He tried to talk to her afterward, to reconcile, to heal the wound between them. But the rape was what she wanted to talk about. Said he never told her the truth about what he did for a living. Said he never told her he loved her. Said she never felt special. Said he never thought about her needs and wants. Said he was a bastard, a heartless bastard.

The knock on the door awoke him from sound sleep, his body curled up on the sofa with a company dossier on his lap and two dog-eared books on Haiti at his feet: Robert Rotberg's *Haiti: The Politics of Squalor* and James Leyburn's *The Haitian People*. It was his female companion for the night. Etienne had delivered on his carnal request and sent a sweet young thing for his nocturnal diversion.

Gruffly, Roy told the girl to disrobe, take it all off, while he remained seated, reaching for the half-empty bottle of rum. What tasty morsel was this? She couldn't be any older than fifteen, sixteen at the outside. Young, almost pure and supple. Possibly only slightly used. Thin girlish face and frame, bee-sting breasts, and a nice little bubble ass. It all excited him in a way his wife never had. His erection pressed rigidly against his taut stomach as he absently touched himself, imagining the velvetness of her sex.

Looking at her standing in the center of the room, he was consumed by the desire to be inside her, while he sat up to take in the wonder of her nubile young beauty. She stood there nervously, watching him. He motioned for her to come to him, and he stroked her smooth black buttocks, then several fingers probed her underneath until she moaned. Tight. Like Claire once had been. His body pulsated with lust and need. He had been with black women in the States, Africa, all over the world, but never one so young. His hands roamed freely over the gentle curve of her small, juvenile breasts, purple nipples jutting and firm, down to the soft, tawny stomach, and the thick bushy delta above her long legs. There was a hint of adolescent curiosity in how she regarded him through her dark brown, almond-shaped eyes.

Before straddling him, the girl jerked back, her face savage and wild. "Tell me what you want, Monsieur Blanc."

"How do you know this name?" he asked. He kissed her thighs, the softness of the flesh there, with cool lips.

"Everybody knows you, knows your name," the girl said.

Roy didn't expect her to allow him to take her in the hard, cruel way a man can vanquish a woman. Yet something about her boldness, her girlish manner, filled his iron-stiff erection with hot, virile blood. She resisted slightly when he pulled her writhing body onto the bed. Her gaze locked on the enormity of him, her eyes widening as he moved behind her. His hands gripping her hips. Claire. The image of her face clear in his mind now. It seemed the girl screamed suddenly during his first full penetration of her, both of them snared in the fevered sexual power of the coupling, and for a second he paused, savoring the sensation of the satin entry before diving back in her shallow wetness again. Claire. He pounded into her with the force of a stag rutting a doe in heat, animalistic and rough. The girl sobbed uncontrollably, all the while grinding her rump against his stone hardness. Claire. His dick stretched her opening with each passionate thrust, mining her deepest regions in erotic desperation. She possessed her own hunger yet she permitted him to ruin her innocence with his bestial longing until his body shook at its peak of ecstasy and then revived quickly for another assault.

Claire. The room was heavy with the raw perfume of sex. There was nothing for Roy as tantalizing and exquisite as the possession and destruction of young virtue. It must have been this way for the first colonialists in the New World. Virgin territory to be despoiled any way imaginable. This had always been his fantasy, yet he didn't like the rage it brought out in him. He wanted to hurt this dark girl, smash her, maybe even kill her. He withdrew gently from her and spurted his DNA across the glistening perfection of her black behind, moaning in sheer rapture. Claire. His vile need to dominate this girl, to control her, compelled him to seize her shoulders and drive into her once more with all the strength left in his body. Little black bitch. Nigger bitch. Six, seven, eight, nine more times into her until he gasped loudly and collapsed on top of her.

The girl hissed at him, rolling her eyes in disgust, and pushed his pale bulk away. He retreated weakly to a corner of the bed, curled up in a neutered ball, and watched her dress quickly and leave. Oh God, his long-lost Claire.

In the morning, Etienne arrived at his door before ten, smiling evilly as if he'd been watching the cruel mating session of the night before. Roy's military contact, dressed in civilian clothes, was accompanied by a pair of menacing Macoutes. He said nothing about the girl. They walked in a solemn group to the car, climbed inside, and drove to a FRAPH lair in Bel Air, a slum in the capital. Etienne spoke with three men, laughing and joking, before moving on for the long drive north to Cap Haitien and the infamous La Prison Civile.

"A group of FRAPH members attacked the Cite Soleil, the slum downtown, last night and a few shanties were burned," Etienne said. "Nothing serious. I asked my friend, Mr. Pierre-Pierre, if he knew anything about it and he laughed and said no."

Roy didn't respond. He was more concerned with the up-country prison, which had received national coverage when some human rights group, examining the files, revealed the death rate of the inmates was too high. Much too high. It appeared that too many prisoners were dying of cardiac arrest, self-inflicted internal injuries, and tuberculosis. In truth, quite a few were tortured with electricity, mutilation, beatings, and assorted other methods before dying in its cavernous dungeon.

Once there, the guards walked him around the facility, describing their efforts to control and contain the prisoners, which they concluded were terrorists. The commandant of the prison insisted he detested any use of violence but was forced to surrender to it to keep things orderly. Roy watched and listened, taking mental notes for his weekly report to the Company.

As Roy was being ushered to the car, a heavily scarred man with no hands, the victim of torture by machete, rushed up to him and spat in his pale face.

"Die, die, Monsieur Blanc, die," the scarred man hissed. "You will not escape the just reach of Voudoun! Neither you or your murderous dogs! There is nowhere for any of you to escape, nowhere."

The guards swiftly threw him to the ground and proceeded to beat and kick him until he was a bloody mass of flesh. Slightly shaken, Roy wiped his face with the back of his hand, glared at his assailant, and slipped into the car.

That night, Roy and Etienne watched a BBC-TV report covering the start of All Saints Day, and a celebration by dancers at the sacred tomb of Baron Samede, a voodoo god, in a nearby cemetery. Roy was amused by the ruckus made by the revelers during the traditional African rite honoring the bond between the living and the dead, but Etienne was not laughing. He explained how it was a tradition brought to the island by slaves and deeply revered.

"What did the scarred man say to you at the prison?" Etienne asked, a worried look on his face. "I couldn't hear him from where I was standing."

Roy repeated the man's deadly curse word for word and dismissed it with a rude joke. "This voodoo mumbo jumbo is fairy-tale stuff. Nobody in his right mind takes it seriously. Your people let Papa Doc use it to control them and in a way he still controls them with it. Even after his death."

Etienne's expression became glum. "Most Haitians believe in Voudoun. They know its power and do not make light of it. It's a way of life here. I would ask you to not make fun of things you could not possibly understand."

"Do you believe in it?"

"I believe in some things. Such as zombies. There are things I've seen with my own eyes that cannot be explained away. Such as Voudoun powders. They have been used as weapons as far back as the late nineteenth century and are quite effective. There are powders that can blind you, cover your face with boils and sores, take away your potency, turn your flesh to stone, even kill. Voudoun is not something you, my American friend, could possibly understand."

Etienne looked around the suite and took a long swig of rum. "Zombies are the living dead, undead flesh under the Devil's own control, forced to act against their will," he said in a torn whisper. "A living death is the worst of deaths. They have no soul, no heart. They have no peace."

"Do you really take this garbage seriously? Old wives' tales, that's all. Nothing more. For God's sake, you're a civilized man, so you should know better."

Sitting up straight, Etienne swallowed twice and spoke slowly and deliberately. "Listen, my friend, I'll tell you something I've never told anyone. Why I believe in zombies. A sweetheart of mine, Elle Douyon, from Cayes, was stabbed to death by her uncle on her birthday. She was taken to hospital but she died. The doctor said she was dead. We took every precaution with her burial—the proper oils, the right preparations, the appropriate holy words. Still, I saw her three days later walking stiffly along the road near the foundry where I worked. Others saw her as well. This is the truth."

Amused, Roy sipped the rum, feeling it work its way down his throat. He shook in jest as if he were frightened out of his wits, mocking the teller of the tale. The Haitian waved his hands, asking if he could continue. Roy nodded yes.

"On the day I was married years later, my sweetheart appeared outside of the church. Even my bride, a neighborhood girl, recognized her from an old school photograph I had of her. Elle came to the village of her mother that night and told her intimate things only her daughter could have known. And this undead thing was someone whom we all saw buried and a large headstone placed on top of her grave. Truly the Devil's work. Frightened by her mother's story, the family had her dug up but the coffin only contained the skeleton of a two-headed dog with a red ribbon tied around its neck."

"No more rum for you," Roy teased. "It's going straight to your head. You're drunk. Admit it."

Etienne got up, his legs somewhat shaky. "Maybe you're right, my friend. Maybe I should go. Remember if you need me, just call. Tomorrow you will meet with some of the general's staff but sleep late because the meeting is not scheduled until two in the afternoon."

They shook hands, and the Haitian wobbled out of the room. Roy remained in his chair, staring at a large spider ascending the wall, moving with a stern sense of purpose. He closed his eyes and let sleep take him away from the day's tensions, thinking only briefly of the group of Haitian children he saw earlier near the pier wearing *Haiti Libere* T-shirts. How defiant they seemed. He was needed here. Shots had been fired into a hospital and a school bus filled with kids was raked with bullets while caught in a crossfire. Where was God if He could allow so much pain, suffering and evil to exist in one small place?

After a few minutes, a loud noise in the hallway awoke him. He went to the door and opened it, only to see an old black man wearing a soiled top hat and tattered waistcoat. The man smiled, showing two rows of large yellow teeth, and lifted a withered palm and blew a cloud of blue dust into Roy's face. Roy fell back inside the suite, howling and rubbing his eyes. Blinded, he could hear laughter and screams coming from the hallway, the sounds of loud thuds, possibly bodies being slammed against the wall or to the floor. As his vision cleared, he staggered to the doorway and glanced out to see several men in dirty rags hunched over an American attaché in a tuxedo, clawing out his entrails while the man tried to fend off his attackers. There were bodies and blood everywhere and these walking corpses going from room to room, and the screams hurt his ears. He knew that smell, the odor of death and decay. A white woman, the German reporter he met the day before, was straddled by one of the undead who rammed his fist through the back of her black cocktail dress to her ribs. After that, she didn't move.

Roy couldn't believe it. He screamed until he was hoarse. There was no escape. Soon the hallway was a bloody chamber of ripped limbs, torn flesh, and violated bodies. He slumped over and threw up, starting to shake uncontrollably. Stepping over another dismembered body, he attempted to utter another anguished cry but it died in his throat. What the hell was going on? What were these things? Couldn't be zombies, just couldn't.

These things were killing everybody in sight, every person on the floor. And it was probably the same throughout the whole hotel. He ran back into his room, slammed the door, locking it, and then reached for the telephone. It was dead. He heard more whimpering, pleading, and begging from the hallway. Frantic, he loaded his gun. There was the sound of pounding at his door and a tearing noise when it splintered under the weight of the invaders. It was their eyes that terrorized him to his very soul, so lifeless, these remote-control killers. He aimed his gun at them, these zombies, these undead, pulled the trigger twice, but the shots didn't slow the things.

One of them grabbed him by the arm and slung him over the sofa to the floor. He jumped up and ran for his gun, which had bounced a few feet away. Their hands were on him, choking him, jerking at his arms, blood issuing from his lips until he finally yanked free and ran for the open door. But he didn't make it. The old man in the top hat materialized from nowhere and pushed him into the circle of the walking dead where he fell to the floor and they surrounded him. Crazed with fear, he tried to fight but he was too weak with one of his arms torn off. He closed his eyes, feeling their weight upon him, feeling his life flow out of his body.

Somewhere in the background, he heard a wee voice, that of the young girl from the cruel night before, singing *Monsieur Blanc. Monsieur Blanc. Monsieur Blanc.* He cursed them all. He cursed Voudoun, he cursed Haiti. The growing stench of death. His death. *Goddamn you all*, he thought as the ugly refrain continued to be chanted by the undead while he bled to death. *Monsieur Blanc. Monsieur Blanc. Monsieur Blanc.*

The last thing Roy saw before his life slipped away was the sinister, twisted faces of Etienne and the young girl smiling evilly, urging on the living dead while they finished their grisly work on him. *Monsieur Blanc. Monsieur Blanc. Monsieur Blanc.*

THE ULTIMATE
BAD LUCK

Outside the moon is full, golden, and bright in the black of the sky. The day faded quickly with no trace of a sunset or dark clouds. Nobody knew what to think. It was all mighty odd. I drove to a nearby roadhouse after working a long, hard day at the cotton mill, the white dust still clinging to my clothes and hands. Weary as a young suckling, I walked with a slight wobble into the rowdy place that was damn near empty, save for the pretty Creole gal behind the bar and a few stragglers. She paid me no mind when I settled on a stool and ordered a whiskey. I handed her two bucks that she took directly to the cash register and rung up.

"Vala, where's your old man tonight?" I teased her. "He let you run things all by your lonesome? That's one brave soul."

"He say you get two drinks and that's all," she said, pocketing my change after putting my drink on the bar. "We can't have you acting no fool up in here. No monkey business. I mean it."

A man I seen at the roadhouse before was sitting three stools down from me, pouring drink after drink down his throat. He had a bit of a gut on him, a wrinkled face that looked like it had been slept in, and the longest nose ever seen on a person. His eyes were devouring Vala's every move, caressing her every curve and contour. The woman was typical of the sweet, young Creole gals who came to the big city—cream-colored; long black hair almost to her waist; and hot looks that would make any gal jealous. The man lifted his drink, winked at me, and tossed it down.

I was feeling my oats after my second drink. "Vala, come heah. I want to tell you something. Come heah, sugah."

She walked over to me, leaned over so she could hear what I had

to say. I spoke softly to lure her to come closer. Her face twisted up
with disgust. There was no fooling around with her. Still, I tried to
be slick, asking her to come closer to let me whisper in her ear. Now,
I'm a big man, real big, dark buck, the kind peckerwoods get scared
of in a hurry, but she wasn't afraid at all. If anything, Vala seemed
always a bit taken with me. We always fooled around, her flirting
with me and me flirting right back. Neither of us knowed what Old
Man Touissant might do if we got randy and messed around behind
his back and he caught us. The old Cajun was at least twenty years
older than she was, and I couldn't figure what she saw in him or
how he kept a hold over her. But one day, one day real soon, I
planned to see what everything was all about, including her. Vala.

"Clem, why you drink so much?" Vala asked me, looking at my
face like she could see right through it. "It's like you sick in the
heart and think that likker gon' put out the pain."

"I like the stuff, the taste of it," I lied, all the time knowing full
well that the real reason I drank was because a fire ate up my wife
and two daughters three years ago and the torment of their loss was
still with me. I tried to save them. Ran up on the porch, opened the
door, and the flames roared out, their yellow and orange fingers driving me back. My next attempt at the windows failed, the glass
shattering in my face at the touch. They were so hot that the heat
cooked the flesh of my arms. Splinters of glass in my neck and
hands. Everything bloody. And their screams, shrill and terrified, off
from somewhere in the burning house. I couldn't get to them, and
their screams remain with me every night.

I didn't want to answer any questions so I got up. Brushed her
soft cheek with the back of my hand. "See you directly, sugah."

"Where you going, big man?" she asked, a lusty twinkle in her
eyes.

"Home, before I get into some trouble." I blew her a kiss and
started out for the door.

It was a chilly night for August. Nobody was out. Weather's been
real strange since they been sending those rockets up into space.
President Kennedy say it alright. They going to the moon, maybe to
Mars, but we should leave that mess alone. I didn't have enough
clothes on for the change in weather. Just overalls and a short-sleeve

red shirt. Shivering, I ran for my old Ford pickup, jumped in, and cranked the motor. It sputtered, shook twice, then finally started.

Once at my shack, I pulled my truck behind it and parked. My feet were fairly unsteady, mostly from being tired and not from the two shots of straight whiskey, but I made it to the door. Crickets sounded in the distance. A hoot owl sounded its blood cry before surprising a rabbit in the thickets. My hand fumbled with the key at the lock for several seconds before the door opened. There was my usual searching in the dark for the oil lamp near my bed, a gift from Aunt Price before she died of sugah a few years back. A match brought the room into light, and I jumped against the wall from what I seen there.

Miz Gertrude, the white woman from over at the Source Plantation, sat on the edge of my bed, all pink naked in just her bra and panties. Her face was all flushed red. She was a husky woman, blonde with clear blue eyes, hook nose, and thin lips. I never liked her, with her flat ass and nasty mouth. Word around these parts was that she was trouble. Loved her some dark meat. Colored mens stayed the hell away from her, for she was the Devil's spawn sure enough. I looked at my place. It looked like a tornado had hit it, everything topsy-turvy, furniture turned over, cabinets emptied, and clothes scattered here and there on the floor.

"Howdy, Mr. Neptune Johnson. Today's your lucky day," the white woman said in a gravelly voice. She was sitting back in the shadows, but I could make out the lower part of her mouth, her large floppy titties, and the large automatic in her hand.

"What you want heah, Miz Gertrude?" I was trembling visibly. "I don't want no trouble. Why don't you just leave and we won't evah speak on this again? I give you my word."

"I've been watching your big, black nigger ass walking around here like Mr. Big Coon Shit for over two years, six-eight, all muscles and dick," she said low and evil. "My brother, Halbert, say you got quite a reputation with the nigger wenches, say you hung like a stud stallion. I mean to get furrowed tonight. I want to see if you as good as they say at pleasuring. I want some of that dark snake between your legs, black boy."

This was the very reason why I'd always stayed as far away from

white womens as possible. Unlike some colored mens, I'd never
been excited sexually about them, their pale skin, no lips, straw
hair, and strange-colored eyes. A lot of the white girls around here
sneak off and meet some buck in the woods and get her first experience of real loving. The cracker gals were curious of colored mens,
what they got down there, or had grown tired of pleasuring themselves with their fingers. But many of them got their minds wrecked
by the colored mens they seduced, sexually put under a spell that
few white mens could break. But Miz Gertrude was a freak, even
the peckerwoods knowed that. She ruined colored mens left and
right, rode them until their nuts shriveled right up, hung like empty
sacks of flour. Totally ruined their nature. After her, the mens could
be nothing more than gal-boys, sissies, letting other mens ride
them like wenches. This cracker woman was real dangerous.

"Take your clothes off, nigger," she ordered, pointing the gun at
my privates. "All of them except your drawers. I don't want to see all
of the goods right off."

I could hear her breathing get all heavy and rushed as I sat on a
chair and untied my boots, slipped off my overalls, and unbuttoned
my shirt. My huge, powerful frame would do me no good here. I'd
met my match and probably my end. Her eyes went over my face
slow and easy, measuring the cut of my African features, strong
nose and thick lips. I stood before her, knowing that she held the
power of my life in her hands, and the terror of that knowing made
my heart race. I felt the knot of fear vibrate in the center of my
chest. What was I to do? I hated this cracker bitch. I wanted to kill
her white ass. If I took the gun from her, I was still a dead man. My
life would never be the same after tonight. *Lawd, just let me get
through this. Please, Heavenly Father, please. I'll say the Lawd's
Prayer every night if you let me get through this alive. Save me from
this white devil heifer, please Lawd.*

She lowered her gaze to the bulge in my drawers. "You ever been
with a white woman? Tell me the truth. I'll know if you lying, nigger."

"No, ma'am. I always be respectful." I put a little coon into my
voice. White folk love to hear that Sambo talk. In this case, I fig-

ured it might buy me some time until I could get away from this crazy cracker woman.

"A woman has needs, more than most mens know," she snorted, motioning with the gun for me to lower my underwear. "Ain't nothing sinful about a woman pleasuring a man she likes. Not a'tall. I believes I likes you, Neptune, you and that long, thick snake you been keeping from me."

I tried to appeal to her good Christian sense. "It's a mite hard to say this but you knowed whut they'll do to me if word gets out about us heah like this. A nigger man who mess with a white woman is a dead nigger fuh sure. You knowed that right, Miz Gertrude. Why you want to kill me, ma'am?"

Her fixed gaze became a hard glare and she spat out her next words. "You mind your tongue, nigger! No back talk. Next, you be saying niggers are human, too, like that Dr. Martin Luther Coon down there in Montgomery. Niggers is niggers and white folk is white folk and the Good Lawd made them different. That's that. I don't hear that niggah shit. I came here to get furrowed, and that's what gon' be."

"It ain't right, just ain't right. This is plumb wickedness." I didn't have a stitch on at this point. My hands were folded over my privates, shielding my sex from this white woman's prying eyes.

She leaned forward, turning slightly in the darkness. "Turn around and bend over. I want to see your butt; your high, round nigger ass. All of the girls talk about how nigger mens have the best-shaped asses, for a man. Round, smooth, and full."

I did as she told me, bending over with my behind open to her view. She was giggling like a schoolgirl back there, but I didn't glance at her. Instead, I stayed in that folded-over position until she ordered me to straighten up. My eyes kept on that gun, and what it could do was sure on my mind.

"Come here, nigger," the white woman demanded. "My father's father and his father's father owned niggers like you. Back in his time, a big stud nigger like you would furrow four or five wenches a night, every day in the week, until the breeding took. You know how many white men would love to be in your shoes? Average white man lucky if he gets with four or five women in a lifetime, and you nigger studs go through hundreds of darkie wenches. Come to me now."

"I don't want to die, Miz Gertrude," I begged, kneeling at her feet.

Her cold blue eyes narrowed slightly. She hummed to herself, waving the gun near my head, slowly and sensuously to the rhythms in her blond head. Then she slipped her free hand down into her panties and began rubbing herself. "It needs licking, nigger. It needs some tongue powerfully bad."

"Please, ma'am, don't do this . . . don't." I pleaded with her to show mercy, to stop this before it was too late for both of us. Nothing was going to come of this, nothing. She reared back and slammed the gun upside my head. It happened real fast, like a sudden blur. Pain shot all up through my face and head. I saw stars, then darkness, and a flash of white light as I slumped over her, trying to get my head to clear.

"Suck it, nigger," the white woman commanded, her thin lips snarling. "Do it right or I'll give you some more of this pistol on your kinky wool nigger head."

Carefully she leaned back and spread her pale, blue-veined legs. One of her hands yanked my head into place at her crotch with my tongue at her pink opening, and then I started licking. The taste of her was bitter, like quinine. She kept her eyes open, began moaning loudly and grinding her sex into my mouth. I listened to her chant "Oh yes, nigger. Lick it, lick it, nigger," while her legs fastened over my head, and all the while the gun was pressing against the top of my skull. Soon she started trembling all over, her legs jerking up and down, reaching her peak, but the gun didn't move. When I pulled away from her crotch, my face was covered with her juices—her oily, bitter juices.

She kicked me in the face, knocking me back on the floor. "You know what I want now, Mr. Neptune, and you better give it to me good. Good just like you'd do with one of your nigger wenches. Furrow me like your life depends on it. 'Cause it does."

My silence made her mad. I was through begging. I knowed how I'd make her pay. As I rose above her, crouching on my knees about to go into her, she raised her hand and slapped me hard across my face. I took it without a whimper, although I thought real brief about her long, slender white neck trapped between my big, strong black hands and me squeezing the life out of her. Grabbing her underneath her butt, I yanked her forward, impaled her on my hard snake, and pounded it into her pink wetness with deep, powerful, hard strokes. Each made her gasp for breath, her mouth open and teeth bared, but the gun was still against my head. Nothing could stop me now. I bent her back, panting and flushed red, punishing her with each deep, thrusting plunge until I spent myself and her, collapsing over her body. She tried to pull herself out from under me but I was too heavy.

"Let me up, goddamnit nigger," she shouted, placing the gun against my right eye. "Is that it? All that meat and you don't know what to do with it. Don't tell me that is all the furrowing I get tonight!"

"I worked hard today, Miz Gertrude," I said, not looking her in the face. "I was tired when I got home. You's done finished me off."

"I want more, Mr. Big Nigger Buck," she screamed, beside herself with passion. "I want more or I'll shoot your big, dumb darkie ass right here and now."

Weakly, I rolled over on my side and glanced down. My snake was wet, slimy with her rank oil, and limp. There was nothing more I could do. Anger changed her features. She was like an evil white witch, all wrinkles and fangs. She started that crazy humming again, getting off the bed, putting on her clothes like she was in a trance. Once dressed, she told me to come to her and stand where she could see me. Tears were rolling down her cheeks. She repeated over and over again, "He took me, he took me, he hurt me down there, it's ruined down there, he took me," and started yelling at the top of her voice. When I moved toward her, she stopped, no more screaming, and pointed the gun at my head. I turned to back away and then something hit me real hard near the ear and the room went black.

When I woke up, the white woman was gone. I could still smell her. I had no idea how long I was laying on the floor, but I knew I had to get the hell out of there. It was only a matter of time before

the pecks would be at my door with rope, dogs, and guns, seeking to
avenge the ravishing of one of their women. The suitcase was
quickly filled with clothes and photos of my dead folks, silverware,
my tools, and a Holy Bible given to me by Aunt Price. I ran out of
the house, jumped into my truck and burned rubber for the highway. They were waiting for me with trucks pulled across the road.
White mens with shotguns and torches blazing red in the dark
night. The truck cut me off when I tried to back up and turn around.
The peckerwoods swarmed on the truck, rocking it back and forth,
smashing at the windows with the guns, showering me with glass. I
prayed in that instant like I never done before. *Oh Lawd, hear me,
hear my cry. Protect me from hurt, harm, and danger.* They dragged
me out and slung me to the ground, kicking and punching me until
I almost blacked out again. Someone yelled, "Don't kill the nigger
right off." I felt someone cut at my face and ear with a knife before
they carried me to a truck and threw me in the back where the
white mens cursed me, hit me, and beat me with clubs.

"Let's take the nigger down to the swamp," one cracker said,
holding a torch so close to my face that the skin started to sizzle
and bubble up from the heat.

The others cheered and hooted. Another man yelled how they
could have real fun out there with the coon, maybe do some bad
things to me before they got rid of me. One of his friends, wearing
a rebel hat and carrying a hunting rifle, suggested that they use a
cane knife to cut off my privates to save as a souvenir, keep it in a
Mason jar at Joe Feeley's repair shop out on Route 8. I didn't say
anything. I couldn't say anything. That was how it was when you're
really so scared that you lose the power of speech. The peckerwood
running the show walked over and placed the cane knife at my
throat as his friends chanted for him to gut me. He slid the knife
down to my crotch, smiling with a mouthful of rotten, tobacco-
stained teeth. The blade bit at my snake through the fabric of my
pants, enough to slice a cut along its length, and I felt blood running down inside my pants leg. I squirmed, holding back a scream,
praying and praying.

For some strange reason, I thought of something that happened to me when I was ten years old, out on the swamp water with my Papa, who was responsible for keeping out folks from certain parts of the area. He worked with a white man, Mel Ryan, an old guy who got around with a cane. A gator took off his left leg and Mr. Ryan wouldn't go near the water no more, so my father did it for him. On this one day, we came upon these pecks tossing meat into the murky water, waiting for the gators to come on shore, then shooting them with rifles. Papa got out with his shotgun and told them to get into their car and go away. They had a large gator, about six feet, with two little ones beside it, trapped in a clearing, taunting it with their rifle butts. It circled, trying to keep them from hurting the young ones, putting its body between them and the hunters. Papa wrestled the gun away from one man but the other one shot at one of the baby gators. I tackled that hunter to the ground. As I lay on top of him, the big gator moved right up to me, its eyes looking at me, memorizing me. It was inches from my face and stayed there for a minute. Suddenly, it turned around, nuzzled one of the little ones and ran for the water where they all disappeared almost without a splash.

Just then, a fist hit my face and I was back with the pecks beating the hell out of me. About to die. "Nigger, I think you need to learn a lesson," the white man with the rebel hat said, spitting in my eyes. "We ain't gon' tolerate no black buck putting his filthy hands on our lily-white gals. That gal you soiled is sitting ovah there in that truck ruined for life. Ain't no decent white man gon' want her now. You destroyed her life, nigger. Admit whut you done."

The bright glare of the torches made it hard to see faces—some of them wore hoods while others were brave enough not to wear anything. They had nothing to worry about. Dead mens tell no tales. They brought Miz Gertrude out from the truck, looking all battered and bruised. Her face was bloody and swollen, her clothes ripped damn near off. One of the mens had to hold her up, limp as a rag doll, her legs seemed so weak. I shouted that I didn't beat her like that. Miz Gertrude whispered in a string of choked words that I was the one who did that to her, took her against her will, hurt her bad, and then she swooned. She should have been in pictures.

Someone yelled "lying nigger," a voice I knowed as my boss at the cotton mill, and something metal slapped upside my face and the darkness came back.

What woke me up this time was hitting the ground and the smell of swamp water. The white men were worked up, shouting and screaming, a blood lust upon them. I rolled over, my hands tied in front of me, and saw what was making them holler. The water was full of gators, maybe fifty of them, most of them older ones. The pecks tossed handfuls of raw meat into their midst and the beasts fought among themselves for the food, some of them moving so quick that you knowed nothing human could escape them. I got to my feet, pleading with them to let me go. My shouts were drowned out by their mad laughter and the loud yells from the crazy white woman to kill me for what I had done to her. The pecks circled me with their guns pointed at my feet, pushing me to run toward the dark water and certain death. When I tried to run for the trucks, they fired over my head and at my legs, forcing me to run toward the shore, where the gators were moving in wild, restless patterns. *Oh Lawd, if you ever wanted to show mercy, now is the time.*

I could see some even bigger ones coming out of the water, their heads up and their jaws working. I ran for the trees, where I might have a chance, toward where the moonlight reflected so strangely. There was the thudding sound of the gators behind me, fighting one another for the meat. Some of the more agile ones, the younger gators, took off after me. The pecks yelled even louder, firing shots over my head to keep me from getting into the trees and higher ground. One bullet slammed into my leg, and I went down. Two of the younger gators were upon me, mouths with rows of big, jagged teeth open before I could scramble up and run. I kicked at them as they went for my legs. Suddenly, one of the largest gators I've ever seen, more than eleven feet long, pushed through the circle of beasts and moved right up to my face. Its eyes searched my features for several seconds. The others stayed where they were, waiting for a signal from the big one. In the background, the pecks were firing at the reptiles, trying to provoke them into eating me, but I laid there, praying and waiting for my death. *My Father who art in*

Heaven . . . Strangely, the big one retreated, pounding its long huge tail on the ground, turning to face the white men. The others turned as well.

What the pecks didn't know was that another group of gators had come up behind them. Still more of the gators waded up out of the water, moving toward the white mens who turned to run for their trucks. I ain't never seen gators go after mens like that. Some of the pecks fell and were lost under the tide of the killing beasts. The gators were on them, tearing and ripping their limbs, fighting over the scraps of human flesh. One white man, the one with the rebel hat ran for the shore but a gator caught his leg, and he fell with a terrifying shout into a mass of the beasts. I saw the jaws of a large one close over his head and heard the sickening sound of bone and gristle being crushed. Two more gators were making a meal of the white woman, twisting their heads with parts of her body caught in their teeth, tearing them away from her torso. The shouts of the mens were becoming less and less as the beasts enjoyed their forbidden feast. With the big gator moving beside me, walking re-gally among the others, I limped painfully toward the truck through the sea of murdering reptiles, stepping over torn and bloody bodies and bits of guts. None of the gators made any effort to harm me.

The big gator watched me find a truck with the keys still in the ignition, get in, not moving until I was safely inside. My hands shook. I saw I'd wet myself from fear. Finally I started the motor, letting the truck run some before I put it in gear and drove the hell away from there. I never looked back. All the while during my time on the road to Memphis, I thought about that day when I was ten and the gators I saved from the hunters. Something else crossed my mind. Something my aunt Price used to say a lot: No good deed goes unpunished. That made me laugh and laugh and laugh.

IN MY FATHER'S HOUSE

Without a second thought, I jumped into a cab as soon as I heard her voice on the telephone that Friday, terse, anxious, and full of terror. Anna loved drama, keeping her friends near her whenever her husband was away on one of his many business trips. "Susanne, please come quick," she said in that breathy voice of hers. "I need you, dear, with me this morning." Gerard, her husband of eight years, owned a successful computer software company based on the West Coast in Silicon Valley and was rolling in money. Not as much as Bill Gates had made with Microsoft but he was not hurting. Unfortunately, Anna loved New York City, Manhattan and its swank shops in particular, so she stayed behind with the kids in their expensive Park Avenue penthouse.

It took me two hours to get cross town with the holiday traffic. I'd gone to the health club for a session with my trainer, followed by a quick yoga class and protein drink in the restaurant downstairs. Nutty Anna, my friend. Society Anna and her ever-growing brood of children, each adopted from this private agency in Chelsea, which always gave her first look at any strays they acquired. Anna was worse than the actress Mia Farrow when it came to this adoption obsession, forever adding another new face to her litter.

I hadn't seen her in six months, since we ran into each other at the charity function for Broadway Cares, the group that provides funding for actors and dancers with AIDS. Gosh, she was radiant that night, dressed in this absolutely splendid Dior dress, and nobody could take their eyes off her. Anna loved every blessed minute of it. Although we didn't see a lot of each other, she called me at least twice a week, keeping me posted on the latest gossip—what

Bobby Short sang at the Rainbow Room that night, what dance troupe was appearing at the City Center, or what opera was being performed at the Met this season. Not that I really cared about any of it.

Park Avenue was always hellish to navigate, bumper-to-bumper cars even during the off-peak afternoon hours, but the cabdriver, an Indian-looking fellow with his head wrapped, did some fancy maneuvering and soon dropped me off in front of her building. I paid him quickly, stepped onto the curb, wondering what I was getting myself into. You never knew what to expect with Anna. The doorman nodded, waving me inside, saying I was expected.

The door was open and I walked in, glancing around for any sign of the cause for the frantic call. There was no way Anna would be at the door to greet me, that was not her style. It was a game she played, Anna's hide and seek, meaning you had to search through the apartment's many finely decorated rooms until you found her. Today was not too bad because I heard her out on the terrace that possessed one of the truly great views of the city, day or night.

If Anna were here, she'd go into the whole routine about how they bought the place for a song at eleven million dollars in 1990 from a woman who bought it from one of the heirs of the Angelli clan, the people who own Fiat. She'd walk you through the palatial digs, pointing out the treasured gilded eighteenth century French furniture and the outrageous art collection that contained a Degas, a Monet, two Picassos, and a Miro. And oh yes, her precious portrait taken by Avedon. But today she was out on the terrace, thank God.

"Darling, are we out of tonic water?" Anna de Rochampbeau, the ultimate socialite, asked as she paced out there.

Anna was always dressed impeccably, as if she had just stepped from the pages of a glitzy fashion magazine, *Elle* or *Vogue*. Her gear today was a silk crepe top, an embroidered silk shirt, and harem pants, courtesy of Valentino. Very chic. Her body was in superb shape for a woman of sixty, very surprising because she never exercised or dieted. Some gossip columnists, including Liz and Cindy, placed her age closer to sixty-five or seventy, but with her, you couldn't tell.

"Did you say something, dear?" a male voice answered from somewhere back in the apartment. It sounded like Gerard, his rich continental accent, but that would be odd since she never called me when he was in town.

"Is there any tonic water or Evian?" Anna repeated. "I'm parched, simply parched." Not a trace of the angst I heard earlier was left in her voice. I always thought she reminded me of the late Tallulah Bankhead, the husky-voiced actress, when she talked.

"Did you call me, honey bunny?" Gerard called out from his perch in the mammoth living room, his eyes on the strip of stock figures rolling across a large TV screen.

He turned to face me when I came farther into the room. Gerard was in his early forties, a man of average height with a full shock of graying blond hair and pale blue eyes. He was dressed very casually, a Yankees sweatshirt pulled over a jogging suit. I found myself standing close to him, thinking he still appeared remarkably youthful and vital.

"You can give me a kiss, you know," Gerard said, suddenly standing and holding out his arms. "You're among friends here, Susanne."

I moved into his embrace and let him squeeze me for a second before giving him an air smooch on both cheeks. Very continental. There was a time when Anna, in one of her paranoid states, thought Gerard and I were having an affair but in reality, nothing ever happened between us. He asked me about the reason for my visit after all these many months, trying to read my face, and I told him about his wife's hysterical morning call.

The telephone rang in the hallway. Gerard slowly walked over and answered it. Cupping one of his massive hands over the mouthpiece, he whispered that the hired help was off today, something to do with a rehearsal for the Puerto Rican parade Sunday on Fifth Avenue. I could tell he was pissed his wife gave Maria and Jorge the day off, especially since Gerard and Anna were driving out to their country home for the weekend.

Suddenly, Anna swept dramatically into the room from nowhere, with Fifi, her white manicured poodle under her arm. "Here, give it to me, dear. It's for me. I've been expecting that call."

"It's probably that quack doctor she just started seeing." It was obvious Gerard was not pleased by this new development.

"Is she sick?" I asked, watching the dog lick her soft pink cheek.

"No, she's been taking Artie, the new black boy we adopted, to see this charlatan," Gerard said, screwing up his face. "I need a drink."

"What's wrong with Artie?"

"I'll let her tell you about it," he replied. "I think he's acting out, faking like he's troubled so he can get more attention than the other kids. Well, I told her he was going to be a handful when we took him."

In the hallway, Anna spoke with the hint of a laugh, showing her expertly capped teeth as she held the telephone to her ear. "Oh, darling, how good to hear from you. Yes, it's just so grand. Everyone's who's anybody will be there . . . the usual crowd . . . Bunny Mellon, Kitty Carlisle Hart, Blaine Trump, Catie Bass, Carroll Veronis, and Carla, you know, the Italian prima ballerina. Uh-huh. You hear about Libet? Oh no, really? Libet wore the most precious white sari to the annual Onyx Ball at the Waldorf . . . Unbelievable? Please, darling, absolutely not. Let me discuss that with Gerard and see what he thinks. I'm sure he'd love to come out there for a few hours before we go to the Hamptons. Did you get my check for the Kurdish Relief Fund? Wonderful. You're such a dear. Sweetie, I've got to go. Yes, Susanne's here. You remember her. Yes, yes. Ciao, darling."

"It's Arthur," she said with a weariness in her words. "We're been through so much with him. First, the business with his parents, then the sickle cell anemia crisis, and now this latest thing. He doesn't sleep, won't eat, and will not talk to any of us. And now he has this habit of just screaming at the most inopportune moments, just screams his head off. We've had complaints from other tenants in the building. Gerard's had it up to here with him, wants to return him to the agency."

The other children. Anna's brood of youngsters rivaled the makeup of the United Nations: a Korean boy, a Swedish girl, a Russian boy, a pair of twins from Croatia, and Artie, the black kid. I recalled when she first brought him home after his parents vanished, spent hours talking to the black woman who works for a family on the second floor of the building on the art of being colored in a white world, and the super who sometimes walked Fifi for her. I was not much help in that department since I am white and have no black friends to consult. But I did buy her a copy of a book, *Raising Black Children* by two black psychiatrists, Dr. Alvin Poussaint and Dr. James Comer. Anna thanked me and carried the book with her everywhere for about a month, marking up the pages and underlining key passages.

"Where are the other precious monsters?" I asked sarcastically, watching Gerard take a Cuban cigar from a Javanese humidor.

"Everyone's at school except Arthur," she said sadly. "He won't go. When he did attend, he wouldn't do the work, just sits there and stares at his hands like an idiot. I don't know what to do with him."

Gerard had doubts about Artie. He put the cigar back into the container and walked toward me with a pained expression. "She spoils the boy, and he loves it. We tried to find two of his kind to invite for dinner a few weeks ago. No go. Luckily, the agency let us borrow a couple for a day. An utter disaster. Those black so-and-sos were so unruly, no table manners, ate like apes."

Overhead, the chandelier made a musical sound, matching Anna's laughter, as its weight shifted. "Don't say that, dear," she chided her husband. "That's not nice. These children are products of their environment, those horrible slums. They don't know any better."

"Darling, you take this angel of mercy routine too far," he said. "You contribute your time to every charity, every organization, every club now. You saw a damn African kid on TV the other night with a swollen belly and flies around its mouth, and the first thing you want to do is to adopt the fucking thing."

"More people need to look out for their fellow man," Anna said, her eyes focusing beyond her husband on some spot on the wall.

I could never figure her out. Her heart was good but she could be a bit of an airhead if the moon was in the wrong phase. Anna was somewhat older than her husband, and most of her friends never let her forget that. As I watched her, she fiddled with her costly David Webb enamel Zebra bracelet, with the same look on her thin face she had the night Gerard gave her a new diamond necklace from Harry Winston. He'd bought that for her to wear to a state dinner where the Secretary of the Interior was going to speak.

On the wall behind her was a carefully arranged set of framed photos: Anna and her first husband, Drew, with Ambassador Adlai Stevenson at a U.N. function; Anna and Drew with Spanish flamenco dancer Antonio and opera diva Maria Callas in Madrid; Anna and Drew with JFK and Jackie at the Camelot White House; Anna with dancer Martha Graham at a café in Paris; Anna and Drew with Bogie and Lauren Bacall at Hollywood's Brown Derby; and Anna sipping hot rum with the wild painter Dali at the famed Russian Tea Room. Oddly, there were no photographs of her with Gerard, as if he was something tacked on to her life after the fact. An afterthought.

"Regardless of what you do with these people, I don't think you can turn them around, redeem them," Gerard was saying, a martini in one hand, his eyes still glued to the set. "They're accustomed to their way of life. I feel, honey bunny, as if we're intruding, pushing our values, our existence down their throats. I never liked this whole adoption business. It's false, artificial. Probably the best thing would be to donate money to one of their Baptist churches and let them handle the situation. As everyone knows, breeding tells."

In a way, he was calling her a hypocrite, and I couldn't stand there and let that happen. "I don't understand you, Gerard," I said. "You were such a liberal once. Your parents even went south to fight along with the blacks during the civil rights protests. Your father even knew Martin Luther King, Jr., and Roy Wilkins pretty well. What happened to you, Gerard?"

"Twenty years of living in New York City," he said bitterly. "Before this current mayor got into city hall, the blacks were killing this town. Everything was going to the dogs. Artie may be a good boy but most of the ones I see on the streets are just plain niggers. Excuse my French."

"I hate that word," Anna said flatly. "Gerard, we've talked about your use of it before. I won't tolerate you using it with Arthur in the house or otherwise. And you promised you wouldn't."

Gerard muttered he was sorry, that yes he'd agreed not to use it, but he wasn't going to let her cling to her rosy view of the world. He sat back down in front of the TV, watching the market figures once more. "These kids are little dolls to you, Anna. Playthings. You know I'm right. Often, I've wondered what would have happened if we'd had children of our own . . . then maybe we wouldn't be going through all of this craziness. I try to humor you but enough is enough, honey bunny."

That hurt her. Anna knew what her husband was implying, that the thing with the rejected kids, especially Artie, was another one of her whims. An expensive hobby. Like her tennis obsession a few summers ago. Or her misguided yen for that Indian swami. Or her brief fetish for anything soy. Artie, her colored kid. Anna made the painful connection, said nothing, suddenly looking very pale and drawn.

Anna had visibly winced when her husband said that, the barbs in his words wounding her again and again. She touched my arm, smiled weakly, and said she was going to check on Artie. It's always painful to witness the underside of a marriage, the real absence of love and the constant bloodletting that comes after all trust and respect have gone. And anger and disappointment have taken their place. Yes, there were things money could never fix or replace.

Artie was sitting on his bed in his room, quietly staring into space, among his video games, books, posters of Brittany Spears and Jennifer Lopez. I wondered if he'd heard any of that lethal exchange a few minutes ago, but if he did, there was no indication of it in his demeanor. He was a thin boy, the dark color of a plum, with bright eyes and the thick features one associates with blacks with no history of white blood. His lips were especially large, lighter in hue than the rest of his face, even fuller than those of Mick Jagger of the Rolling Stones. Still, I'd always found little Artie very smart when he chose to talk and quite adorable in his own way.

"Arthur, you remember Susanne, don't you?" Anna asked the boy. "Remember she went with us to see *Antz*. Remember?"

He nodded quietly and held out his tiny hand, and I shook it, smiling as if there was no need for this type of formality. Sometimes

I wondered what it must be like for him, living there, a stranger in a stranger land, so removed from everything he'd previously known and loved. An alien. Snatched away from his own kind, never asked what he wanted, and dropped without warning into this circus. Maybe Gerard was on the money when he said one day, "It was like an endangered species plucked from the wild by misguided animal lovers, trying to domesticate it to act tame and passive among humans who had no real understanding of its true nature." Also, Gerard and Anna, for all of their good intentions, were not Ozzie and Harriet or the Bradys.

"Arthur has always been a little shy," Anna said. "Get your coat, Arthur. We're going to see Dr. Bitto this afternoon. Come on, dear, we can't miss this appointment. We missed the last one, and we can't do that this week."

Artie rolled off the bed, completely emotionless, and walked to the closet to get his coat. I'd never seen a child with such a lack of joy in him, nothing there, a blank. I thought it was sadness or grief at first, but that was too easy. Mechanically he put on the coat, never looking at either of us, then followed us like a zombie out of the room past Gerard, who was still engrossed in his stock-market data.

I waited patiently with the boy while Anna kissed her husband on the forehead and chirped that we'd be back in no time.

When we were in the cab headed downtown to Soho, I asked Anna what happened to poor Artie's parents, if he knew what happened to them. She was silent, watching the small black boy peer at the city going past the windows, sitting quietly with his hands folded in his lap. Again, the neutral expression on his shiny oval face.

"Something to do with some strange church cult," Anna said thoughtfully. "That's all we know. He won't talk about it."

Cults. That crap always frightened me: Charles Manson, Jim Jones and that bunch in Guyana, David Koresh and his group burning up in the house in Waco, the forty-eight members of the Order of the Solar Temple who set themselves on fire in Switzerland, and those forty young guys dressed in white found dead on beds in that California mansion a few years ago. No, cults gave me the willies.

Looking at Artie, I couldn't imagine him being mixed up with something like that in any way.

Later, at Dr. Bitto's office, Anna told me a few more things about Artie's background, the cult business, and his missing parents who were members of this strange, mysterious church that had big congregations in Harlem, Mississippi, and Alabama. I'm not an expert on black churches or their music; it all seems too frenzied, hysterical, somewhat over the top, totally at odds with a refined Presbyterian or Methodist service. From what I understood, the church's leader, this bishop guy was doing quite well for himself and his flock with two used-car dealerships in Mississippi, an auto parts store in Harlem, a frozen-food plant in Alabama, a chain of restaurants, a hog farm, and four funeral homes.

Anna believed the church, like the newspaper said, did a lot of good among the blacks, giving them some direction and self-respect. But she was alarmed by the rumors and reports about the church's bizarre rituals and practices all centered around the worship of the bishop as some kind of mystic or messiah. Creepy. None of this was ever proven so it remained just hearsay.

Dr. Bitto, who looked like a pudgy Jackie Gleason from his *Honeymooner* days, took Artie into his session room, a cramped space with a couch, two chairs, and nothing on the white walls. Quite Motel 6. It seemed Anna wanted me there too. Dr. Bitto put his arm around Artie's shoulders and walked him to a chair, trying to loosen him up before delving into matters of the mind. But the boy didn't speak here either, just nodded yes or no. I told Anna on the way over that maybe Artie needed to be committed or to be put on some meds, like Prozac or lithium or something. That ticked her off. What else got her miffed at me was when I asked if this Dr. Bitto was certified to handle complex cases like Artie's. She never answered that. All she said was the good doctor was referred by a friend who spoke very highly of him.

"Artie, we're going to try the hypnosis again today," Dr. Bitto said, patting the boy on the arm. "Remember we did it once before? And it didn't hurt. But we need to get to the bottom of what's got you all bottled up."

My guess was that Artie wanted to get this over with real quick because he kept nodding yes to everything the doctor asked. It took no time for the doctor to put him under, but then something remarkable happened. One minute Artie was simply sitting there, eyes shut tight, and the next he got up and walked to a corner of the room and began taking off his clothes. Soon he was naked, kneeling on his pants, facing the wall. Anna rushed toward him but the doctor stopped her before she could reach him.

"Where are you, Artie?" Dr. Bitto asked in a soothing tone. "Where are you? What are you doing?"

"We is in church, everybody there—Sister Mahalia, Deacon Moss, the bishop, Mama and Daddy, everybody there." Artie said it like he was reading something off a cue card. "Sunday school is over and the adults is praying and the bishop is saying God has turned his back on black folk 'cause we has turned our back on Him. He say we's lost our closeness to the land, joined hands with Satan and lost our souls. He say we all waiting for handouts, waiting for somebody to deliver us from our troubles, waiting for somebody to save us from ourselves. He say we need to do for self, to be what we was and walk away from wicked ways of the world."

"Arthur . . . Arthur," Anna called to the boy until the doctor motioned for her to be quiet.

The doctor asked Artie what else he saw but the boy didn't answer. Instead he covered his face with his hands as if it was best he didn't see what was there, as if he was repeating things he was warned not to mention, not to anyone.

"The bishop is dressed in all white and the sisters have white robes too," Arthur said. "The bishop say the Holy Ghost is among us, that no sinner will be spared in the moment of righteous judgment, the clapping starts and the choir is singing the hymn, 'Nothing to Do in Hell,' and somebody yells 'Oh, sweet Lawd Jesus' and the whole church is moaning. The bishop say the Maker gon' demand an accounting of every soul in the flock and nobody can escape the power of the Word and nobody can be in God's army lest they be ready to make a sacrifice. That too many of us had left the holy life and chose the way of Mammon and there was no way back to the fold except to render unto the Lawd that which is His. The bishop say the wages of sin is death but the gift of God is eternal life. And everybody is rejoicing, including Mama and Daddy, as we start the next hymn, 'I Cannot Live in Sin.' "

We moved around so we could see his face because I guess, even the doctor hadn't seen anything like it. The boy was shivering like a leaf in the cool autumn wind, his tiny limbs moving to and fro in some kind of crazy rhythm, yet he was covered with sweat from head to toe. Believe me, I'd never seen anything like it. Twice he'd opened his eyes, the lids slowly coming up, and all you could see were the whites, no pupils. Real creepy.

"Tell me, Artie, what happened next." Dr. Bliss stood behind him, his face close to the entranced boy's ear. "Where are you now?"

Like a bolt of lightning had struck him, Artie sat straight up, his back stiff like a soldier on review. The swaying stopped, all movement ceased, and no one in the room stirred. He stayed like that for almost five minutes before he started to talk again, very quickly and nervously.

"I didn't want to go, I didn't want to go," the boy said. "I tell Daddy that. I tell him that I was scared. He say he wasn't scared and neither was Mama because they was in the Lawd's hands. In the bishop's hands. We drive all day to get where the Night of Redemption is being held, where folks from the bishop's Harlem church is. The Temple of the Redeemed Inner Light. It is dark, pitch black when we get there, park out back where the other cars is, and then the big fires is lit, and the hymns are sung and people act like I'd never seen them act before, like they is all possessed by the Spirit. Everybody, all dressed in white, hold hands and lift their arms over their heads chanting 'Hosanna, Hosanna,' while the bishop talk about the Great Day coming, of the return of the Son of God, of the Devil's tricks and the flames of Hell. The church members is divided into two large circles, men on one side and women on the other, and a tall, gray-haired man, somebody from one of the down South churches, takes Mama and Daddy off somewhere, leaving me there by myself."

"Where did he take them, Artie?" the doctor asked softly.

"I don't know but the members keep feeding the fires until the flames is almost as tall as the trees, and everybody starts clapping real fast and yelling 'life everlasting, life everlasting, life everlasting.' Three men, deacons, is in long white robes with a bleeding heart on the back of each one and someone shoves me out the way just as I hear Mama's voice shout 'Oh Lawd, Oh Lawd,' and I see her face for a second and then her whole naked body as the deacons hold her up wiggling in the air. And my Daddy shouts something real loud about no man has the right to play God but a hand goes over his mouth and he can't say nothing else. I see a whole bunch of men press down on Mama, moving between her legs while some others hold her down and everybody chanting 'life everlasting, life everlasting, life everlasting.' In the background, the bishop is holding his arms up like he is receiving a message from on high, all the while chanting 'waste not the seed, the precious seed, waste not the seed, brothers.' When the last of them did what they had to do, the sisters come out and wash her down with spices and holy water and oils before they take her away."

Not one of us took a breath. What he was saying was unbelievable, something out of the Dark Ages, some pagan sacrifice rite. I thought if Gerard heard any of this, he'd immediately say it was just what he expected from these people. Barbarians. Heathens.

"Did you see your mother after that?" Anna asked, the shock of the boy's revelations etched on her face.

"I thought I did," Artie said in a drained monotone. "I hid outside the church one night later and the elders brought this woman in and she looked just like Mama but all her hair, including her eyebrows, was shaved off. I moved closer and saw it looked like her eyelids and her lips was sewn shut. Stitched together. Swear to God."

Everybody gasped. Artie remained in the trance, kneeling with his hands together, tears shiny on his dark cheeks. The doctor kneeled beside him and asked about the fate of his missing father. "What happened to him? Why do you think neither body was ever found, Artie?"

Artie laid on the floor, naked, his eyes blazing yet unseeing. "After Mama is taken away, they drag my Daddy into the middle of the circle and he fights them, the elders, and Bishop gives him the sacred kiss on the lips and three of the Chosen sisters is brought out to get on top of my father when he is tied down. I see Sister Una mount my father, her head goes back and her titties bounce as she rides him until she falls out, then another straddles him and another. The elders give him something to keep him strong down there, a drink. These sisters is the ones who didn't have kids or a man. All the while, the members chant 'life everlasting, life everlasting, life everlasting. Waste not the seed.' I hear my father moan loudly and there is no more sap in my Daddy. He lay there spread-eagle as Deacon Moss brings out the large ceremonial knife and each man member kisses it before it is handed to the bishop who tells my father to be still."

"What then?" It was Anna who spoke now. Her face was flushed.

The boy's eyes widened even more, his voice seemed trapped in his mouth. "The bishop lifts his robe and climbs over Daddy, then lowers himself down near his face. And that was when I see the large curved knife rise, the spray of bright red blood and hear the roar of the congregation. My . . . Mama . . . and Daddy."

Trembling even more, the boy curled up in a knot, his arms locked around himself. Each shudder harder than the last. We kneeled in a group beside him, seeking to hear every tortured word from his quivering lips.

"I run, run, run, and keep on until I get deep into the woods," he rasped. "Deep into the dark, deeper, deeper, deeper where they can't find me. They say nobody would believe me anyway. Say if I say anything that the wrath of the Almighty will be visited upon me. Two sinners washed in the Blood of the Lamb. Washed in the Blood of the Most High. They killed them. They killed them. Killed them."

Suddenly the boy started praying some ancient, unintelligible prayer, saying words that none of us understood. His pain was greater than anything we'd ever known. He cried, cried until he heaved one last great sigh and lay completely still. Every vein stood out in his face, neck, and arms. Some blood appeared in his ears and mouth. The doctor immediately positioned Artie on his back, put his ear to the boy's chest, then checked for a pulse. Artie's oval face was ashen, contorted as if he'd seen a terror no words could describe.

"He's dead," the doctor announced, saying what we already knew. "I don't know what to make of it."

"White liberal guilt, my ass," Anna said bitterly while we watched Dr. Bitto call for an ambulance and the police. She could hear Gerard now, saying the colored boy was a little con artist, a hustler, that his story was a pack of lies: "Anna, he knew how to push your buttons. I know the type, honey bunny."

"I don't know what to make of it," the doctor repeated. "I've never seen anything like this in my entire life, so very strange. This whole damn affair, so very strange."

And neither had I. I knew there was more to this pitiful slum kid than we could possibly understand from one tragic outburst of memory. Maybe his story was true, all of it. We'd never know for sure, for the police hadn't located his parents in six months. Now Artie was dead too. I placed a coat over him so Anna wouldn't have to look at his face like that, but the sight of him dead on the floor got to her anyway. She covered her eyes as the body was loaded onto a gurney, the police and ambulance staff standing there. My guess was that Anna had never had the harshness of real life come right up to her like this. Not this close.

On the way to her apartment in the cab, Anna, still in shock, told me, "In a way, I killed Arthur. I took him out of his environment, just like Gerard said, without knowing how to care for him. Gerard was right. Sometimes you should leave things just as they are. I killed Arthur just as sure as those people killed his parents. I'll never forgive myself, Susanne; sometimes you should just leave things just as they are."

THE INHUMAN
CONDITION

The last thing Casey Dossey, the promising Columbia University law student on leave, told his fiancée before he drove off into the blinding winter storm was, "We'll pick out the rings on Friday, you and me, something old fashioned but classy."

Dressed in a custom-made white shirt, jeans, leather coat, and wingtips, Casey added he'd come by later that night if he was not delayed by the snow. A truly tall and lanky black man who couldn't play basketball or dance, he first wanted to meet with Richard, a friend who was doing a stint with Legal Aid, and help him map out his case involving a young Hispanic boy with organic brain disease who had suddenly stabbed everyone in his family to death while they were sleeping. Friends said the boy had been smoking angel dust for six days straight and was not himself. That morning, the day of the storm, Richard called Casey to confide that he was considering a temporary insanity plea for the kid since he was only fourteen and his medical condition was already known to doctors.

In the midst of the intense white-out, Casey was pushing his old Buick sedan hard and fast along the snow-covered highway near Lake Erie in Cleveland. *Damn, I'll never get there. I told him that I'll get by there before it got too late.* Richard could only wait at his office until three-thirty. He was running super-late, speeding along the snowy road, making good time. He tried to dodge the stalled cars and tractor trailer pile-ups causing delays in the downtown lanes, moving his foot back and forth between the accelerator and the brake. Visibility was especially bad because his windshield wipers were old, frayed, and needed to be replaced. His car's tires fought for traction on the ice but couldn't keep their grip.

Inside, Casey struggled to maintain control of the steering wheel against the sheer might of the gale-force winds coming off the frigid water in solid bursts. *Careful, don't push it too hard.* Occasionally, he touched the beautifully wrapped gifts on the front seat near his leg, some tokens of love for his sweetheart, a cinnamon-colored girl from Alabama with a smile so dazzling that you forgot she was so country. And oh man, what a body! His family thought she was quite backward, uncultured, without class, but none of that mattered to him. Love never takes those things into account.

His beloved had warned him about being late so much. It was a pet peeve of hers. He'd promised her that he would leave in enough time so he would not have to rush in the bad weather. That afternoon, he promised he would see her with time to spare. But he was doing it again, rushing and taking risks, racing like a fool over treacherous icy ground with very little regard for his safety. Also, his mind seemed to be wrestling with a thousand things at once, and he tried to focus his attention on the driving but he was failing miserably. Maybe he should get tickets for the Browns game next Sunday against the Giants. Richard would dig that. Herbie Hancock was playing this Tuesday at Severance Hall with Wayne Shorter, two good jazz guys, and those tickets might be reasonable if he bought them early. Gotta get some snow tires at Sears while they were on sale. Dad seemed determined to break them up. Maybe he could talk some sense into his father if he could get him alone, away from Mom. The worst thing that happened during the week was finding a vibrator in his fiancée's purse, and just what did that mean? Was he not satisfying her in bed? Had to talk to her about that before she did something stupid with another guy. None of it made sense. Maybe the associate dean of the law school could get him a summer internship somewhere.

Suddenly, the wheels twisted under the car and the vehicle slid completely around, going back toward the oncoming traffic. *Oh shit!* Casey battled to keep the car away from the others rushing toward him through the dense white fog, frantically fighting the steering wheel but nothing helped, and a large van crashed into his Buick, sending it through the railing toward the lake. The last thing he remembered after the neon flash of impact was the car flipping over and over down the side of the hill into the frigid water.

Casey didn't remember how long he had been under the water or where he was taken after he was removed. Everything was like a bizarre dream, a twisted vision, hazy, as if he was watching himself from outside of his body, and there was this man with a radiant face and an unbelievable grip who pulled him from the wreckage and the lake. He recalled that much before he blacked out again. Soon he had the strangest sensation of flying above the ground, above the police searching for his body with divers and rescue boats, the brave men going down between slabs of ice into the bone-numbing water to the submerged car. Somehow he didn't feel cold despite the fact that he was soaked. In fact, he could barely feel his body, the weight of it, the mass of it. But he did feel these arms, these powerful arms clutched around his waist and soaring with him, above the wind-whipped city, above the cries and screams of his family and sweetheart, who waited by the phone for any word of him.

After two weeks of searching, authorities said any hope of finding his body was lost and ended their effort. The family planned a memorial service, which was attended by most of his professors, friends, and fellow students. His sweetheart came to the church with a new male friend, something that didn't sit well with Casey's father.

It was almost a year later that Casey suddenly awoke in a strange bed in a shabby bed-and-breakfast in a rural part of the state. Stunned, he had no knowledge of how he got there or who paid the bill or cared for him during the long time he was asleep. Or dead. All of it a real mystery. His savior with the luminous face was nowhere in sight. He rose and stretched his arms, immediately noticing their dull gray pallor. Ashy limbs in need of lotion big-time. His legs also looked and felt odd, as if they were not really his, an entire body on loan. In the mirror, the face spoke of a slight hint of decomposition, staring back at him in a state of arrested erosion, but then it was the aroma of something dank, something decaying that caught his attention. His glance went back to the anguished visage reflected in the mirror, his hollowed cheeks, deep-set eyes, and mournful expression. A living ghoul. He didn't mind any of this, really. He was *alive*, not in a grave. He had cheated Death.

I should be made a saint, for I have power over Death, he thought, his black lips pulled back in a sardonic smile.

That afternoon, Casey washed thoroughly and dressed in one of the clean sets of clothes he found neatly hung in the closet, perfect fit. Everything he needed was there: dress clothes, sweat suit, jeans, sweaters, and shoes. On his way out for a walk, he ignored the stares of the other patrons at the inn, as well as the comment that he looked as if he needed some sun from the fat woman behind the counter. What did she know about anything? His adventure took him to a nearby supermarket within view from his room, and there the man with the luminous face appeared next to him in the produce section.

"What are you doing here, following me?" Casey asked the man, who looked past his resurrected friend to a man with two little boys as if he could hear what they were thinking. "Are you an angel or what?"

The man crept closer to the father and his boys, putting his hand over the man's head, sending a thin beam of light down into his skull. "You want to know too much, Casey. Just enjoy what you got, a second chance."

"Are you from the other place?" Casey asked, continuing his questioning. The light coming from the man blinded Casey, preventing him from getting a good look at his guardian.

The angel shook his head, suddenly materializing right at Casey's elbow, leaning close to his charge's gray face. "There are rules that come with your new life. I've been commanded to tell you that you are not to see anyone in your family or loved ones for seven days. No one you know must see you for a week. No one. If you break this command, the consequences will not be good for you."

"What are you saying? What do you mean . . . no one?"

The angel offered him a patient smile much as a benevolent coach would do with a disagreeable rookie on a junior varsity football team. "Heed my words. No one in your family, especially your parents, must see you for seven days. Neither your fiancée nor old friends can look upon you in that time as well. Heed my warning well. Also, you should be wearing a coat because it's somewhat chilly outside." With that, a light yellow jacket materialized in the angel's hands and he handed it to Casey, who stood near the cabbages and broccoli with his mouth agape in astonishment.

Nervously, Casey glanced around to see if anybody had witnessed this miracle, this magic, but the people seemed caught up in their own small lives, not concerned with this angel and Lazarus. When he turned back around, the angel was gone, vanished without a sound. He remained there for several moments, trying to figure out what had just happened, looking in all directions in disbelief. This was getting weird. Totally weird.

He slipped on his jacket, ordered his sluggish legs to take him away from the place and back to the inn. There was always the telephone and room service. On his way into the building, he stopped to chat with the fat woman, asking her about the bill. She laughed and patted his arm, cooing to the surprised man that the bill was paid up for another two weeks.

Back in his room, Casey paced the floor, hoping that movement would clear the fog in his head. How much of any of this was real? Where had he been for a year? Did he die? Was this Heaven? Or a bad dream? Sure he'd wake up in his car, struggling with the steering wheel on the icy road like one of those creepy *Twilight Zone* episodes. The angel's words filled him with a frightening mix of sadness, remorse, and anger, largely because the warning was quite clear and so adamant. A strong warning with no exceptions. No contact with anyone, not his family, not his beloved Alicejean. This was crazy. What was he supposed to do? What was the guarantee that this guy was an angel and not a *messenger from Hell?* Or maybe he'd suffered a head injury in the accident and was having a hallucination in a nuthouse somewhere. Who knew?

As the days went by, Casey slowly became agitated from boredom, isolation, and the tight restriction on his movements. It was torture. Trapped in the room like a caged animal. He thought briefly about praying, but only briefly, since he wasn't especially religious and not a person to be screaming and shouting in some Baptist church on Sunday. God had forsaken him anyway. He really didn't want to think about what happened after Death or the final tallying of sins. All bullshit. But the notion of going to the Other Side did sometimes intrigue him. Did you face Judgment Day immediately after dying? Or did they let you linger around for a while while they figured out what to do with you? This was all fantasy, for what interested him now was the present, the immediate, the promise of the new day, not sitting in this place. There was no way he was going to stay cooped up in this room when his family and sweetheart were only a bus ride away.

However, there were other complications. Casey wanted to go out but there were other forces at work, powerful ones. Twice he tried to leave the furnished room, yanking on the doorknob, but it wouldn't open. Once, the doorknob fell off, bounced on the thickly carpeted floor, and rolled under the bed. He squatted and searched for it, finally overturning the entire bed in anger. No doorknob. To his shock, the knob was there back in place, shiny and intact, when he glanced back at the door. The second time was even stranger. He tried to walk out but his legs suddenly locked, total paralysis from his waist to his toes. Casey resembled Lot's wife in the Bible, a pillar of lifeless flesh instead of salt, a stiff penalty for divine disobedience. Only when the thought to leave for his parents' home departed from his mind was his ability to move restored.

Abruptly, Casey fell on the floor in a heap of unruly gray flesh, cursing and grumbling at his sorry fate. Cursing all the angels in Heaven! What was the point of this second chance at life if you were locked up like a damn prisoner? This was a living Hell for him. He cursed the angels again, struggled to his feet, only to be startled by the sudden appearance of the man with the radiant face once more.

"Don't you ever knock?" Casey wisecracked. "I'm being held here against my will. That's not right."

The angel leaned against the wall. "You've been given another chance, so you should be grateful. We won't stop you if you want to go but you've been warned. Remember that." Having said that, Casey's heavenly guardian disappeared in the blink of an eye.

Casey was determined to resume his old life despite the stern warnings. To hell with the angel! He was going to see his folks regardless of what it might cost him. He prepared himself for the trip home by better grooming and hygiene, perfumed soaps, potent deodorants, and whitening toothpaste. Something new was going on with his body. He noticed there were new elements, the dull gray tinge to his skin was worsening, the dark thickness of his hair resisted scissors or blade, and his flesh healed regardless of the type of injury. He was immortal. The dead cannot be killed. He could never be killed again. But why the second chance? Had someone made a mistake somewhere? Maybe the names got mixed up like in a movie he'd seen. The wrong black man sent back, right?

When he started the trip, it had seemed like a good idea. But there were too many hours on a cramped seat on a Greyhound bus, layovers in small towns, loud-talking passengers with babies who cried without ceasing, and finally the arrival at the city depot. Everyone stared at Casey and tweaked their noses when he walked past. The stench of the undead. He decided not to call his parents. Any previous attempt to call the Dossey home only brought harsh static over the receiver, but the phone rang this time and he hung up upon hearing his father's voice. With halting steps, he limped to the curb where a row of cabs waited in an orderly line and slid into the backseat of the first one. The driver squinted at him in the rearview mirror, cleared his throat, and asked where he was headed.

The doorbell to the Dossey home rang three times before his mother came out and collapsed at his feet. She hit the ground solidly, with a thud that brought his father running to a dead stop when he saw his son—or what he thought was his son—standing before him. After they assisted Casey's mother to the living room sofa, the two men embraced warmly, his father pinching his nose slightly, and then laughing as if the occasion were a holiday.

"Do you smell something bad, son?" his father asked, not wanting to come out and say his boy smelled like damp earth or worse, like something rotting in the summer sun. "Anyway, where have you been all this time? God, boy, we had you dead and buried. Literally."

"Not really dead or buried, " Casey answered solemnly, looking at his mother still unconscious on the couch. "It's a long story. I'll tell you someday but now is not the time."

His father stared at his eldest boy's gray skin, feverish eyes, and sick face. "Casey, you look worn out. You should lay down and get your strength. Want some Kool-Aid, juice, or something stronger? We can talk later. Where's your luggage?"

"I don't have any." His reply made his father shake his head.

Ah, the return of the Prodigal from the Valley of Death. A refugee from the grave. Casey laid across the bed in his old room, a vault of childhood memories, tried to rest but couldn't. The sound of conversation between his father and revived mother was easily heard through the thin walls; they were happy to see him come home but both decided something was strange about his appearance. His mother wondered where he'd been all that time. Was he in a hospital? Why hadn't he called before? Why did he look so bad? As he listened, he heard the sound of an aerosol can spraying something, possibly some kind of pine room freshener, to kill his scent of the open grave.

When Casey finally emerged from his room hours later, his parents greeted him lovingly. His mother, a middle-aged black woman with graying hair, worked on him with questions. Between dabbing at her nose with a paper napkin, she wanted to know everything. "Leave nothing out, baby," she said. "Tell me every detail."

"Moms, I was dead," Casey said proudly. "But I'm back now, just like Lazarus in the Bible. Live and in color."

His mother didn't find that funny at all. "The only one to come back from the dead was our Lord, Jesus Christ. Don't blaspheme in this house, Casey. Don't play with God."

But his father was amused by Casey's fanciful story and asked him about Death, resurrection, the afterlife, God, the Holy Ghost, Gabriel and his trumpet, and the final Judgment Day. None of these issues could be settled by Casey because he remembered nothing of what happened after the car hit the water, and what snatches of memory he possessed were not believed by either parent. He had questions too. What happened to Alicejean? His father told him Alicejean was married and pregnant with her first child. The father of the baby was his former best friend and law buddy, Richard.

During the next few days, his family kept Casey in the house, waiting for his appearance to improve and the bad smell to subside.

Neither situation got better and soon they began talking about sending him south to stay with Aunt Dorothy in Florida. Aunt Dorothy had Alzheimer's and was slowly losing her mind so he could keep her company in her final years. Some small town outside of Tampa. They were ashamed of him, ashamed of how he looked and smelled, and were careful not to let their neighbors or any relatives know he was alive.

One night, Casey got the family car and drove down to the red district of town, found a big-breasted girl for hire and rented a motel room. He stripped off his shirt and pants, revealing a body covered with deep bruises, purple blotches, and grim scars. His body was continually going through changes. The woman lit a cigarette, looked him over, and debated whether to take him on. She blew a thick plume at him and he immediately erupted into a series of hacking coughs, the type with congealed, heavy phlegm. His allergy to cigarette smoke was another consequence of his sudden emergence from the grave.

After reflection, the rented woman exhaled some more smoke and said without any emotion: "Damn, what kind of freak are you? Well, don't expect me to kiss nothing or have you up in me. Not looking like that."

Casey was miserable, almost on the brink of tears. He got dressed, paid the woman, and disappeared into the comforting shadows of the night. He prayed no one would see him. What had he done so wrong? Why was God punishing him like this? On some days, he swore he could feel a slight, feeble pulse and on others like this, there was no sign of life in his rank, gray husk of a body.

Another night, Casey was sitting in a bar on the other side of town, and he used a borrowed Swiss Army knife to cut off a hand while two guys looked on. The hand turned to dust right before their eyes. Both men fainted, their heads striking the wood floor at the same time. By the time Casey finished laughing at the unconscious disbelievers, another new gray hand had taken the place of the severed one.

A week later, a young thug tried to rob Casey but he had no money so the kid stabbed him twice, hard in the chest, so hard that the resurrected man's knees buckled. Before the kid could run away, Casey ripped open his shirt to let his assailant watch the wound seal itself and close with new gray flesh. The kid screamed at the top of his lungs, yelled that the dude was a monster, a damn Frankenstein monster.

It was a curse, this second life, this second self. He was a monster. The undead. What fun was any of this? His parents fed, washed, and cared for him, but they kept their distance otherwise. Wherever he went, all eyes were on him. The freak. The ghoul. When there was nothing to occupy his mind, he sat on the windowsill in his room, sitting very still, watching the clouds move across the sky, happy to be above ground. He developed this curious habit of waking early in the morning before anyone was up, to see the sunrise. That soothed him somewhat.

But sometimes Casey wished he was dead, really dead. He wished that someone supernatural would come upon him, kill him again and release him from this hell. He craved the comfort of the damp earth, worms, and a tombstone. Sometimes the boredom became too much and he would slice off a finger or a toe and watch them grow back. Sometimes he wished he didn't know Death's first name, the afterlife or the miraculous touch of the angel. Just wanted to be a mere mortal. Just wanted to die and stay dead.

The pain in his soul was so intense, so great, and there seemed to be no release, no escape. This was not life. Not the sweet life he knew before.

Two days before his twenty-fourth birthday, Casey got a call from Alicejean, who wanted him to come over. Richard wasn't home. He was out of town on some business trip. She said marriage was quite an adjustment, not like she thought it would be. She missed the intimacy and laughs she'd shared with Casey and needed to see him once more.

"I heard a rumor you were back," Alicejean said, her voice light and gentle as a soft first kiss. "Where have you been all this time? Sweetie, I need to see you. I really do. My marriage . . . you heard I was married? It's a bust. A total mistake. He's never home, out all night with his job or his boys."

"I don't want to see you, Alicejean," Casey said, slow and deliberate. "Not now, not ever."

"I won't take no for an answer," she insisted. "As soon as I hang up, I'm on my way over there. I've got to see you, sweetie. Got to."

Once the call was finished, a panic came over him with the memory of the hard impact of the car colliding with the truck and tumbling into the lake. Alicejean couldn't see him like this, no way. It would be the ultimate humiliation, her ridicule and rejection of him. The monster she had once loved. This couldn't happen. He needed guidance, advice. Where was his angel? Where was the man with the luminous face? His divine guardian.

Slowly Casey sunk to his knees, tears on his cheeks, praying in earnest. "Dear God . . . I don't know why you did this to me . . . a second chance and all . . . but I want to be released from your gift. Give me back my death. All I have brought on everybody is shame, embarrassment, and fear. Set me free from this torment."

The angel appeared near the door, wearing a solemn expression, with profound sadness in his eyes. "You understand what the consequences for your disobedience were. You were warned. It could have been much easier for you. I feel sorry for you. I really do. You were my assignment, my responsibility, and I have failed."

"No, I failed. I should have followed the rules. I did dumb shit. Excuse my language. I could have lived an honorable life but I didn't. I wasted my first chance at life. I wasted my time. I get a second chance and screw that up too. Tell your Boss I'm sorry, so sorry."

"You got any cigarettes?" the angel asked. "It's one of the few vices from Earth I miss. That and butterscotch sundaes."

Casey dug into his shirt pocket and removed a pack of Newports. He'd started smoking again even though it often left him coughing like crazy. He handed one to the angel, who lit it without a match and smoked it quietly, looking at the pitiful figure before him.

"Yes, we dropped the ball on this one," the angel said to no one in particular. "I've been commanded to set things right. To let you try to work things out from another angle. The Boss says this is how I can redeem myself. But I've not figured out how to do this yet."

"Could I have my old life back?" Casey asked. "I'll be good. I won't smoke, drink, no women, no cards, no TV, no radio, no movies, no bright-colored clothing, no food with salt in it. Nothing. I'll do whatever your Boss says. Whatever He says."

The angel sat down on the edge of the bed, his full wingspan of white glowing feathers apparent, and asked for another cigarette. "Yes, we botched this up badly. If they could see me smoking right now, they'd be mad. It's a violation of the Code. Anyway, let's put our heads together and see how we can straighten this whole thing out."

Both men smoked in total silence for several minutes, lost in thought in the small, cramped room until the angel stood, folded his wings, and ordered Casey to stretch out on the bed. The man with the gray face did as he was told. He listened for further instructions from the Divine Being. "Don't open your eyes until I tell you to. Don't let the heat surging through your body frighten you. Relax. Surrender to it. Clear your mind of everything and feel yourself float. This won't take long." Casey sensed himself being hoisted up by an invisible force until he felt weightless and formless. Floating above the clouds. Like a spirit. Like an unfettered soul.

In an instant, Casey was inside the Buick again, struggling to control the car, the steering wheel unruly in his grip. The tires went in an uncontrollable spin, cars and trucks speeding at him, and suddenly the van came out of nowhere and crashed into him. A blinding white light, just like before. He tried to turn the wheel, to guide the car out of its wild ricochet, but it smashed solidly into another car before coming to a stop. He slumped over the steering wheel for several seconds, his face smeared bloody, but he was alive. Lucky to be alive. Three people rushed to his car door and peered inside. He heard their voices, urgent and terrified: "The ambulance is on its way. Are you hurt?" They yanked the dented car door open, helping him to his feet, assisting him to a leaning position against the side of the demolished Buick. One woman, her face distorted with concern, put a blanket around his shoulders, saying "You're lucky to be alive." Another voice shouted, "Look at his left leg, it's all mangled." Casey really didn't care much about the leg. He didn't even feel it. He touched the deep gash on his forehead before he slumped forward into the arms of the woman, the woman who he would eventually date and marry. Paula. His last thoughts before the darkness arrived were that he'd paid a considerable price for this terrible new knowledge he had gained. *Value your life. Waste not even a minute. Life is a precious and wonderful gift.* Yes, he was lucky to be alive, damn lucky.

BORDERING ON
THE DIVINE

There was another flash of lightning, the sound of the howling wind, and the shutters banging against the building outside. In a converted building in lower Manhattan, Edgar Allan Poe stood ramrod straight, then he spoke in a high-pitched, excited voice over the clamor of busy tongues. He truly wished he could chase his guests from his cluttered hideaway and be alone once more. There was only a little time left before the owner of this hideous cell wanted it back for his own use.

"Sometimes I see myself doing all manner of things, and I have no way of explaining them," Poe said nervously. "This other person is myself. I may respect him but I also fear him as well. He is a mystery, delightfully so, or to use Lady Bledsoe's favorite word, *odd*. Often I look upon him in wondrous awe, much as a parent would do with a peculiar child."

He walked among them, his two guests both seated on a strange assortment of chairs, squirming in discomfort. The couple assembled there were dressed in their formal best, as if geared for a sophisticated society ball of some importance, reeking of the moneyed class. They had detoured from their prearranged outing to visit their eccentric friend, humoring him and pretending to eagerly sup on his every animated word and gesture.

"What do the critics know?" Poe continued, motioning wildly. "How can they say my work is flawed, too melodramatic with overdone language, funny and absurd at the wrong moments, too much revenge in the stories, pointless and morbid? I wish them a starving maggot in their brains, the whole lot of them. They know so little of the horror that creeps daily upon a person, so terrifying in its infec-

tion of the soul. That is especially the fate of anyone who puts pen
to paper. Nothing can please them, the asses, the dolts!"

Mr. Bledsoe, the scent of liquor on his person, glanced at Poe's
Negro servant standing in the doorway and asked a meek query of
his host, the chalky-skinned man with the sad, haunting eyes.
"Sounds like some critic went at one of your books with a meat-ax.
Is that it, Poe?"

Poe was pondering something else. "The more I strive to be normal, the more elusive it all becomes, so it becomes uppermost in
my aims to achieve this end. But now the role I play in life is inex-
orably linked to the world I place on paper."

"How do you like New York these days?" Mr. Bledsoe asked. "I
know you were away for a time. Has it changed for you?" His wife
sat mute, staring transfixed at her dusty surroundings, which were
far below her social status and usual preference.

Lady Bledsoe heard the uneasy trembling in the timbre of her
husband's words. No doubt he was remembering how somber the
tall, silent black man had been when he led them down the long,
dark corridor containing stacks of stained-glass windows along its
length to this room. The three of them were compelled to walk
sideways to avoid stumbling or falling down on the hardwood floor
as there was very little room to maneuver.

"I think New York is still a queer place with a few minor distrac-
tions," Poe said as he hurriedly left the room, temporarily astonishing the couple with his abrupt departure. Sometimes he could sit
still like the Sphinx, solid, unmoving. At other times, he was a
whirlwind, restless like a young colt, moving about the room in a
blur.

After Poe departed, the Bledsoe man and his wife boldly walked
over to the rolltop desk stationed in a corner of the room, ignoring
decorum as they examined the used quills lying among the crum-
pled, discarded wads of paper on its well-worn surface. The entire
place was thick with cobwebs and dust. It was obvious that this was
not a locale that the writer frequented regularly. Lady Bledsoe
turned up her nose in disgust, holding a scented cloth to her face.

Quietly, Poe came from another room, more pages of script in his
thin hand, walking in his customary fast, nervous steps. His cloth-

ing was most unusual. His guests watched him with both surprise
and annoyance, for he still had to acknowledge their presence with
a formal greeting. After inviting them to his new lair, he was being
his usual erratic self.

Back to his clothing, the writer was now attired in the gray uniform of the West Point Cadet, circa 1831, the single-breasted coa-
tee, black silk cord in Austrian knots, Jefferson shoes, round black
hat civilian style, silk cockade with gilt eagle, white gloves, and
sword. The uniform fit him poorly.

Mr. Bledsoe arched his eyebrows in mock surprise, then winked
at his slightly plump wife. Her appetite for pastries and sweets was
well-known and the talk of the gentry. Both knew anything was possible with Poe. The man loved to shock so the suit was not especially out of character.

"Edgar, you are always so busy," Mr. Bledsoe said flatly. "A bundle
of energy, I dare say. Quite a celebrated figure these days. I hear tell
the abolitionists approached you to speak at one of their damned
conferences but you turned them down."

Their host remained silent, toying with the sword, doing imagined thrusts on an unseen foe. He eyed them suspiciously while he
adjusted his hat just so on his head. His occasional glances followed
Mr. Bledsoe's every movement, the looks intense and somewhat
glum as he moved toward them near his desk. Lady Bledsoe tried to
read one of the pages scattered about on it, straining her eyes and
holding the paper close to her face. The script was contorted, barely
readable, and to make matters worse, the lighting in the tiny room
was feeble at best. There was better illumination in the average
crypt. Two oil lamps were lit, their wicks turned very low. Lady
Bledsoe also noticed there was nowhere for one to sleep, not even a
pallet, unless there existed another unseen chamber.

"I sense your admiration for my exquisite costume," Poe said
with a snide laugh. "There is a party downtown. I shall be celebrat-
ing the anniversary of my expulsion from West Point. That was not
a place to frolic. However, ingenuous outfit, is it not?"

Suddenly put on center stage, Mr. Bledsoe nodded in agreement,
but his wife only tittered, which drew an immediate sneer from the
writer. She was not his idea of a suitable woman, pretentious and

full of airs. While he measured her with a casual look, a rat, large and gray, scurried around the fringes of the cell-like room, causing both guests to leap with a shriek at the sight of it.

From the hallway, Silas, the Negro, wiped his gleaming black face, the proud countenance of an African of Ibo ancestry, and suppressed a grin. Whites were a constant source of amusement, especially Mr. Poe. He quit the room with stealth and returned with a tray containing cups and a teapot. Lady Bledsoe wrinkled her nose when he walked past her, his imagined scent too pungent for her genteel nose. As Silas served them, he felt her stare upon him, examining him thoroughly as though he was yet a young buck on the auction block. Quietly, he moved to a position near the door where she could not see him yet he could keep her in full view.

Toying with her bonnet, the woman asked Poe, "Have you ever tried to end your own life, Mr. Poe?" A wicked reference to the writer's supposed emotional distress. Her husband quickly glowered at her for asking such an insolent query.

Not a sound for a time. Then Mr. Bledsoe said as if to cover the damage of his wife's ill-conceived question: "Edgar, some of your work is simply sublime. I can think of one line you once wrote in an essay that I absolutely adore. 'Can it be fancied that the Diety ever vindictively made in his image a manikin merely to madden it?' What a startling thought?"

Poe was neither vexed nor amused by the question. Still, the famous Poe half-smile flashed for an instant, and he went out of the room, coming back several minutes later with a flask of spirits and glasses. This act aroused great alarm, for it was common knowledge that the writer was not one to tolerate the power of strong drink well.

Outside, the storm continued its fury, more bolts of lightning, shadowed by the loud rumble of thunder. Walking like a petty thief, Poe crossed the room and addressed them familiarly, with a diabolical death mask where his face had formerly been. The shadows of the dark room contorted its features evilly. He would get his revenge on the doughy wench, the Lady Bledsoe. Bah, no one could insult him in his own dwelling!

So the sinister drama began. "The smell of damp earth frightens me," Poe said in a low, raspy tone. "After my wife's untimely death, I sought to embrace death, to woo it. I began drinking heavily, which is a form of suicide, slow death. I even tried to welcome death's embrace another way when I was depressed. But some passersby found me unconscious in the road, although I do not recall how I got there. I had consumed a large dose of laudanum but luckily I did not die. Or unluckily."

The Bledsoes wore morbid looks, totally uneasy now, saddened but unnerved by the tale of private misery. They took their seats once more.

Lady Bledsoe volunteered with much false gaiety in her words, "Mr. Poe, what you need is a woman to help you forget your sorrows."

Poe poured himself a drink and downed it. His reply was not long in coming. "I do not know the reason for it, but I seem too fond of widows." He passed into gales of uncontrolled laughter, alternating laughing with crying. Silas shook his head with pity. Between tortured breaths, Poe poured drinks for his guests and handed them out.

"The single-purpose life is an encouragement to boredom and early death," the writer muttered. "We invent our manner of death in each action, in each choice, in each second of the day. We plot and construct our deaths. This, dear friends, is mine." With that, he poured another glass of spirits and gulped it down.

"I am a poet by choice," Poe mumbled to himself. Lady Bledsoe picked at a spot of dried mud on the hem of her elegant, multi-frilled dress. Poe cleared his throat rudely as he watched the anguish of her deeply cleaved bosom, and at length, remarked to her husband accusingly, "She will be your death, my good man."

Both Bledsoes turned crimson, violently perturbed. Realizing the barb in his statement, the writer walked over to the man and leaned in mock friendship on his arm. He said that it was all in jest, and the tension eased somewhat.

"Now, what about the Negro question, my dear Poe?" Mr. Bledsoe inquired before taking a sip of the spirits. "Where do you stand on that? You have given so many answers to the question that many say they do not know what you believe."

"Please, no vile politics today," Poe answered impatiently. "No talk of slavery or states rights. Please. Is that what you came here to visit me about? Possibly getting my signature on some document?"

Mr. Bledsoe blushed again. "Most certainly not. We came in friendship, to see you, to hear what you are doing." Not commenting on the fact that they had been invited, he pondered his question to the troubled soul standing before him.

"Why were you expelled from West Point?" Lady Bledsoe asked suddenly. Worried, Silas moved further into the shadows, back out of the way, watching all three.

Annoyed by his silence, Lady Bledsoe stood and returned to the desk, lifting an open book to the light. "What is this? I do not understand Spanish that well. What does the inscription mean? *Ninguna otra cosa me pareció tan agradable, como la de obsequiarte este libro, porque al menos sé que cuando termines de leerlo, vas a recordme.*" She acted somewhat embarrassed, suddenly realizing she had asked two questions back to back without getting a reply for the first.

The writer, watching them over the extended blade of the gleaming sword, replied slowly, "As for your first query, I was expelled for what they termed 'behavior unbecoming of a cadet.' I shall not go into that tonight. As for the second one, the gracious inscription was from a Spanish writer, who I met at a dull party. All it means is that he enjoyed my book. Quite flattering, is it not?"

The couple looked at each other in dismay, then stared at the small, feverish eyes of Poe, which were buried in deep purple circles. They were up and down in their chairs, nervous with the expectation of the writer's antics.

"Mr. Poe, I do admit you are still very much the maverick," Lady Bledsoe said coyly, fingering the spine of a book. "That reputation for being overly curt with your acid tongue and quick wit is not unfounded. However, your career would be much better served if you were not so inclined."

Poe pretended to be engrossed in something else. He could feel the woman's eyes upon him. She watched him as if he were a ghoul of some sort. Meanwhile, her husband stroked his full face of unruly whiskers, occasionally mumbling to himself while he continued to search through the debris on the rolltop.

"Bledsoe, will you tell your wife to stop regarding me in such a manner," Poe said with one of his most cruel smiles. "Tell her I shall not harm her. She has nothing to fear from me."

Her husband chided her bitterly. "Darling, please. What did I say about that?" The woman dropped her head much as a misbehaving tot would do when scolded. Poe laughed under his breath.

When the writer saw she had begun to stare again, he stifled further laughter with his hand and hummed in an eerie voice while he walked across the floor toward her. "Lady Bledsoe, have you consider the taste of human flesh? Of course not. You are much too civilized for that type of thing." The woman squirmed tensely in her chair, gripping its sides so tightly that her knuckles were pale.

Her husband was familiar with Poe playing this role at social affairs, horrifying anyone who would dare indulge him in his morbid charades. What good did it do to protest until the madness ran its course? The man could be intolerable when he was like this. There was no doubt that Poe was afflicted in some way.

Poe stood in the center of the room, waving his sword over his head, ranting, "Lady Bledsoe, as you may know, the Roman emperors recorded their deeds for all to read. Are you familiar with the Roman games? If you are, then you know they were a combination of lust, terror, and unspeakable violence. Children and young women like yourself were often raped and mutilated by both man and beast for the amusement of an appreciative audience. Cruelty was the national sport of the Roman Empire. Be glad that you did not live during those times. Why, it is said the Emperor Tiberius tortured men by forcing them to drink large amounts of wine, then he would have their genitals bound so they could not relieve themselves."

Mr. Bledsoe's hands went to his privates in an almost reflexive action. Poe saw the gesture and smiled lewdly. Lady Bledsoe looked ill.

Angered at seeing Poe take advantage of his wife's weakness, Mr. Bledsoe said coldly, "Edgar, I do not believe my wife wishes to hear any more. She is not interested in the barbarism of Ancient Rome. Why can't we talk about the pressing matter of states rights? What are you afraid of, my good man?"

It was not Poe's way to abandon a job half done so he carried on with his baiting. "In a moment, we will get to that. But now imagine that time of supreme decadence amid the splendor of the Eternal City. Now when I ponder on it, maybe the reason for Tiberius' unquenchable fury was his wife, Julia, and her libertine ways. Neither five nor five hundred men could provide her with the physical satisfaction she so desperately craved. She was the daughter of the Emperor Augustus, beautiful and very worldly. Julia was given to exhibiting her body publicly, so the rumor goes."

"Stop it, Poe," Mr. Bledsoe growled. "Enough!"

"Let me see, there was Claudius, then Nero," Poe continued. "Now there was an interesting one for you, Lady Bledsoe. The man was said to have a special penchant for making human torches of Christian prisoners to light the games and garden parties."

Lady Bledsoe shuddered involuntarily, her thin lips trembled. Her husband was not at all pleased by the writer's performance.

A solemn boat whistle could be heard from the nearby pier, mingling with the chatter of workmen hurrying in the rain. Poe stopped abruptly, pivoted slowly, and smiled calmly at the couple. What was he up to now? What new game was he conjuring? Unfortunately, Lady Bledsoe appeared at the peak of uneasiness, her face damp with the sweat of terror, and teetering on the verge of fainting.

Her husband pleaded with the writer for the sake of his wife. "Edgar, please, I have asked you to restrain yourself once before. I will not ask you again. I am shocked by your behavior."

Poe put the sword away, grinning. "I do not understand your complaint. Surely, your wife is not that fragile that mere talk would affect her so."

Lady Bledsoe viewed it all as a matter of pride and straightened herself in her chair. "It is perfectly alright, my dear. Let him speak as he wishes."

"See there, Bledsoe, she is much stronger than you care to admit," Poe said, moving ever closer. "Where was I? Ah yes, I know. Would you believe Cain slew his brother, Abel, for savaging sexually one of their sisters, and Ham was disgraced and cursed after abusing his father sexually . . . I read that somewhere."

Lady Bledsoe jumped angrily to her feet and shouted at Poe, "I think you go too far when you bring the Bible into your stupid games. Your books should be banned and burned. Yours is the kind of illness that could poison young minds and send them to eternal damnation."

"It's truly regrettable that you should feel so," Poe replied. "So anything unpleasant or truthful should be ignored, silenced, or rooted out? Is that what you are saying?"

No one said anything for a time. Lady Bledsoe returned to her seat, sitting motionless with her gaze firmly planted on Poe, who was pouring another drink. There was no doubt that he was deriving great enjoyment from it all.

Mr. Bledsoe stepped forward, getting inches away from the writer, his eyes passing from the face of his wife to that of Poe. "I think we have heard enough. You are drunk and obviously not responsible for what you are saying." Then he leaned over and whispered in his wife's ear, "Life does not always have a soft heart." She giggled.

It was in the back of Mr. Bledsoe's mind, the presence of the nigger, Poe's servant. Somehow no matter how much he tried to alter his views on their humanity and worth as one of God's valued creatures, the reality of their foreign appearance and their dark skin overruled any effort for total acceptance of Negroes. "Maybe the Southern planters are right about those nig—" With a loud clap of his hands, Poe interrupted him and said that was a word he did not want to hear under his roof.

Outside, the thunder sounded like the crisp crack of a whip. Poe folded his hands on his chest and watched the couple for several seconds, then he said, "Did I tell you my good fortune? I finally met the Great Man, Charles Dickens. Seven years ago. God, I have not seen you two in quite a while."

His guests looked at each other with some degree of surprise, stunned at his sudden shift of mood and subject. "Edgar, you never stay in one place too long," Mr. Bledsoe replied, coughing from the thick dust in the air. "We cannot chase you about. Now, what is this story about the illustrious Dickens?"

"The rumor on Mr. Dickens," the writer started to say before slowly bursting into guffaws. "The rumor on Mr. Dickens at the time was that he engaged in a strange relationship with his wife and her younger sister. He fornicated with both of them and they lived together in the same house for some time. Well, the younger woman, nearing her fourteenth birthday, had a heart seizure one night in her bedroom and died. No one will say if Dickens was with her at the time. Anyway, the Great Man took a ring from her finger that he wears to this very day."

"Have you seen this ring?" Lady Bledsoe asked.

Poe lied innocently. "Yes, with my own eyes."

The woman was visibly upset with her host. She was perturbed that Poe seemed to possess no sense of loyalty or kind words for anyone. As she scrutinized him, the slender writer paced the floor in his ridiculous uniform, drinking again hearty gulps, refilling his glass to the brim.

"How can you repeat such filth about someone you so admire and respect?" she asked. "How can you?"

The answer was short and biting. "Very easily."

More silence. More drinking. Then Poe was talking again, rambling, incoherent from the spirits. "Believe this, my friends. There is so very little in me but bitterness, sadness, and loss. I miss Virginia so. When I walk the avenue behind charming couples holding hands, oh, how her memory comes back, so full and strong. My heart swells with agony. She was nineteen when she started her decline. The hemorrhaging. Now she is dead. That is the reason for this place, so removed and out of the public eye. I never go out except to go to the cottage out in the country. Sometimes I talk to Silas here. He can be quite entertaining and good company with his fables and tribal folktales. Yet there are other times when the sting of solitude becomes too much for me. Do you grasp the meaning of what I say?"

The Bledsoes nodded in unison, a yes, assuring him that they understood totally. In truth, they possessed no idea of what he was talking about.

"How long have you had Silas with you, Edgar?" Lady Bledsoe inquired.

"Several months now," Poe replied, glancing warmly at the black man. "He is a good man, regardless of his hue."

How did Silas meet Massa Poe? The black man thought back to the occasion when he first spied the slight, shadowy figure walking with his head down through a graveyard one day. About five minutes later, he saw Poe come out of a general store, carrying a bag of dry goods, and when he walked around the corner, there was Poe again, the same man, crossing the street, talking with another white man. How could he be in so many places at once? Yet when he saw Poe again four days later, he asked him for a job as a manservant and got it.

"Silas, were you ever a slave?" Mr. Bledsoe asked the black man brazenly. "Were you ever in bondage?"

Poe frowned as if the white man had violated some unspoken law. "Silas, show him your back. That should answer your questions once and for all, Bledsoe."

Silas walked soundlessly into the center of the room and stripped away his thin white shirt, revealing a network of deep, ugly welts running the length of his broad back. The Bledsoe couple winced at the disturbing pattern of twisting scars marking the dark man's skin. Lady Bledsoe gasped and covered her blanched face.

"My God, man, what happened to you?" Mr. Bledsoe asked with some alarm. "What did you do to deserve such horrible treatment?"

"I refused to dance a jig for my massa's pleasure," Silas said. "The white folks dragged me across the yard from the Big House behind the slave cabins, then chained me to a post. Mr. Davis, the white overseer, ripped my shirt away and began laying the whip across my back. He whipped me until my skin tore away and the pain became so great that I could no longer scream and my legs lost their power. God was merciful and I passed out."

"Maybe you forgot your place and deserved the punishment," Mr. Bledsoe said. "Order must be maintained."

Silas spoke up bravely, his eyes blazing defiantly. "No human being deserves to be treated like a mule or a horse. You don't know what it's like to be examined like livestock, standing butt naked before a group of white folk. A finger in your mouth, hands lifting up your privates, weighing them, being forced to kneel, to spread your butt cheeks for the buyer to see if you got piles. All in front of anybody standing there. Nobody deserves that, no suh."

"That is enough, Silas," Poe said quietly. "Go on about your business. I will call you if I need you." He then apologized to his guests. "Drink goes to my head rather quickly, and I get carried away. Do you accept my apology, my good lady?"

The mood of the visit had changed with the former slave's admissions. Mr. Bledsoe, with a wrinkled brow, stood and walked to the window to see if the rain had stopped. "Edgar, you spend too much time alone. It is changing you. Someone looking at you from afar would accuse you of a haughty, superior affectation. You were not always so."

"Not so, my dear Bledsoe," Poe retorted sharply. "You are entitled to your opinion. Moreover, it matters little to me what you or anyone else thinks. I live my life as I see it."

Silas stepped from the shadows. "More drinks, Massa Poe?"

The writer said nothing. He felt a peculiar pain in his head. Much like the day before. A shift of expression on his face occurred from the worsening agony, and his lips parted in a sardonic grin. "Possibly there is a certain amount of madness in us all. Just as there is perverseness in every human heart; the fact that a lifetime of love can be so easily forgotten in a moment of hatred or revenge is perverse. Am I not correct, Bledsoe?"

"I do not know." His guest admitted his ignorance and glanced at his wife. "All I am saying, Edgar, is that this way of life breeds madness. It is not good to be alone too long."

"Who are we to say what madness is?" Poe asked, biting his fingernail. "Madness may be the highest form of enlightenment. What about slavery? Is it not a form of madness?"

"Speak plainly, man."

"What I am saying, Bledsoe, is that I propose that we are in a system of existence where the totality of things is compelled by a dual process of being endlessly created and destroyed. And therefore . . ."

Bizarrely, Poe stopped in mid-sentence as if hearing voices. Words only he could hear. He started walking toward the door, halting again with his head oddly cocked to the side. A queer sound issued from his lips. He raced from the room into the narrow hall and out into the street and the raging storm. He sprinted across the puddles on the cobblestone road, pursued by the Bledsoes and Silas. They screamed for him to stop, pleaded for him to come back to shelter out of the deluge, but he continued to run. Soon a mongrel, its mangy coat heavy with mud, joined in the chase. Growling, it rushed the trio and Lady Bledsoe fell away in a dead faint, her exquisite dress ruined by the muck. A woman walking by stopped to help her while the others turned the corner in full flight. Sailors laughed at the follies as the cur gave chase to Mr. Bledsoe and the servant, staying hard on their heels.

Silas dodged the beast when it rocketed past him after Poe in his soiled West Point Cadet uniform, the writer's legs windmilling, pumping. Everybody was laughing at him now from underneath their parasols. Even Silas propped himself against one of the buildings and doubled over in a spasm of chuckles. They could see Poe running full out, down the street, darting past people on horseback and in carriages with the dog in determined pursuit. The Bledsoes caught the fever of mirth as well as they watched him fall in the mud, losing one of his coveted Jefferson shoes, up again, falling once more, up again, then stopping to kick at the snarling dog. The mongrel ripped his pants cuff and yanked part of it away, revealing his bare bony leg. Suddenly, the writer was off running again until he disappeared from view as a flailing dot on the misty horizon, still chased by the animal.

That was three days ago. Since that time, all who have called on the writer have been turned away. His friends are worried. Silas greets all visitors with an over-rehearsed long face and the practiced lie: "Massa Poe is away in Baltmo. He be back Friday week."

To himself, Silas mutters and shakes his head, "Crazy white man, crazy out of his mind. Lawd, jes tell me. How did these crazy white folk get to rule everything? Tell me that."

HAVOC AFTER DARK

Don't pity me. I don't need it. I brought this on myself.

This is no lie. I was always the kind of guy who stayed in bad relationships too long, even after the thrill was gone, even after the lovemaking soured. Of course, I could have found me some new young thing if I wanted to invest the time because I'm a lounge lizard by trade. Love the clubs and the nightlife, always have.

Ava, that's the woman I'm seeing now, and I go out every weekend to the elite clubs, hot spots like Sky, Life, Exit, Moomba, Veruka, and sometimes The Tunnel. We used to go to Limelight before the drug busts became a regular event there. But the places we frequent now are the places where models, show-business types, music celebrities go to be seen and get their pictures in the gossip columns of the tabloids. Bad publicity is better than no publicity at all.

None of these joints have the glitz and glamour of the old Studio 54, but they're fun to go to, and you never know who might turn up, people like Donald Trump, DMX, Wynona Ryder, Madonna, Will Smith, Leonardo Di Caprio, Foxy Brown, Lil' Kim, or Maxwell. All the beautiful people. Occasionally, the A-list clubs let wildly dressed nobodies like us in there to add a little spice to the evening, so that's why you see so many people from Jersey waiting patiently behind the velvet rope to enter.

This one night, we went to Purgatory, this club everybody was talking about. Ready to boogie. I'd planned to break it off with Ava that night because I was tired of putting it off and suffering in a relationship that was going nowhere. I knew Ava was difficult when I met her but I thought I could change her. Tone her down some. She was a real hottie, dark, tall, with a killer shape. It was strictly a sex thing with us. She possessed the face of an angel but had the mouth of a Cuban sailor. And the fiery temper to match. You couldn't talk to her. She'd start yelling if she didn't like what you were saying. If you showed any deep emotion, you were a punk and weak. Probably the last straw happened three weeks ago when we had a threesome with another girl, her former roommate, at her urging. I know that's some guys' dream but I'm not with that. I did it reluctantly and now she keeps wanting to do it again. Real lezzie shit. Something's up. Time to bail out of this.

Ava's on the dance floor getting her thing on with some guy, and I'm cooling out at the bar when I noticed this incredible woman sitting on a stool down from me. She was the color of mocha, black but with a hint of dark Spanish features, sultry and irresistibly beautiful. Dressed in a sheer lingerie top and a black latex miniskirt with black stiletto heels. Every now and then, she'd flick her long braided ponytail—the jet-black cord hung down to her ass—glance around, and take another deep drag on the cigar she was holding.

Definitely smitten, I tried to make eye contact but she didn't see me. Or pretended not to notice me. The woman had this weird aura going, this strange power. A few of the other brothers picked it up, too, gliding past her and whispering their best lines into her ear. Her magic. It was in her posture, manner, and dress. Almost regal. None of the real players, the bona fide Romeos, could muster the nerve to approach her and stood watching from the sidelines. But I jumped right into the game. What was I thinking?

I kept my voice full of Barry White cellar bass. "Hello, I'm Curtis. Is this seat taken? Do you mind if I join you?" I swiftly dropped onto the stool before she could reply. Yes or no.

"No, go ahead." She inhaled the cigar smoke and let it out through her nose. "I'm Milan."

"What are you drinking?" It looked like the hard stuff.

"Bourbon. Neat, as the British say."

Needless to say, Milan was more beautiful than Ava ever could be, more alluring, more seductive, more mysterious. How do you talk to a woman who looked this good? The usual gimmicks or jive pickup lines don't work. We went through three rounds of drinks watching the club fill up, and Ava never left the dance floor, but I could feel her eyes on us. The DJ was playing all kinds of stuff, house, techno, hip-hop, reggae, even some old Motown tunes I hadn't heard before from its golden days. Driven by the beats, the crowd was rocking, bursting loose.

"Is that woman your lover?" Milan asked suddenly, nodding toward Ava who was wiggling her ass in front of some black stud in a red muscle shirt and baggie cargo pants.

"She was. Not after tonight."

Her voice became husky, even sexier. "Good. I hate complications and intrigue."

We drank as we talked, sometimes glancing at the dancers cutting up on the floor. I learned Milan was a serious film buff. She mentioned she worked nights but was very vague about the type of job. But what sparked things between us was how passionate she was about the cinema, as she called it. As a film student at NYU, this was the easy part, the hook, so all awkwardness vanished when she launched into this long rap about Ingmar Bergman's movies, *The Seventh Seal, Persona, The Ritual* and *Shame.* The man's deep sense of sorrow and regret, the grim Swedish angst, and total empathy with women. She continued with a lengthy mention of her appreciation of Hitchcock's work, his mastery with tension and suspense, especially *Strangers on a Train* and *Vertigo.* I figured I'd let her dominate the conversation rather than show off with a lot of trivia, although I disagreed with her opinion of Polanski's *The Tenant* and *Repulsion* as masterpieces. Vastly overrated. I favored one of his other films, *Knife in the Water.*

We both agreed there was nothing much currently happening in black films, except looking back at Spike's early stuff, *She's Gotta Have It* and *Malcolm X,* Singleton's *Boyz in the Hood* and *Rosewood,* a gem called *One False Move,* and yes, the very creepy *Eve's Bayou.* Her flawless face lit up with a smile when I said I was a big fan of Bertolucci's *1900, Last Tango in Paris,* and *The Conformist,* warming me behind my zipper and giving me a twitch. She winked all cute as she revealed her fantasy of devouring Dominique Sanda, the actress from the Italian director's anti-fascist film after we mentioned Brando's famous butter scene. Maybe it was my imagination but I'd swear she blushed while chatting about the bloody scenes in Peckinpah's western, *The Wild Bunch,* and the mayhem in his rarely seen *Straw Dogs.* This woman was astonishing with her knowledge of film. Sure, this was another form of seduction, going for the mind rather than the stomach. But it worked with me.

"Name your three favorites," Milan whispered as if asking me to lick her nipples. My armpits dampened.

I finished my drink and ordered another. "Anything by Kurosawa, especially the films with Mifune. Kubrick's *A Clockwork Orange,* all of Fellini's work, Ken Russell's *The Devils* and *Women in Love, Citizen Kane,* Scorsese's *Raging Bull* and *The Last Temptation of Christ.* That's more than three, isn't it?"

"Yes, it is. I bet you like *The Third Man* and *Metropolis,* too, right?" She crushed out the cigar in the ashtray, sliding her stool closer to mine.

"Milan, whose films do you hate?" The entire time we talked, I was not only amazed by how much she knew but how easy it was to be with her. I realized a conversation like this was impossible with Ava, the chickenhead who didn't know one director from the next, cross-cutting from a closeup.

Probably by mistake, Milan's hand touched mine, and a slight electrical charge passed through me. We both laughed, savoring the brief physical contact, and then she went on with her answer. "I hate Woody Allen, too whiny. And he's not even funny. The other one I detest is Truffaut, the French director. Too soft, no balls."

That made me laugh. On the dance floor, the folks were getting their grind on to something slow by Luther Vandross, pelvis to pelvis. This was my cue, my reason to ask her to dance. Though I expected some resistance, Milan got up immediately, walked out to the floor, and slipped smooth and easy into my arms. She was a superb dancer, matching me step for step, dipping and sliding on the sensuous parts of the ballad when I held her tighter. There was no sign of alarm in her face while she moved against me suggestively, setting off an embarrassingly stiff reaction. It even felt as if she brushed her fingers across it intentionally to measure its length and girth. But maybe that was all in my mind. Women don't do that kind of thing, right? We were floating above the floor, that's how it seemed. The others on the dance floor didn't exist, only dim shadows in the background. When the music changed tempo, she turned in a graceful swirl, tossed her head back, the ponytail whipping around like a black snake before she pressed her full body against me. Now there was no doubt what she wanted from me.

The next thing I know, Ava was all in Milan's face, screaming and yelling, "Bitch this, bitch that." She really put on a show, her finger jabbing into the other woman's cheek. "I don't know what you think you're doing, skank. This is my nigga so you better back the fuck up before I get in your shit here and now. I don't play that shit."

Milan squeezed my hand and winked at me, as she surveyed the room. Very cool. She let Ava go off totally, hands on her waist, head bobbing like the hood sista she was.

"He's my man, my man, get that, bitch," Ava shouted loud enough for the DJ to stop the music and the dancers to halt their jamming across the whole floor. Everything stopped. A catfight. The brothers love that, two women going at it.

It was not to be. Milan offered a hard smile, giving my former flame the coldest look I've ever seen. It was scary. Her words, spoken very softly, could barely be heard. "Be quiet, worm, before I silence you for all time."

Now this was the shocker. Ava shut the hell up and walked away like a whipped dog. I was stunned. Because Ava was from the projects, a real hood rat, and running away from a rumble was not a part of her vocabulary. Still, she disappeared into the crowd without a whimper, and that was that. The crowd clapped, cheered, and went back to dancing. Following that little scene, Milan gently took my hand and asked if I wanted to go. We got our coats and left.

Outside, we walked along the snowdrifts in the dark streets, the white mounds glittering and powdery. Winter in Gotham City. It was cold and windy but I barely felt it. My footsteps made a loud, crunching sound on the frozen sidewalk while hers were strangely silent. Like she was a ghost hovering above the ground. Since it was late, there was no one out on the streets in this part of the city.

"How does it feel to be a free man?" Milan asked, locking her arm in mine. "She was beneath you, a different class, not your equal."

"I don't think Ava'll disappear just like that. She's not the type. She'll make my life hell for the next few weeks."

"Personally, I think you've seen the last of her. She won't be bothering you anymore. I know she'll decide it'll be in her best interest to move on. She's not as dumb as she seems."

As cold as it was, every time I spoke, a small cloud would appear before my lips but oddly none materialized whenever this strange and beautiful woman uttered a word. I wanted to mention it but I didn't. Truthfully, I was just happy to be with her.

She saw the cab before I did and stepped out in the street to hail it. The driver pulled over, and we got inside. I could have sworn the driver looked at her in the mirror, nodded submissively, and turned out into the street. We said nothing, only held hands lovingly as the cab found its way over the ruts and icy patches to our unknown destination. I never heard her give him her address. When the cab stopped, it was in front of a large brownstone on the Upper West Side, a nice address in a nice neighborhood.

"It's quite late, maybe I should head on home," I said it but I didn't mean it. Both of us knew where I wanted to be, upstairs, with her in my arms.

"Come up, just for a little while. I want to talk to you about something important. It can't keep until tomorrow. Then you can go home if you still want to."

With that decided, I paid the cabbie and followed her up the stairs to her door, watching her magnificent legs. The door opened as if by magic, because it slid back with a creak, and I never saw a key in her hands. Her apartment was located on the second floor, a roomy two-bedroom show palace with a cozy living room, eat-in kitchen, and sizeable bedroom. Her fabulous scent filled my nose briefly before she reached around to close the bedroom door after the grand tour.

"Let me get us some coffee," she said, smiling.

"I'll help you." I followed her into the kitchen and watched her pick up the coffeepot, then place it on the oven. She showed me where the cups and saucers were in the cabinet, pointing, still smiling. Our faces were inches apart but we didn't kiss. I felt very alive, nervous, my breath suppressed.

"Is there a man in your life?" I took the tray with the cups and saucers into the living room.

Milan stared at me, and I felt a tingle of deep apprehension. "You might be right about your woman. Maybe she won't let you go so easily. She knows you're a good man. Decent. Hardworking and honest. Women know that's the kind of man you don't just throw away."

"Are you involved with anyone right now?" I asked again.

"Oh, you smell really good," she said, pouring the coffee.

"I'm not wearing any cologne tonight. Maybe it's something else."

A spine-twisting chill went through me when she put her head near my neck and sniffed at my collar. "No, Curtis, it's you, your body," she said, smiling again. "You're healthy, pure, abnormally healthy. No infection, no diseases. I can smell it."

"About your lover?"

"Yes, I had a beloved but he's dead." Her tone was cold and sharp as the edge of a knife. She refused to meet my dark, questioning eyes.

"You really miss him, don't you?" A Klimt print on the far wall caught my attention for a short time.

"Yes, some days more than others." Milan said it with an aching sorrow in her words. "Losing him made me see that nothing in life is in our control. We act like it is, but the truth is that it is not. I understood everything when I accepted that death is a part of life. Or at least it was back then."

My heart drummed madly like Elvin Jones running amok on the skins behind a long Coltrane solo. The roar of my pulse could be felt in the tiniest capillaries in my brain where the sensation of fear echoed the strongest. *Get the hell out of here. Something is not right with this sister. Run, fool, run.* But like the idiot I am, I stayed, curious to solve the puzzle of her.

"Don't be afraid," she said, chuckling. "I won't eat you."

My hands barely brought the cup to my lips, the tremors worsening noticeably despite her assurances of my safety. "What do you remember most about your man?"

She sat down on the couch near me, gazed at her cup still on the tray. "I remember it all. Our lovemaking, our fights, our makeups after the battles. He'd say he was sorry, get me flowers, fix me something I loved for dinner, then afterward push me gently against a wall and start kissing me."

Abruptly, Milan rose, covered her face with her hands, sobbing. She ran into the bathroom and locked the door. I could hear the water splashing in the sink and my shouts and pounding didn't persuade her to come out. Minutes passed, a half hour, still no Milan. I was worried. I didn't want a suicide on my conscience.

When Milan exited from the bathroom wrapped in a yellow terry-cloth robe, she was upbeat, her mouth twisted in a wicked smile. "Can you be faithful? Can you be committed to just one woman and not play the field?"

Sexual infidelity. I was never a player. I've always believed in serial monogamy, one woman at a time. That didn't mean there hadn't been times when I wasn't tempted to step out with somebody. Other men feel like I do but we don't get much credit. Still, I understand that infidelity was more the rule than the exception in the new millennium, regardless of the threat of sexually transmitted diseases or the other complications that arise. As my father once told me, any relationship is a constant battle between loyalty and freedom. It was a conflict that so many lost.

I replied that I wouldn't enter a relationship unless I wanted to explore it fully, completely. We argued over whether a person who loved his partner would have an affair, opening the door for discontentment, betrayal, lies. I told her that a loving husband or wife might have an extramarital fling if the opportunity was there, but that didn't mean all was lost. Many marriages survive cheating since sex can be just that, sex. Just release. It can be other things as well: power, control, lust, obsession, perverseness, or just full of contradiction.

"No," she said flatly. "Love means sex and intimacy are reserved for your beloved. If it is handled any other way, then it isn't love."

I didn't understand why she was so emphatic about infidelity. "What's this thing you have about cheating?"

"I am what I am . . . because my man cheated," Milan explained. "He went out into the streets and brought something back. This curse, this infection, home with him. He's dead; he's free. But I'm not."

No black man in his right mind would risk everything for a few quick thrills, especially with a woman like her at home. Hard partying is one thing but nothing is worth death. Or screwing up your health for good. I was grateful that she warned me of her condition before we got into the bedroom and started some serious loving.

"Curtis, it's not HIV or anything like that," she said. "I'll explain later. But back to cheating. It corrupts something special, destroys the magic of your love, by the giving of part of that joy, either sexual or emotional, to someone else outside of the relationship. You spoil everything by bringing another person into your heart, into your bed."

With the AIDS question answered somewhat, I played along with her, assuming the Devil's advocate role. "What is cheating? Going on a date if you're married and kissing and cuddling? Touching each other intimately without penetration? Or is it just plain fucking?"

Milan caressed my neck, stroking the tender skin there. "Honey, it's all cheating. Meeting in secret, not telling your partner or lying about it, telling your new lover things you wouldn't tell your beloved. Cheating is anytime a friendship crosses the line to become a close emotional intimacy deeper than your real relationship. After that, the chemistry changes from flirting to this thing that says: 'I'm available, open to anything.'"

Maybe it was something in the coffee, maybe something in the musky air of the apartment, or maybe the gallon of drinks in the club, but I found myself unable to move.

My limbs would not respond. Paralyzed. She regarded me with this quizzical look that filled me again with fear. So weak, so tired, so dizzy. I couldn't move at all so she reached under me, hoisted me up like an eager groom would carry his bride over the threshold. Like an oddball hallucination. There was no tension in her arms, no muscles showed any strain. Snatched me up as if I were a ten-pound sack of potatoes.

"Humor me, Curtis," Milan said, stopping to put her soft, icy cheek against my warm one. "I'm tired of talking. I need your love. I need you inside me."

"What are . . . are you?" I sputtered in total terror. "What are . . . are . . . are you going to do to me?"

"Be patient, love." Her voice was syrupy sweet. "I've been watching you for a long time. Months. It was no accident that I was there tonight. I was waiting for you, Curtis, just for you."

Talk about optical illusions, special effects. Soon I was naked on her bed without ever having unbuttoned a shirt or shed my pants. Everything happened so fast, in the rapid shuffle of color slides projected before my eyes, snatches of images, or it could have been that time was compressed while I was delirious. I heard her say, "What do you wish, my love? What manner of woman do you like?"

In the dimness of the shaded lamplight, Milan transformed herself into a quick catalog of desirable beauties as we lay there, enjoying the magnificent sensation of entwined flesh. She could become any woman I ever craved. Any woman! Imagine kissing a young Lena Horne just at her blooming best, caressing a willing Dorothy Dandridge at her ravishing peak, matching lips and tongues with an aroused Halle Berry or Whitney before her Bobby Brown days. She could produce these women in the blink of an eye and then morph into someone else just as quickly. As a movie buff, my lust was insatiable for actresses. For a change of pace, she let me sample Ava Gardner from her MGM sex goddess period, Rita Hayworth as Orson Welles first saw her, and Marilyn Monroe at her ass-wiggling apex. I was in heaven. Milan was the eternal vixen, the ageless siren, the ultra-female, all women in one. An endless dream of sensual delights. The ultimate male fantasy of sex, limitless and invigorating, with every desire indulged and fulfilled. Willingly, I let her make me her slave that night. Without any resistance.

In the red mist, Milan shuddered under me, cradled my sweat-drenched face in her hands and kissed it all over. Her body, like an elusive shadow, folded under my bulk, and my senses flooded with the overpowering force of her. Again, the images came, my mouth on her luminous breasts, my hot lips to her hardening nipples, the spreading of her moist thighs and the tasting of her there in the silky thatch of black pubic hair, feeling her swollen bud yield to the intense rhythms of my tongue. Milan bucked violently against my face, locking her legs around my head, while the bright burst of climax exploded inside her, and the room could barely contain the sound of her excited gasps and wails. I didn't cease my oral assault, now feeling her series of orgasms coming in an unending rush of lengthy, almost tortured spasms until she finally pushed her panting self away from me, her black hair in long, wet strands over her gleaming mocha face.

On all fours on the bed after an extended slow session of tender lovemaking, Milan reached out and seized my engorged meat, squeezing it, "I knew you were the one. This is mine. I never share nor do I forgive. Curtis, you are a very unselfish lover. But listen carefully. You must never betray what we have. If you do, the consequences will be extremely grave for you. I will not tolerate cheating in any form."

I was still winded from the sex. "So you're the jealous type, Milan?"

"Yes, very much so. And possessive. I can't stand losing. I hate to lose anything . . . anyone."

Somehow, the question I dreaded asking popped back into my mind. "How did your husband die?"

Her head lifted in slow motion, and her stare was indeed riveting and bestial. Red, burning eyes upon me. "I killed him. He betrayed me. He deserved to die. I'd rather not talk about it."

Gently, Milan pulled me by the legs until I was partially off the bed, watching me with a stern expression while she moved into position to engulf my organ with her extraordinarily long tongue and hot mouth. She worked on me expertly, causing me to grip the sheet, grinding my hips into that indescribable sensation. I clung to her for dear life. Her head bobbed and weaved over me, and I became aware of nothing but euphoric bliss, the crazed thrashing of my limbs, and the crashing of thunder in my head. *I love her. I love her.* To hell with the consequences.

Suddenly, Milan stopped her soft, tender kisses, her cool, clammy flesh on top of me, and her lips opened in the shimmer of the moonlight. Then I saw them, her pearly white teeth, those of a carnivore, the long canines. Her tongue traced the steady pulse of the artery in my neck; I felt the slight pressure of her sparkling fangs as she asked to drink of me. I knew in that terrible instant what she was, what my fate would be. I felt a burning wave of pain mingled with pleasure course through me, a light prick, then a harder bite, heard a sudden sucking sound and experienced the dizzying feeling of being emptied, drained.

Upon finishing her feeding, Milan sat back, sated, droplets of blood trickling from her mouth and chin to the stark whiteness of the sheet. "Sweetheart, would you like to be inside me again?"

It was my fault, that it, my baptism of blood, had gone so far. My lust for her had dulled my reason, pushed my fear of her into the background, and delayed my departure. Just look at what happened. I was so terrified of her, so scared, but fascinated, obsessed beyond my will. A beautiful, murderous monster. Now I understood what had happened to her husband, the man who had infected her with this curse of living death, dooming her to roam the earth in search of blood. And she killed him because he had betrayed their love and eternally damned her. I felt no pity for her or him. I wanted her dead. I wanted to see the end of this heartless monster for bestowing her dark, merciless gift on me.

Her touch was gentle and loving as she washed my thighs with a soft, wet cloth. "Don't try to understand. You never will."

"What have you . . . done . . . done to me?" I still couldn't believe it. A vampire, a damn bloodsucker.

"Curtis, you're not just another pretty boy who will steal my heart, use me for your pleasure, and leave," Milan said, licking a smudge of blood from her arm. "I've taken steps to prevent that from ever happening, ever. My hell is to be immortal and alone. I've outlasted so many lovers through the ages. Do you know how many men I've brought home for dinner, sexed, and not one left alive? You are the first man since my husband to survive the night."

Looking more radiant than ever, Milan ran one slender finger around the red, puffed puncture wounds on my neck, touching the bites with great care, saying we were one for all time. My butt was sticky from the pooled blood on the soaked sheet underneath me.

"I'll teach you everything you need to know," Milan said cheerfully. "How to feed, how to walk about the day without letting the sun sap your power or burn you to death, how to transform yourself into vapor or any animal or human you wish, how to sharpen your survival instincts. All the tricks, Curtis. But your new life will not come without the price of loyalty and fidelity. No infidelity will be tolerated. No exceptions, no excuses."

My eyes devoured the wondrous distraction of her body, and my manhood started to stiffen once more. I was totally confused. Unquenchable lust. Milan was mine, totally mine. I couldn't get my fill of her. I wanted to be inside her once more. Unadulterated lust.

"I'll never leave you," I rasped.

"Darling, I know you won't leave. You have no choice. You need me as much as I need you. Believe me, I sometimes hate what I am and what I must do, but I had no choice in your case. I knew that when I saw you months ago."

"I don't understand any of this," I said, the horrifying image of my blood on her lips in my mind. "What about Ava? She won't just leave us in peace."

Lighting a cigarette, Milan explained what had happened to Ava when she slipped away from me earlier to go to the bathroom. Milan had returned to the club, waited for Ava, rushed the woman in a single blurring move, knocked her to the pavement. Ava tried to run, but the vampire was everywhere at once, before and behind her. Then Milan snatched the struggling Ava high into the air, her legs pumping, her mouth open in a last scream, then bounced her hard on the street and closed her jaws in a viselike grip on her victim's long brown neck. She drained Ava quickly, efficiently, as one would do a squeezed orange and cast her aside. No more competition.

"Are you afraid of me now, like the others?" Milan asked in a low, guttural voice. "Your friend didn't suffer. I just want your love. Are you afraid that you still want me now?"

I knew I was whipped, completely vanquished. In another minute, I entered her again on the bed, plunging deep into her body, joined at the groin, until the vortex of desire tossed us spent ashore on the blood-soaked sheets. Sex had never been like this. Her mouth was nestled at my torn neck the entire time. I could feel the fire of her deadly kiss through my whole being. Exhausted, we fell asleep. I listened for her breath, imagined her labored song when there was none. Silence. There were only my shallow, troubled breaths.

Worn out, I staggered to the bathroom, switched on the light and washed the clots of dried blood from my wounded neck. The image of myself in the mirror was truly sobering. Gaunt, skeletal, I didn't recognize the face before me in the glass. Dark circles around the eyes, parched lips, hollow cheeks, and pale, almost parchment skin. And this was just the first damn night. Burned out. I couldn't survive this for long. Pain, maybe that was what love really is. But I'd be dead in a few weeks at this pace unless . . . I became like her.

It took all of my strength to drag myself back to the other room, struggle into my clothes, and slip on my shoes. I quickly made my decision. I wanted my life back. Not this distorted version of eternal life. A tortured existence of endless predatory nights hunting human snacks. Like a crackhead seeking that next nourishment, that next high. Never ending. Twice I glanced over to see if Milan was still asleep, and once I thought I saw her eyelids flutter. Maybe she was awake. She could suddenly rise, rip out my throat or snap my neck like a stalk of celery. I was afraid, really afraid moving toward the door and the outside world, but I regretted nothing. What was done was done. It was morning, redemptive morning, and a warm, golden sun was already up over the brittle snowdrifts. I walked nobly toward it. No regrets. Soon I'd know peace, sweet peace, peace everlasting.

THE
BLASPHEMER

Of course, there was nobody I could tell my secret. It concerns something Winston Summer, the columnist with the tabloid *The New York Courier*, wrote a few weeks ago. The newspaper was a staple in our household for a long time, since my father thought it carried the best sports section in town and my mother read it religiously to find out what the rich and famous were doing in Monte Carlo, Newport, Paris, and the Hamptons. My mother, who worked much of her life cleaning wealthy white people's apartments until her retirement three years ago after a bad ankle injury, always turned to Summer's column, "The Summer Report," first thing every morning. There she sat at the breakfast table, her nose buried in the paper, devouring his every word while my father groused about the President's latest lie or the slumping Yankees baseball team or the rising cost of gas.

"Honey, I don't know why you read that trash," my father said every morning. "I believe that man makes that mess up. Nobody can be everywhere at once. Probably most of it is lies and something he dreamed up."

My mother would remain quiet, ignoring him and drinking her coffee. I'd read his column as she was finished with the paper and imagine what Summer's glorious life must be like. I couldn't imagine how it could be to have such rich and powerful friends. To know everybody worth knowing. To be feared and adored.

Then there was that dreadful morning when all of the newspapers ran articles about the tragic suicide of his young model-wife, a queen of the runway and print ads, on their front pages. Even the subdued *Times* gave the bloody death major play, detailing how

Claudette, his alluring twenty-four-year-old French wife killed herself at the peak of her fame. She ate a cup of yogurt, a brownie,
drank a small bottle of Evian water, undressed, locked herself in the
bathroom, put a .45 automatic in her mouth, and pulled the trigger. The beautiful model was the third Mrs. Summer. The other
two marriages ended in divorce. The *Post* called her Summer's
"child bride" and ran a grainy photo of the columnist leaving the
morgue, wearing dark glasses and a fedora pulled down over his
face. His own paper, *The Courier*, said he was "inconsolable" and
"in seclusion."

My father dialed me at the job and asked if I could stop by the
house before going to my apartment near Lincoln Center. The de-
tour was out of the way, inconvenient, because my parents lived on
the once-fashionable Sugar Hill in Harlem. Something was bothering him. I could hear it in the tone of his usually cheerful voice, his
choice of words, and his abrupt manner.

"What's happening, Dad?" I asked. "Is it Mom? Is she alright?"

He didn't say anything, only that she was taking the death of
Summer's wife really hard. Too hard, if you asked him. She didn't
even know this young white girl. But then she had been distraught
for days when Jackie O and Princess Diana died. Couldn't eat,
couldn't sleep, barely got out of bed. You would have thought these
folks were relatives, kinfolk cut down in the prime of life by the way
she mourned them. Deep, heartfelt grief.

"It's that damned Summer and his column that's done this to
her," my father snarled. "I told her to not take that shit so seriously.
That white man don't give a damn about her, and here she's a
wreck because his crazy wife blows her brains out. I don't get it. But
we've been through this before with all of the Kennedy deaths. I'd
probably have to commit her if something happened to Dr. Ruth,
Judge Judy, or Oprah. Damn that Summer to hell. Damn phony.
Thinks he's God."

For the most part, I agreed with my father, because Summer
seemed to know everyone and everything. When I was in the
eleventh grade, Summer was asked to come to my school to speak
about the importance of the press, and the entire student body

filed into the musty auditorium to listen to the well-dressed man
with the matinee-idol looks. Clad in his stylishly tailored dark blue
Italian suit, Summer spoke in his typical fast-talking way used in
his nightly radio broadcasts, every word off the top of his head,
without any notes, then he answered questions from the kids.
Usually with a quick quip, practiced wisecrack, or a smart-ass joke.
But he made a big impression on me. Maybe that was why I joined
the esteemed fraternity of reporters after college, entering the field
of journalism with the highest of hopes. That school visit occurred
more than twenty years ago, and it still comes to mind whenever I
see his column.

A certain aura of mystery surrounded Summer. Whereas everyone else seemed to grow old, the black-and-white photograph of
Summer never did. It seemed unnatural that the newspaper didn't
update the photo since it was the same one used above Summer's
byline from my childhood. Even his recent TV appearance shot at
the morgue showed a man who looked much the same as the one
who spoke to my class two decades earlier. Not a wrinkle more, not
an extra ounce of weight. Personally I thought the whole thing was
more than a minor oversight or error of judgment; it was dishonest,
almost criminal. Not that the newspaper wanted to hype the fact
that its prized columnist was getting old but there was such a thing
as truth in advertising. And the other thing was this man was at
least sixty-five, if he was a day, and the publicity photo showed a
man in his mid-thirties, robust, in the prime of health.

As a young man in my twenties, I was first assigned as a reporter
to a general assignment post at the *Daily News*, covering fires, library openings, shootouts, robberies, bad weather, people falling
under subway trains, gang warfare, church vandalism, and the like.
I rather enjoyed it, starting from the bottom, proving myself to the
ever-watchful veterans and editors. In the past, a young reporter
could work for years before being promoted to one of the special-
ized departments such as entertainment, business, sports, or City
Hall. When my father complained that the quality of the newspaper was below my talents, I usually tuned him out because there
weren't that many jobs for blacks at newspapers back then. Add to

that: the number of newspapers was dwindling rapidly all across the country. Why couldn't Dad be thankful that I was working in my chosen field? How many black men could say that?

Something remarkable happened one day several months ago. I was covering the umpteenth anniversary of *Cats* on Broadway and was walking from the subway to the gala celebration. There had been a police action on the train, meaning the cops were arresting some rowdies, so I was running late. And there was Winston Summer, in the flesh, walking near the Helen Hayes Theatre on West Forty-fourth Street. It was unbelievable. Summer looked just as he did in the timeless publicity photo from his newspaper column. Unlined face, bright eyes, thick black hair, smooth ivory complexion. Damn, he didn't even look thirty-five up close. I suppose the term *ageless* not only applied to Johnny Mathis and Dick Clark, but to Winston Summer as well.

I watched him stop to stare up at the marquee while some tourists slowed their step to gawk at him, but none of them went over to speak. They knew better. He had a reputation for being a real bastard if approached on the street. He loved his privacy when dealing with the common man. Still, I took a chance and walked over to him, pulling out my *Daily News* reporter's notebook to give myself some credibility. And courage.

"Mr. Summer, uh . . . uh . . . uh my name is Greg Harewood," I stuttered, extending my hand. "I'm a reporter at the *Daily News* . . . uh . . . uh a long-time fan of your column. I just wanted to meet you, sir."

He looked down at my hand but didn't shake it, making a sour face. "Glad to meet you as well. Always good to meet a loyal reader, even if he's employed at a rival paper. Got to run. Take care."

You've got to understand, this was Winston Summer, the master of contemporary gossip columnists, carried in more than 250 newspapers with thirty million readers nationwide. He was also an influential radio host who was frequently a late-night TV guest on *Letterman, The Tonight Show,* and that Conan guy's program. He was big, bigger than Walter Winchell, Ed Sullivan, Dorothy Kilgallen, or Hedda Hopper in their heyday. A living legend.

I tried not to think about the slight of the ignored handshake, the sneer, the whole prejudice bit. After all, Summer was a white man and played the part to perfection. In fact, I was amazed at how briskly he walked through the midday crowd in Times Square, head up, shoulders squared like General Patton reviewing the troops. As if he was superior to everybody and everything. The filthy masses.

It was the middle of winter two years later when I saw him next, sitting in a secluded corner booth in a Greenwich Village bar. He looked just as he had when I saw him last in the theater district. Unchanged. Dorian Gray himself. Timeless.

This time he noticed me. "Mr. Greg Harewood, am I correct?" He slurred the words. It was obvious he was drunk, from the uncontrollable tongue, the glassy eyes, the tremor of the neck, and the row of emptied glasses on the table before him.

I was shocked to see Summer so juiced in public, for everybody knew the man had a long list of enemies, powerful ones, who would love to get a photo of him like this for publication in a rival paper. He seemed so vulnerable, almost human. Lucky for him, this bar was off the beaten path, on a dark side street. A cozy neighborhood tavern. Maybe that was why he chose it to let his hair down. Carefully I eased over to his table and extended my hand. This time he shook it warmly and asked me to sit with him.

"What are you drinking, Mr. Harewood?" he asked between sips.

"I don't know. What are you drinking? Maybe I'll have some of what you're having. I'm surprised you remembered my name. It's been awhile and you meet so many people."

"I never forget a name or a face," Summer replied with a dry smile. His eyes were yellowish, cloudy from drinking. "That's important in my business. Know what I mean?"

I was impressed since my memory sometimes failed if someone I met during a story just ten months ago walked up and introduced themselves. So many stories, so many names. Everything was just a blur now. Lost to the whirlwind of time.

"Vodka," he announced wearily with a loopy smile, holding up a half-empty glass. There was something pathetic in the way he said it.

I ordered the same, and the drink arrived in no time. He eyed me for a moment, silently weighing my intentions, then continued drinking. Only a real lush could down the stuff the way he was doing it. A real hollow-leg man. The way he was sizing me up made me uneasy. I didn't know what he had on his mind.

"How much do you know about Winston Summer, Mr. Harewood?" Summer asked, leaning back in his seat, his fingers laced behind his elegant head. "I mean, about Summer the man. Not the celebrity. The damn man."

"Probably as much as most people, from his columns."

"There's so much more going on there than what you read," he said, snorting mysteriously. "A real scoop. A fucking story big enough to get you a job at *The Times*. You could write your own ticket. Man, could I give you an earful."

He stopped suddenly and rested his head on his arms, the liquor hitting him solidly between the ears with almost knockdown force. I knew that feeling well, the spinning sensation, the throbbing at the temples, the queasiness in the stomach. The out-of-body feeling. It was one of the reasons why I was never a big drinker—the aftereffects, the vertigo, the pounding headache of the morning after. He ordered one more drink for him and another for me.

"Greg, I want out," he lisped. "I'm sick of what I do. It used to be fun but now it's tedious. Boring. It's a chore now."

"Maybe you need a vacation, some time away."

"I can't leave, they won't let me," he said mournfully. "It's not about what I want. It's what they want. And they want me to work until I can't anymore. I'm a damn slave."

"Who is . . . they?" I couldn't imagine the Great Summer bowing down to anybody, his bosses, his editors included. With his large readership, the newspapers needed him, not the other way around.

"And I miss my wife, my Claudette so. They don't miss her, only me. Only I understand what she went through before the end. She suffered greatly but they didn't care. They didn't give a damn about her or what unhappiness she was forced to endure. One day, they'll pay for everything they did to her. Everything."

Suddenly Summer glanced up and saw a large bear of a man in a chauffeur's uniform standing at the door. I thought my eyes caught a momentary expression of panic and fear crossing his smooth face before he caught me looking at him. With the cool style that was the Summer trademark, he finished his drink, occasionally glancing in the direction of the chauffeur, before finally asking me to call him in two days at a phone number he gave me. Private line. "We need to talk," he added in a whisper, "seriously talk." He repeated the number twice to guarantee that I had it right. Then the Great Man rose gracefully from his seat, straightened his tie and walked out to the limousine at the curb.

The grip of the mystery surrounding Summer worked on my mind for more than a month without letup. Though I was curious, I steered clear of the columnist; the tease of the puzzle persisted but I decide not to get involved. Eventually my curiosity compelled me to check into something about the man. Summer understood the power of the press and mined rumors and hearsay for everything they were worth. Scandal, his stock in trade. Doors were slammed in his face during the early days of his career. Twice his victims beat him down after he ruined them. He prowled gatherings, parties, and openings, looking for exclusives. Only A-list events. His prominence grew with each passing year. All around town, press agents and publicists kissed his butt, hoping to get a word about their clients in his column, a good mention rather than a snub or worse. He never seemed to sleep, eternally haunting the night. He kept an ear open for dirt from police calls. Since he was lavish with tips, he could milk a lead from hat check girls, headwaiters, men's room attendants, waiters, and busboys.

Summer was a strange one to figure. Only the truth, right? He never retracted a wrong item, never seemed to fear legal retaliation, never worried about smearing innocent parties. Totally hard-boiled. Libel and defamation of character were not in his vocabulary. Or fear. Even a whacked-out mob chieftain threatening to break all of his bones didn't rattle Summer after he ran an item about the man's wife leaving him for a rival capo. A Cardinal, who shall remain unnamed, called him a loud-mouthed SOB after a blind item about a group of priests having carnal relations with their altar boys in a town outside of Chicago. Nothing was private, taboo, or off limits.

The owners at *The Courier* tried to cover their backside by saying there would be prompt redress given to anyone victimized by an unfair or inaccurate story. No exceptions. That never happened. Summer wrote columns that drew blood and cut the legs from under the careers of anyone foolish enough not to dodge his evil eye. When his first wife, Blanche, left him ten years ago after a rival columnist revealed his three mistresses, his style became mean, even ruthless. No quarter given, no mercy shown.

One of the usual items from his column would read something like this:

> So-So, that MGM designer, is broke and cracked up in a nuthouse in Paris . . . Talk has it that a sexy R&B songbird is that way with girls and her bad-boy hubby doesn't mind . . . Locals expect the black Congressman in Harlem to resign before spring with a liquor problem . . . A certain A-list actor's mistress has X-rated photos and is demanding her lover leave home or she's going public . . . A well-known show biz couple, popular for their work in the Bard's plays on the Great White Way, are unhappy in their union and the mister wants her to stay close to home. She says no way . . . One of the heirs of the mighty Van Eyck fortune loves dark meat and Daddy's threatening to cut her off unless she stays out of the jungle haunts uptown. . . .

Following one long night waiting out a hostage situation, I dragged myself home, thinking of a nice cool drink, a hot soak in the tub, and zoning out on the tube. The key turned silently in the lock and the door opened with a tiny yawn. What the hell! It was an image I would carry to my grave, Summer sitting on my sofa, calmly smoking a cigarette. He'd found where my booze was stashed and had helped himself to a drink. My entrance into the apartment did nothing to shatter his nonchalant pose. He took a deep inhale on the cigarette, drawing the nicotine into his lungs, and turned to face me, with the smoke issuing from his nostrils.

"How in the hell did you get in there?" I asked, slightly salty. I remembered the door was locked, not jimmied.

"Greg, you didn't call me so I had to look you up," he said. "I hope my visit doesn't inconvenience you but it was important we talked. Is that okay?"

I was angry and smooth talk wasn't going to soothe my nerves. "No, it's not alright. How did you get in here? I don't appreciate people breaking into my apartment. It doesn't matter what their intentions are."

Summer smiled. "I gave your landlady a small tip and she let me in. Now that the subject of my crime is out of the way, can we talk as friends?"

"About what?"

"The scoop, the big story I promised you. It won't cost you anything. I need you to trust me. Will you do that? Can you forgive what I've done with the landlady and trust me on this one? You won't be sorry, I assure you."

"Maybe. What do I have to do to get this big scoop?" I didn't want him to think I was desperate, that I would do anything to get it.

Summer got to his feet, went over to my cabinet, removed the bottle of Scotch and poured some into a glass on the table. The glass was already there so this was planned. Smiling, he walked to me and handed it to me. The drink felt good going down. I sat on the sofa and watched him take a cell phone from his pocket and dial. He spoke softly, telling someone that we'd be right down, to have the car ready.

Upon finishing my drink, I asked Summer what was next. He walked behind me, picked up my coat, and helped me into it, all the time wearing that sinister smile. Then he said it was time to go. We walked to the elevators, got inside and said nothing until we got into the long black limousine waiting in front of the building. In the car, the man leaned over, whispered for me to close my eyes, then secured a blindfold over my face. I listened to the sounds of the city as the limo sped through the streets—sirens, car horns, irate shouts of the driver at other cars—until finally we came to a halt in an underground garage.

Slowly, I was helped into the building and ushered along a hallway to an elevator before they removed the blindfold. The driver nodded and walked back the way we'd come. We continued inside and Summer pressed a button and up we went. What was all this about? Why the secrecy? Was this some kind of setup? Was my life in danger? What was this guy planning to do? I braced myself, getting ready for whatever went down.

Summer moved quickly through the hall and finally stopped before a door, knocked three times, paused, then knocked three more times. A secret code? I almost jumped out of my shoes in surprise. The door was opened by a man who resembled Summer down to the last detail, every facial feature, every strand of hair. He even moved like Summer as he crossed the room where three other duplicates of the writer sat around a table playing cards. I must have stood with my mouth open because the Summer replica who had brought me there smiled warmly and mumbled, "Now you know."

"Now I know what?" I shouted. "I don't know a damn thing."

The four other Summer duplicates, all dressed similarly to the first one, returned to their card game quietly, totally ignoring us. I glanced around the apartment, which was magnificently furnished with the kind of classy furniture one would see in *House Beautiful*, nothing cheap or vulgar but completely understated and elegant. The first Summer waved for me to take a seat, and I dropped wearily on a chair. Nothing had prepared me for this.

"Let me start from the beginning. Winston Summer always wanted to be important," the first Summer said. "If you knew him in those early days, he was temperamental, high-strung, excitable, and quite nervous. But he had two faces like the Greek god, Janus. On one hand, he could be easygoing, calm, understanding, and tolerant. But there was another side, the self-destructive part of him. Everyone knows he smoked four packs of unfiltered cigarettes a day and you can imagine what his lungs looked like. He pushed his body to the absolute limit."

I sat back in the chair, staring first at the Summer duplicate in front of me, then at the quartet of other Summers gathered at the table. "I don't get it. What are you guys? Robots, clones, androids? What?"

"We'll get to that in a few minutes," he said. "The strain of doing the daily column, the late-night carousing, the squabbles with his wives, the battles with his editors, the lawsuits, all got to him after awhile. They all took a toll."

"You speak of him as if he's dead," I said.

"No, he's not dead. But there are plenty of people who wish he was dead. Summer was one mean, clever man. He'd win your confidence, get you to talk, to forget yourself, tell you it's all off the record and then you'd see your innermost secrets in his column the next day. He's ruined thousands of lives. And he never cared."

"Where is Summer if he's not dead? Where are you hiding him?"

The first Summer duplicate stood gracefully and nodded for me to follow him. I glanced at the others, expecting some kind of reaction, but they sat stone-still at the table, still engrossed in their cards. We walked down a long hallway toward the open door of a room where the sound of medical machinery, the whir and hiss of life-prolonging technology, could be faintly heard. I stepped into the room behind the duplicate and saw a little, frail old man with a wizened, wrinkled face outstretched on a bed, attached to a portable oxygen tank and other devices. He was dressed in finely embroidered red Chinese silk pajamas.

"Sir has been like this now for several years. His mind is in a complete fog," the duplicate said. "The final stages of Alzheimer's disease. He knew something was wrong with him when he started misplacing things, forgetting names, places, and appointments. He tried to act for years as if his mind was not slipping but finally he even lost the ability to write."

I stared at the old man in shock. He looked like he was ninety-something, fading fast at Death's door. The duplicate looked at me sadly as the wrinkled form thrashed on the bed and started to shriek. Dementia. I felt unsteady for a moment. The Great Secret. The Scoop, this was it! The duplicate went over to him, speaking softly like a mother would do with an agitated child, comforting him. After a few strokes of a gentle hand across the old man's furrowed brow, he quieted and closed his eyes.

"Does anyone know he's like this?" I couldn't believe it.

"No one except Mr. Agnew, the corporate high-tech mogul," the duplicate explained. "Mr. Agnew, the owner of a robotics firm in California, built all five of us some time ago as a gift of gratitude for a kindness bestowed upon him by the writer. The whole affair was conducted in the utmost secrecy. Each of us is an exact replica of the young Sir in every regard."

I was numbed by the revelation. "That's why everyone thinks he's damn ageless."

The duplicate laughed, the first time since I'd met him. "It's a rather cruel joke, isn't it?"

"And you guys take turns playing him in public?" I asked, watching the old man stare at me with intense, frightened eyes.

"Before Sir became seriously ill, a colored woman used to look after him but he fired her," the duplicate said in a monotone. "He felt she knew too much of his business. I think Sir knew he was becoming senile and didn't want anyone outside of Mr. Agnew to know it. And us, naturally. He didn't want people to know he was old and dying. Remember he was a very, very vain man. He didn't want people crying over him, recalling old stories, or staring at him like he is now. So he made the woman disappear."

I felt bold. "Like you did with his third wife, Claudette."

"No, we didn't kill her. She killed herself after finding out our little secret. It was all too much for her. She was never too stable anyway."

I sagged against the wall. "Where do I fit into this grand scheme of lies and deception?"

"You're the future, fresh blood, fresh ideas," the duplicate said, putting his arm around my shoulders. "We need you. We want to update the column, jazz it up. And that's where you come in. You'll be the new Sir, so to speak. We'll do the legwork and you'll put together the column, choose the items. We'll work for you."

"But Summer's a white man and I'm black." I shook my head. This was crazy.

The duplicate smiled, another rare moment. "So damn what! That doesn't matter. We're equal opportunity employers here. Nobody will know anything about your connection to the column."

I shook my head again, not believing any of this, staring at him in horror. They could never let me go with what I know. If I tried to leave, they could never let me live. I was trapped, doomed by my own stupidity and greed.

"But I have a life," I pleaded. "I have a family and friends. People know me. They'll miss me. You can't do this!"

The duplicate patted me on the cheek with his big, soft hand. "It's a done deal. We've already discussed you joining us and everybody agrees. You'll live here like a king. Your every need will be met. And the column will be better than ever. We've always wanted to feature more colored personalities in it . . ."

I corrected him, "African-American personalities."

The duplicate gave me a tolerant look. "Yes, more African-American personalities, and you'll help us do that. Sir could be somewhat prejudiced. He didn't care too much for the colored . . . ah . . . ah . . . African-Americans."

"No, no, this is bullshit." I pushed him away from me. I'd never known real terror in my life until that moment. *They could make me disappear, vanish like that woman, and no one would ever know the truth.*

While I was quickly losing my composure, two other duplicates entered the room, moving efficiently and swiftly as if performing a pre-arranged football maneuver, and walked over to the bed. One duplicate turned off the oxygen. The other covered the twisted face of the confused, frantic ex-columnist with a pillow. The duplicate put all of his weight on the pillow until the skeletal old man stopped fighting and went limp. I went berserk after seeing that and ran for the door but the other duplicates blocked my way and wrestled me to the floor. I screamed that they couldn't do this. I'd be missed! They wouldn't get away with it! Someone would come looking for me, and their secret would be discovered. One duplicate placed a hot hand over my mouth as another one shot me up with something that made me woozy. On cue, the quartet stood like robots in a row, rigid, with their vacant, lifeless eyes on the first Summer clone. He nodded and they went back to their game.

Quietly, the first clone kneeled next to me, cradling my spinning head. He cooed gently to me that I shouldn't worry, that everything would be just fine. They would take care of me. Slowly the drug totally seduced me, and I fell asleep in his arms, wrapped in a plush, luxurious nightmare from which there was no escape.

ARBEIT MACHT
FREI

Spring 1945

There is no terror like that of war. No one who has ever faced the hell of battle is ever the same—the sprawl of the bodies on blood-drenched soil, the whistling of the bullets seeking their target, the roar of explosions, and the agonizing screams. The screams of men wounded and dying. I was nineteen and totally confused. As a colored soldier, I was glad to have a job driving a jeep with Lieutenant Minot, the white officer in charge of our convoy. Minot was good as white men went, a far sight more humane than the cracker officers who tortured us during training down South. They were no better than Klansmen, with their racist catcalls, cruel punishments, and red-cheeked rage at the sight of "rank smelling nigger apes" in U.S. Army uniforms. Most of the colored troops didn't go off post for fear of getting killed. Hell, I would have never joined the service if it were not for my father and his patriotic speeches about making the white folks see that we have an investment in the country, too, that we were ready to die for America.

Colored couldn't eat or sleep or work anywhere they wanted but we were ordered to die for the very folks who hated us. When I said this to my father, he slapped the hell out of me and walked off. The push was on to sign up colored soldiers. The Army even had Joe Louis and Bojangles Robinson saying we should join up. Dr. Mary McLeod Bethune, who had pull at the White House, was saying it too: "Don't act like they expect us to act" and "be proud to serve your country." General Benjamin Davis said the same thing but their words didn't stop the abuse or the white folks' spit sliding down our faces. Some of the German prisoners of war were treated better than us. Someone asked General Ike about the mistreatment of the colored troops and he acted like he didn't hear the question.

The High Command always sent the colored soldiers where the fighting was heaviest. It was one of the worst battle zones in Europe after D-Day. We were waiting for the first signs of light so we could press on through the area where the Germans had their most seasoned soldiers outside of Russia. The convoys accompanying the advancing Allied troops met stiff resistance, and took big losses, coming under intense mortar fire and snipers. The Krauts shot up another convoy carrying medical supplies, strafing the trucks, killing a doctor and four nurses.

Fortunately the assault was moving too fast for the Krauts to launch a serious counterattack. And the Russian soldiers were moving faster than we were. Hitler miscalculated when he got them stirred up. The Reds often plowed ahead, taking heavy casualties, sacrificing large numbers of men and material, but never giving ground. In fact, we often had trouble knowing where the front was. Occasionally, Nazi warplanes would swoop down out of the clouds and strafe the roads. The trees offered no real protection from their deadly machine-gun fire and anyone caught in the open was a sure bet to be killed.

As we moved up along the road, Minot told me to drive off into a field, toward a cluster of trees, and onto the high ground so he could see the terrain. We could see black smoke billowing into the sky in the distance. He shouted for the other jeeps and trucks not to bunch up. One of the other officers came up, and the two men consulted their maps, looking up at the angle of the sun and glancing down at a compass.

"Sir, I think we should recon the area up ahead," the other officer said to Minot. "It might be crawling with Krauts."

"No dice," Minot replied. "I got orders. I've got to get these supplies and men to Sector Six before nightfall."

"That could be murder, sir," the other officer said. "At the speed we're going, we'd be dead ducks if the Krauts decide to hit us. We're out in the open."

Suddenly, Minot gave the order for us to haul ass out of there, and the convoy started again over the road toward our destination. I looked at the two white men still jawing over what should be done. The enemy was still dangerous, although we had him on the run. We had been chasing him for three weeks, and all of the men were dead tired. The Germans were retreating, destroying bridges, laying mines along the roads and sometimes ambushing our front guard before disappearing in the dark again.

"I don't like it, sir," the first officer protested.

"Neither do I but I got orders." With that, Minot jumped back into his jeep.

As I was about to start the jeep, I heard the whine of incoming artillery. The first blast took out two trucks on the road and the other vehicles scrambled for cover. We dived on the ground beside the jeep as another shell whistled over our heads and landed in the midst of a group of men running. There was smoke, flames, and parts of bodies raining on the field. Screams came from all over. Another shell crashed about three hundred yards from us and tossed a truck up into the air like a child's toy. All hell broke loose. More shells came over and Minot yelled, "The Krauts have us in range, run for cover." I was crawling, hugging the ground, when I heard the whine of another incoming shell and felt the texture of the air change as it drew closer. Everyone ran as fast as they could away from the jeep. I was kissing the ground when it hit nearby. Someone screamed he'd been hit, yelling about where were his legs. The officer who had been arguing with Minot wiggled past me on the ground, with streams of blood running down his face under his helmet.

"They got the lieutenant," he said in a rasp to me, his eyes wild.

The barrage picked up in intensity and soon we were up and running. All of the survivors ran every which way, shouting, cursing, and praying. There were a lot of dead and wounded and no time to pull anyone to safety. I got dirt in my eyes, and my helmet cut into the back of my neck, but I didn't stop running. The song of the next shell was so close that its sound seemed to fill my head just before the thing hit and shook the ground, throwing dirt into the air all around us. I dropped down, put my hands over my face, drew my legs up under me, and waited to die. From where I was hiding, I

could see three of our men running across a gully, dragging another
wounded soldier with them. Then there was small arms fire, a machine gun barked, and the men disappeared from view.

"I told him," the officer with the wild eyes said sadly. "The SOB
wouldn't listen."

Despite the murderous gunfire, I grabbed my M-1 rifle, gasped
for breath, and ran for the gully where the men disappeared. It was
the only safe spot left where we were crouched in the open field.
The wild-eyed officer followed me in a low trot, head down.
Another truck took a direct hit, exploded and rolled over on its side
in flames. Men were trapped inside it, screaming and clawing at the
doors. There was nothing anyone could do because the Germans
were advancing behind the artillery fire. We watched and listened
to the men fry. We couldn't make it to the gully because machine-
gun bursts were raking the earth at our feet. With the shells drop-
ping and the bullets kicking up ground, we turned and ran back the
way we had come, with our hearts pounding from fear.

"Haul ass, soldier," the wild-eyed officer yelled as he ran ahead of
me. Suddenly, a burst of automatic fire twisted his body, slung it to
the ground and the man laid there with two large holes in his chest.

I jumped over him, running in a crouch through the hail of bullets, some of them so close they burned my face as they whistled
past. Another soldier ran right by me, a big colored guy, doing his
best Jesse Owens impersonation. Man, could he run! I followed
him, almost matching his Olympic stride, up a small hill, down a
little path, into the trees. Two of the German planes, Stukas, came
in low, strafing as well as bombing, shooting at the scurrying dots on
the ground. We could see a large supply truck racing along the road,
weaving among the burning wrecks, trying to drive through the barrage of gunfire to safety. The planes went after it, and then there
was a loud explosion and the truck vanished in a fantastic roar of
fire, splintering glass and folding steel.

Finally, we reached a trench on the other side of the road and discovered it was full of dead and wounded. Soldiers had bits of them
torn or burned away. Nearby, a grime-covered sergeant shouted at
the soldier who had been running with me, mainly curses, but his
words were drowned out by the angry chatter of the enemy guns.

We were getting the shit kicked out of us. Just as the sergeant began yelling again, a shell landed in the trench not far from him. He tried to move out of the way but something shrieked past us, taking his head with it. His body continued in motion for a few seconds more, one foot before the other, while a geyser of bright red blood shot up from his shattered neck. Everything was happening so fast. I was beyond fear in a place inside my head where it all seemed unreal.

The soldier who had been running with me said he wasn't sticking around. That sounded like a good idea. He stood, slid his rifle under his arm, and adjusted his helmet. The sky was strangely quiet, very eerie. No more diving planes. No more incoming artillery shells. That didn't last long. It all started up again. Another barrage with more force than before. It was the Krauts' last gasp. They knew it and we knew it.

The two of us ran along the trenches, hopping over the mangled and bleeding men, up and over the side. Not once did we look back. Behind was Hell or the earthly version of it.

"What's your name?" the soldier asked as he flopped on his stomach and began crawling.

"Emmitt," I answered, wiping the stinging smoke from my eyes. "What's yours?"

"My friends call me Ted," he replied, pushing his rifle ahead of him. He was tall, nut brown, solid, and talked in a mild voice.

We didn't say much after that until we had worked our way along the small ridge where we could look straight down on the vista of destruction. Fire, wreckage, smoke, and bodies everywhere. Beyond the grove of trees and bushes down below was a railroad bridge, partially destroyed and smoking. Behind us, we could still hear the shells coming down and the diving German planes having their fun. I didn't want to think about all of the men dying back there.

"We can wait until things ease up a bit, then go back," Ted said. "It'd be crazy to go back there now."

I said nothing, fingering a slight wound on my right arm.

Ted turned and looked at me. "I didn't want to be in this mess anyhow. Remember the Detroit riots two years ago? The white and colored workers fought in the war factories because the crackers didn't want us getting decent housing. I'm from there. Detroit. Couldn't get any work. Plus, I had a young wife, just married for a year, so I joined up. I trained at Camp Lee. Do you know the place?"

"In Virginia. A lot of colored come through there."

He lit a cigarette and took off his helmet. His big hands shook so much that they looked like they were vibrating. "I wanted to be an officer, make money to send home, even applied to OCS. Didn't do me any damn good. Still ended up handling food, supplies, and ammo. The honkies try to keep us away from battle, or at least keep us where we won't shoot a gun but we still end up in harm's way. The last thing they want is a brave nigger. Shit, we segregated and still getting killed. Where you from, kid?"

"A little town in Pennsylvania, near Pittsburgh. Steel country."

"Did you go to England?" Ted asked, putting out the butt on his shoe heel, saving half of it. "How did they treat you? Bad, right?"

"Yeah," I said, thinking of how difficult it had been for us there. The white American soldiers told the English all kinds of lies on us, how we had tails, how we had dicks so big that we would cripple their women, how we were unclean and could make them sick if they got too close to us.

Ted read the frown on my face. "But the Limeys knew what the story was. Especially the women. I got more loving there than I did back home. Those English girls love dark meat."

"I didn't mess with them," I said, averting my eyes from his face.

We lay there quietly, watching a platoon of German soldiers walk along a road below us, and then that old familiar whine of a shell coming over our heads. It landed near the Krauts, who ran for cover, but some of them didn't make it. More shells dropped among them. We cheered. Our side was finally shooting back. No more retreat.

Ted got up and grabbed his rifle. "I want some Kraut blood."

"Let it stop shelling," I called to his back as he ran off. "Hold up! Wait for me!"

He led the way down the ridge, zigzagging among the bushes, and hopped a fence onto the same road where the Germans were earlier. It was deserted except for two overturned, burning jeeps and the bodies of dead enemy soldiers. We started along the curve when we heard the sound of a motor coming up fast behind us. As it neared, we ducked for cover, rifles ready. It was a German staff car with two Krauts on motorcycles escorting it. Ted motioned in sign language for me to shoot the two Krauts on the bikes and he'd get the driver. I nodded and waited for the Germans to come into view. The bikes roared up, with one rider glancing back, obviously distracted by the shells coming in. I put a bullet right between his eyes and he flipped over, taking the bike with him. The other Kraut glanced in my direction a couple of seconds before the second bullet found his throat and he skidded off the road. We heard the crash of his bike. Meanwhile, Ted drilled the driver of the car with one long automatic burst and the vehicle jerked to a stop. We ran toward it, guns at the ready. I pulled back the door and yelled for whoever was inside to get the hell out, with his hands up.

This very tall German, blond and blue-eyed, stepped out of the car, the full Nordic look. He carried himself like a general, all proud and arrogant, but he was dressed in civilian clothes. What the hell! He looked at us, two black beasts, and sneered. Ted pushed him with his gun into the side of the car, and we searched him for weapons. He didn't like us touching him. Our dirty nigger hands soiling his pure white flesh.

"Look out!" Ted suddenly shouted.

I turned quickly and saw the German with the neck wound lunging at me with a knife. I tried to sidestep him but he got under my gun and nicked me on my bad arm with his knife. He swung at me with the knife once more, and I smashed him in the chest with the rifle butt. I whirled and put two bullets in his stomach. He twitched, rolled over, and stayed down. I searched the car while Ted kept an eye on our prisoner. We tried to ask him a few questions but he pretended not to understand anything. We walked back toward the way we had come. The German started smiling. That bothered Ted, who nudged him roughly with his rifle in the back.

"What the fuck are you smiling at?" he snapped. "Wipe that smile off your face or I'll do it for you."

Instead of turning off the smile, our boy decided to make a run for it. He took off like a scared rabbit for the trees. Ted raised his gun and got the German lined up in his sights but I knocked the gun down. I told him we needed him alive. We ran after him. The bastard was in damn good shape. He was covering ground with long, easy strides. I was closer to him than Ted who was running with his mouth open, barely keeping up. I was close enough to tackle him when Ted fired a shot into the air.

I stopped. So did the Kraut. I walked over and grabbed a handful of his collar and yanked him along. His face was pale. For once, there was fear in his cold blue eyes. Ted came toward him. I thought he was going to shoot the man. Instead, he reared back and punched the German in the stomach, bending him over. When the German straightened up, he looked at Ted with a vicious snarl on his face, his head up in open defiance.

We started across the field toward a group of deserted houses. Suddenly, we heard the distant sound of an airplane coming closer and hid ourselves in the bushes and waited until it passed over us. Ted helped the German to his feet with a shove. Our prisoner closed his eyes, heaved a sigh, and then bowed toward his American captors in his Aryan way.

All of the houses were seriously damaged, bombed, or burned. However, we were thinking only of getting some shelter for the long, cold night. The next day, we would rejoin our units. Ted pushed the German into the shattered quarters of the second house, the one with the least damage. The first one we passed up because it lacked a roof. This building provided some comfort with four walls intact and a partial roof. Also, it gave us a good view of the field in case we had visitors.

The chilly late afternoon wind was getting stronger as the sun started to go down. We forced the German to help us carry some of the debris inside the house. If it got too cold, we had some wood, scraps of cloth, and paper. The fire had to be kept low to prevent its smoke from giving away our position. What pleased Ted was a stove built of sheet iron but we could not use it. The Krauts might see the smoke. In a corner of the room was a long, heavy oak table with three stools.

Calmly, the German officer sat down on a stool, his face blank, emotionless yet watching us. He stared most of the time at Ted as if he was pondering how he would settle an old score. Revenge. I was rubbing my arm where the other Kraut got me with the knife. It stung and throbbed like hell.

"How bad is it?" Ted asked.

"It's OK." I looked at the wound but was quite aware of a strange tension in the room, as if something bad was about to happen. The wound looked nastier than it was. I took my canteen and washed it with water, and Ted dabbed a little antiseptic powder on it, then bound it with a bandage.

"What's your name, Kraut?" Ted asked the German, who ignored him.

"What's your rank?" Ted asked next. "Speak English?"

The German officer sat there arrogantly, impassively, shutting his eyes for a moment.

I walked to the window and looked out over the field. The sun's dying rays gave the countryside an amber glow, like a pretty painting. Far off, I could hear the artillery kicking up again. There was no way of knowing whether it was ours or theirs.

"We'll take turns sleeping and watching the German," I said. "Do you want to sleep first?"

"You sleep first after we eat some rations," Ted said, lighting a cigarette. "Boy, could I use some coffee. Even that brine they serve back at camp would go down good right about now."

"If you're tired, I can watch him while you get some shut-eye," I said, glancing at the German sitting there with his hands behind his head and his eyes closed.

After we chowed down on the food, Ted started a small fire in a big pot. The German didn't eat. The Master Race did not need nourishment. It was still a little chilly in the house. I stretched out on the floor, put my helmet under my head and moved my rifle closer to my body. Just in case.

"I meant to thank you for warning me today," I said to Ted. "You saved my ass. That Kraut bastard would have gotten me, for sure."

"Think nothing of it. You would have done the same for me."

"Don't be so sure of that," I joked, and we both laughed. The German opened his eyes and looked at me this time. Then he closed them again.

We were both burned out, totally exhausted. We had walked a long way from the front. It had been a tiring, draining day. In the last two days, I had gotten a total of maybe five hours sleep, not even quality sleep. In no time, I was asleep and dreaming of home. I was with Harriet on the sofa in our living room, telling her how I wanted to marry her when I got back from the war. I asked her to wait for me. She was a shy, quiet girl. Some people might consider her plain-looking but to me, she was as pretty as a movie star. As I talked to her, telling her of my dreams, she said nothing, just listened with a pleased look on her face. I wanted to kiss her so badly. Her father was an undertaker and very strict about his two daughters. The dream was taking forever. Harriet was teasing me, letting me hug and kiss her neck but when I moved closer to her lips, she would turn her face away. For some reason, I awoke, and my eyes opened slowly to a most horrifying, unexpected scene. A shiver went through me, making me gasp for air. I stood and tried to focus. The German officer, with a sinister grimace on his face, had a struggling Ted by the hair, about to cut his throat. I raised my rifle to shoot the Kraut SOB.

"Put your gun down, Blackie," the German officer said in a low, evil voice. "Do it now or your friend here dies."

Damn, the Kraut spoke English! He had the best hand. What the hell would I do now? I couldn't let Ted die nor could I let that bastard escape. I stood there, weighing the choices in my head: Never throw your weapon away. Never compromise with the enemy. Never give up. I held my weapon on him, steady in my decision, no surrender, and the German held his ground with the knife to Ted's throat. There was a heart-breaking look in Ted's eyes like he knew this was not going to end well. He was fucked. The German stared at me, inching the knife closer to the big vein in his captive's neck. Ted kept gulping, trying to breathe, trying not to panic.

"I said put the gun down, nigger," the German repeated. "I won't say it again."

Everybody worldwide knows that damn word, our label, our eternal curse. I hesitated, still thinking how I could rush him, and the German bastard calmly plunged the knife into Ted's neck and ripped it across in a bloody line, slashing his windpipe and jugular in one swift stroke. Ted gagged, gurgled, and slipped to the floor. It all happened so fast. The blood shot out over the front of Ted's uniform, spraying with each pump of his startled heart, and he shook on the floor, clutching his torn throat. I raised the rifle, aiming it at the German's head.

"Don't shoot him, American!" a voice, with a strange, harsh accent, said from the darkness behind me.

The German's eyes widened and shifted from my face to a point over my right shoulder and the knife in his hand lowered. Now he was frightened, maybe even terrified by what he saw. Or heard.

I turned slightly and faced a man, the skinniest human being I've ever seen, holding a Luger. He was all skin and bones, with a shaved head. He was pointing the gun at the German who, when I turned back around, was sprawled on the floor, nearly unconscious. Another living skeleton, a man, was standing over him, holding a thick piece of wood. Next to him was a woman, her bony head wrapped in a dirty bandanna, with matchstick arms and legs. Her face was covered by a thin layer of yellowish skin drawn tightly over the contour of the bones. You could tell she might have been attractive once.

I kneeled next to Ted. There was nothing I could do. He was dead. I wanted to kill the Nazi. I wanted his blood. With hate in my heart, I pivoted with the rifle and aimed it at the prone German on the ground but the stick woman grabbed the barrel.

"No, you cannot kill him," she said in thickly accented English. "It's better that he lives, this beast. This butcher."

"That Kraut killed my friend," I said, gritting my teeth. I wanted to do something, had to do something. The guilt of having gone to sleep and leaving Ted to watch him ate away at my conscience. I had to get even. He must die.

"This thing before you is not a man, he is a monster," the woman screeched, pointing at the German. "I know him. He is *Obergruppenfuhrer* Otto Dorr. I remember him from Warsaw. He has killed thousands." The bony arm she pointed at the German was tattooed with a number that I couldn't read in the dim light of the fire.

The Aryan god said nothing. He simply stared at Ted's dead body and smiled with no teeth showing, a satisfied grin. I wanted to kill him right then. But she gripped the rifle, determined to temporarily save the man's worthless life, and wouldn't let go.

"So this creep is some Nazi big shot, huh?" I asked the woman.

Before she could answer, the man with the club sagged against the wall, so weak and feeble. Finally, he wobbled over to a stool and sat down with a heavy sigh. I noticed a brutal scar along one side of his face, which he kept partially hidden with a bony hand. He glared evilly at the Nazi with sunken, lifeless eyes but said nothing. It was as if he was waiting for the chance to kill the German too. Waiting and watching for the opportunity.

"I was there in Warsaw when Herr Dorr came with his army of butchers," the woman said, one eye twitching. "They took as many of us as they could. The rest they tried to kill. We fought them from the roofs, windows, sewers, everywhere. We made them pay for every life they took. They tried to burn us out. They drove into crowds with tanks, crushing women and children under the treads. Blood flowed in the streets like water."

I looked down at Ted. "We can't leave him there like that."

The thin man with the Luger suggested we wrap him in something and bury him. He spoke in German to the woman, saying something that made the Nazi very nervous. I thought sadly about burying Ted out there so far from his home and family, but I knew we couldn't drag him along with us when we started back. That was impossible. So we made the German dig a grave with a board and his hands, and buried Ted behind the house in some soft dirt, marking his grave with a piece of wood.

"Who are you people?" I quizzed the woman, keeping the rifle aimed at the German.

"I am Sophie Halevi," the woman replied when we went back inside. "The man with the pistol is Dov Lebowitz. You wouldn't know it but he was once one of the greatest Jewish doctors in Germany. The other gentleman is Theodor Bach. He was a cantor, a singer. The Germans cut his vocal cords at Auschwitz. He cannot speak now. This German you captured is *Schutz-Staffel*, an SS leader."

"You were at the Auschwitz death camp?" I asked. "We heard talk of that place, a terrible place."

She said something to the others in German, and they looked at me for a second, then resumed talking among themselves. Theodor never took his eyes off the German. The club remained in his hand, ever ready. The whole group of them resembled ghouls. There was hardly any flesh on their bones, scary. It was hard to look at them. They were like corpses who had dug themselves up from their graves and again walked among people. The undead.

Dov spoke to Sophie in German and she translated for me. "We must make sure he cannot escape again," she said. He forced the German to squat in a corner of the room, facing the wall, with his hands clasped on top of his head. That was a good idea. I would have to spend less energy dealing with him. He did as he was told, remaining there as meek as a lamb.

"How old are you, young American?" she asked me.

"I'm nineteen, twenty my next birthday in three weeks," I said proudly. "What else did he say?"

Sophie said something to the men, and Dov smiled, showing a row of rotten teeth. I think they were discussing my age. They talked for a while, with the men becoming quite animated, considering their weakened state. Finally, they realized I felt left out and included me in the conversation. Not that I could speak their lingo.

She found a seat after checking up on the frail man with the club. "No, we were talking about being young and the innocence of youth. He was talking about your question about what Auschwitz was like. I don't really think you want to know about that place. Dov was forced to help the Nazi doctors with their medical experiments at the camp. Young Polish men and boys were strapped down on the operating table and their scrotums cut open and their testicles removed. Herr Dorr knows what I am talking about. He knows what his kind did there. He was there, the monster. Butchers. The fiends would not give the boys any painkillers so they could see how long they could survive the shock of such a procedure."

My stomach rolled up in a knot. "Oh my God!"

Evil like this was beyond my understanding. Such malice and contempt for life. I faced the German, no doubt with disgust on my face. How could one human being do these things to another human being? But then, I recalled the accounts of some of the lynchings in the South where white folks had picnics, took pictures while the men carved up and roasted colored men hanging from trees. So savage. White people. There was a bestial side to them that most colored people didn't understand, a blood lust, a thirst for inflicting pain and suffering that defied the laws of God and nature. You never heard about colored people doing this kind of stuff. Sure, we killed one another but we never tortured, maimed, or killed like this. In the end, I couldn't figure which was worse: the actions of these Nazis killing people in bulk or the lynchings by these cracker white folk still fighting the Civil War. Could you judge something like that?

Sophie was still talking. "And many of the women had strong chemicals, acids and the like, injected into their cervix and vaginas to sterilize them. They did that to me. I can never have children. Young American, how old do you think I am?"

They all looked at me, waiting for my answer. "About forty," I replied, truly guessing.

"Twenty-five, still a young woman, and look at what else those butchers did." Her hands trembled as they pulled her tattered blouse open. It seemed as though her breasts had been burned away, leaving four charred, jagged lines across her wasted chest. There was nothing there where her titties should have been. I shuddered to the core of myself, fighting down an urge to vomit.

Dov said something to her in German and she closed her blouse quickly. She narrowed her eyes, leered at the Kraut officer, and suddenly spat at him. He flinched but didn't react otherwise.

"The SS came to our house during the Sabbath, smashing everything, destroying Mama's precious Seder set, breaking the Tree of Life menorah, slapping and beating everyone," Sophie recalled, her face drawn and tight with emotion. "I had a pendant around my neck, given to me by my grandmother. It was sterling with the inscription: *b'shem sh'chai l'olam*, which means 'In the name of the one who lives forever.' The Nazi beasts ripped it from my neck, hit me in the stomach, and took me as a man would do his bride right before my parents. One after another, all six of them. I will never forget the hurt and shame in my parents' faces, never, never, as long as I live. Never."

Dov glanced at Theodor, who had moved closer to the German.

It was obvious that the silent man was thinking of harming the officer if he got the chance.

Sophie was breathing heavily, reliving it all as if she was there again in Warsaw in the Jewish ghetto. Surprisingly there were no tears in her eyes. She, too, glared at the German, the big veins pulsing in her forehead.

"When I arrived at the camp, I came with my two sisters, one older, one younger," she said solemnly. "My younger sister, Naomi, had a birth defect, one leg shorter than the other. They—the SS swine—took her away to the gas chamber almost as soon as we got there. I never saw her again. One of them saw my older sister, Tova, had her small baby with her and walked over and ripped it from her arms. She ran at this man. He shot her and she fell near her baby, crawling to it, tried to shield the baby with her body. But one of the SS butchers killed her and stomped the baby. Killed them right before my eyes. How can you tell me that these Germans are not the spawn of the Devil? How can you?"

"Enough for now, Sophie," Dov said in a whisper. "This is no good. No more talk of that evil place. Enough."

I removed all of Ted's valuables from the corner where they were stacked, along with his dog tags, which I had taken from him before we put him in the ground. Dov lit one of the cigarettes from Ted's belongings and offered the pack to Sophie. Meanwhile, the mute skeleton lurked just out of view near the German, waiting, watching.

While we shared rations, they told me more about their escape and the death camp. The details of the killing there numbed my senses. I couldn't believe it. The trains would pull into the camp, Sophie said, and the prisoners would line up into two columns. The left column walked off to their deaths. She said you could hear the motors of the fans in the crematorium stir and the roar of the flames being whipped to a level where the bodies would burn. The incineration room was neat and clean, whitewashed, with thick concrete doors. There were fifteen ovens, with polished iron doors, working day and night.

Outside, the SS guards, she added, lined up the doomed and the big doors swung back. Men, women, and children. Babies, fussy from lack of sleep, clung to their mothers. The people, marked for death, walked slowly, unaware, prodded by the guards. They walked along the cinder path to the iron ramp, which led to a series of steps, then to an underground room with an enormous sign that read: BRAUSEBAD. Or shower bath. This message was repeated in Greek, French, and Hungarian. Many prisoners laughed at themselves for having worried about their safety. They entered a large room with benches and numbered coat hangers. Signs told them to carefully bundle their clothes so they could find them after their bath.

"About how many could they fit in there at once?" I asked, amazed at how efficiently the Germans had made killing.

Sophie repeated the question to Dov, who answered in German and continued smoking. It was as if she felt compelled to tell me everything, like she needed a witness. Someone who had no idea of what horrors they had faced and survived. She told me they could cram three thousand people into the death chamber. In less than ten minutes, everyone was undressed and the clothes hung on the numbered pegs. More swing doors opened, and the crowd was led into another room. The door closed behind the prisoners, the lights turned off and the green gas canisters dropped into the concrete pipes sticking out of the ground. Minutes later, all were dead. The electric ventilators were switched on to dispel the gas. Other inmates arrived to cart off the shoes and clothing. Sophie herself was one of this morbid detail who gathered clothes. Another group entered the death room where the bodies were stacked in a confused pyramid toward the ceiling. There were indications of frenzied panic in the final moments, trampling one another. The instinct of survival. The bodies of the old, women, and children were at the bottom of the stack. The weakest died first. The men were at the top. All of the corpses were covered with bruises and scratches from the last desperate moments. All of the faces were blue, contorted, and bloated. The smell of urine and feces overpowering.

Damn them! I watched the German officer staring at the bloodstain on the wooden floor where Ted's body had lain. What goes through the mind of a fiend like him? Where is the part of God within him? Or is there nothing of the Divine there? His face bore no emotion.

The German suddenly stirred. "Everyone knows the Jew is a parasite," he said quietly, his voice a thick hiss. "Wherever the Jew flourishes, the people and culture die. The Fuhrer said that, and the world knows it is true."

Ignoring the German, Sophie continued her terrible tale. The room, she said, was hosed down and the corpses taken away by other prisoners to the ovens. They stole gold teeth from the dead and dropped them in acid-filled buckets, where the solution ate away all bone and flesh. Necklaces, wedding bands, pearls, and rings were also taken. The bodies were stretched out on sheet-metal pushcarts, the oven doors opened, and then corpses were lifted into the roaring flames. It took twenty minutes to cremate a body. Afterward, the ashes were sifted, loaded into trucks, and driven off for disposal. I sat there, completely dumbfounded.

"We here, the three of us, crawled out of a pit after the soldiers shot us, left us for dead," Dov said, his eyes burning with hate for the Germans. "Each got hit somewhere. Nothing serious. The Nazi butchers smoked, laughed, and joked, and took turns shooting into the pit at anything that moved. We waited among the dead for a whole night before we fled. Theodor was attacked by a vicious SS dog just before we got away. That is the place on his leg where the skin has been ripped away to the bone."

I looked at each of them. Sophie sucked on her cigarette, got up, and walked over to where the German sat with a smug smile on his face. She didn't strike him, only stared at him much as the mute Theodor was doing. This trio of ghosts before me weighed about sixty pounds each at the most. What madness! I felt so bad for them and the others like them still dealing with these devils every day.

"*Deutschland Uber alles*, my ass," Dov said, smirking. "Germany over all! What a crock of shit! *The Ubermenschen*, the super race, ha! I'd watch Herr Dorr here up at the watchtower machine guns, laughing while his men shot at the prisoners in the yard for fun. He would order his men to soak the gypsies in water and make them stand in the snow and freezing cold until they died of exposure. Even the little ones."

Standing behind the German, Sophie puffed on her cigarette. "Do you know what the sign said as you came into Auschwitz? *Arbeit Macht Frei.* It was the cruelest of jokes."

"What does it mean?" I almost didn't want to know.

"It means 'freedom through work,' " Sophie said angrily. "Work would set us free. What a cruel lie. Only death would set us free."

Suddenly, without warning, she grabbed the German's face and pushed the lit cigarette into his cheek. He tried to evade her but Dov held the gun to his head. I stood up, waving my hands, saying, "No, don't do this." Both of them warned me not to come any closer or they would kill him. Blow his damn brains out.

"Stop them please," pleaded the German, his pale skin crackling like frying chicken under the glow of the cigarette. "*Wunsche ich seinen Tod?* Stop them, American, please, before they kill me."

"What did he say in German?" His lingo went right over my head.

Sophie said the Nazi officer asked if I wanted him to die. Good question. At that moment, I really didn't know. From what I'd heard about what they were doing in those camps, he didn't really deserve to live but I wasn't God. But to talk about life and death was crazy in war because it was all around you. Nobody got a free pass during all the killing and dying. Oh, damn! She ground the cigarette into his face once more and he howled in pain.

"*Ich bin allein,*" the German said sorrowfully. I am all alone.

"What kind of human being are you?" I shouted at him, thinking about what had been said. "How could you do this to women and children, to anybody?"

The German swallowed hard and touched his seared cheek. "I was just a soldier. I must plead *fuhrerbefehl.* The orders came from the Fuhrer. My role was a small one."

"Murderer, killer, butcher!" Sophie screamed curses and spat on him.

The German didn't attempt to wipe the spittle away. It rolled down the side of his face. "I never killed anyone. I never ordered any Jew killed. Things sometimes got out of hand. That is all."

"We should torture you the way you tortured so many," Dov said, rubbing the Luger near the German officer's ear, making him wet his pants. "I would watch you strut through the camp in your uniform with the skull-and-bones insignia on your tunic. You are SS. Your mission was the total extermination of the Jews. Admit it, beast!"

"How could you ever understand the German mind?" the officer asked flatly, a hint of terror coming into his voice. He sensed they would kill him. "I'm not ashamed of being a German. I followed orders. I am a soldier. I did as I was told. The responsibility for the extermination order lies with Himmler and the Fuhrer. Not me."

"*Seig heil*," Sophie mocked the German and slapped him hard across the face, once, twice, three times. Dov finally grabbed her hand.

The German called the entire situation *furchtbar*. Terrible, his word according to Sophie. His words were almost pleading. "We wanted a peaceful solution to the Jewish problem. We let a lot of them leave but too many stayed. Then that Jew shot Van Roth, our secretary at the embassy in Paris. It was like they were telling us they didn't appreciate us treating them like human beings. It was their fault what happened after that."

"We are human beings!" Sophie shouted at him.

"Can I have a cigarette?" the German asked.

"No," both Dov and Sophie answered at the same time.

"You hate me and for no reason," the German said. "I am a soldier. I follow orders. We didn't create the hate of the Jew. It was here long before the Fuhrer. Even your precious Zionist Herzl admitted that. Wherever there are Jews, there are people who hate them."

"You were with Eichmann at Auschwitz," Dov said bitterly. "You killed Jews. It was your work."

"Every race has the right to protect itself," the German said, holding up his head. "You Jews have done it for years. Why can't anyone else do it? Look at America. Whites there do not want to mingle with the blacks. They don't want you niggers. You think what the world sees here will end the hatred of the Jews. No, it won't. The Jews will always be hated. And the blacks as well."

"America will change one day," I said angrily, hating that he saw fit to drag me into the argument. "Jim Crow can't last. White people will have to accept us colored to make the country go forward. They must."

"Not so," the German replied quietly, as if to make his point. "You cannot make someone accept a race he feels is inferior. *Afflinge*. Or in your language, monkey race. Like you and the Jews here. We know of the lynchings. We have many friends there. Is that acceptance? They will never accept you. How can you fight for a country that treats you like that, Blackie? That allows you to be hung."

I was quiet, seething. His words hit home. The Jews looked at me.

Dov blinked hard, grimaced, and moved his gun down to the German's neck. "Enough of this. Let us take him outside. You must not stop us. He must die. He is a killer."

"I cannot let that happen," I said forcefully. "You will have to kill me before I allow that. He is my prisoner." I had my rifle on the two of them. What I had not counted on was the other one, the mute Theodor, who had slipped out and recovered Ted's weapon from the doorway. I felt him behind me before I saw him. The weapon poked me in the ribs and I lowered the rifle.

For the first time, I got a real look at the marred face of Theodor, the young silenced cantor, now standing where he could get a clear shot. Half his face was so torn that the inside of his mouth, the teeth and gums were exposed. The look in his eyes frightened me. Things were totally out of control. I was responsible for this Kraut, especially after he killed Ted. That meant something. I knew these Jews, these living skeletons, had a legit gripe against this murdering bastard. War, huh. Let them have him. It was the least I could do for Ted. I knew how our white troops sometimes treated his kind. The Kraut would be treated like royalty. No, let them have their way with him.

"You can have him for five minutes," I said, walking toward the door. "Do whatever you want to him but don't kill him. I want the asshole alive."

The Jews talked in a huddle, agreed to my terms. The German screamed for me to do something. That I couldn't do this. That I wasn't his judge or jury. That I had no right. Maybe not. But fuck him. I left the house when I saw Theodor club the German, his body hitting the floor with a thud, and then Dov walking over to the fire with a knife, singing some Yiddish song. I stood outside the door, smoking a cigarette, listening to the German yell with a scream that raised the hairs on the back of my neck. *Gott im Himmel,* he kept repeating. Later I learned that meant God in Heaven.

That next morning, we walked over the fields to the Allied camp. No, the Jews didn't kill the Kraut but they beat him some, blinded him with the hot knife and did something to his throat where he couldn't talk. I think that was Theodor's doing. Often, I think about whether I did the right thing but I then I remember about the bodies stacked high, starvation, torture, and mass murder. And about Ted. Whether it was justice or revenge. Whether I was evil like the Kraut. I don't know. Hell, I became a man that day and now I sleep like a baby. I had looked the Devil in the face, smelled his filthy breath, felt his claws about my throat, and never blinked once or backed down. I know I was right. And soon I will be going home with a whole different mind-set. I am a man now.

SPEAK NO EVIL

In a crowded back room of a smoky Chicago blues club, J. D. Shines listened to the warm-up band as he admired himself in the dressing room mirror. He had the room with the gold star on the door. He was tall, dark, almost bony, with a wiry body that obeyed his every command. Often, his hand patted his shiny, conked hair, reminding all who saw him that he was of the old school, back in the day of Lightnin' Hopkins, John Lee Hooker, Pinetop Perkins, Muddy Waters, Jimmy Reed, and Howlin' Wolf. If someone told a funny joke, he'd wiggle his pencil-thin mustache and display the two gold front teeth that were his trademark. One had a diamond in it. Dark shades covered his eyes. Even his manager thought he was good-looking for a man his age, someone who drank and womanized as much as he did. But his standard sharkskin suits, thin lapels, narrow pants legs were a dead giveaway. He was stuck in a different time, a time long gone.

"Don't tell me nuthin' 'bout pleasuring no woman," J.D. said, smirking. "I got a degree in it."

His bass player, a chubby boy from Tampa, giggled. "What 'bout that gal in St. Louis? She say you left her hangin'. Didn't finish the job."

"She tried to get me kilt, had some Negro waiting out in the alley for me," the bluesman shot back. "I don't play that. It's got to be on the up-and-up for me to mess wit' it. I don't write no checks my ass can't cash. 'Member that, Junior."

In the old days, he had to beat the women off, all colors, plenty of fine young things. But now he was older, more picky. More often, the groupies who dogged him were white, Barbie dolls with inflated breasts and nice flat butts. Like that blond gal who brought him the cup of Earl Grey tea a few minutes ago. There was a time when he'd lock the door, toss her over an amp, and punch that grinner right out.

"I knowed there was going to be problems wit' the gal from the moment I laid eyes on her," J. D. mumbled, pouring a finger of Jack Daniels from a hip flask into the steaming cup of tea. "I don't need any grief wit' the law, no suh."

"What do you think of the boys playing on stage now?" the bassist asked.

"Sounds like a lot of noise to me, crying guitars and screams," the bluesman said, toying with the turquoise amulet hanging around his neck.

In truth, his mind was somewhere else, back on the Cuban girl who got into his dressing room before the Detroit show the night before, dressed in a long Burberry raincoat with nothing on under it. She was a luscious collection of curves. He recalled how she said nothing to him, only dropped on her knees before him, took his bone out of his pants, and began working on him until he was almost on the edge of orgasm. Unfortunately, once he got behind her, starting to get going, her smooth round brown ass slamming hard into him, the manager popped his head in the room and said he was on in five minutes. He pulled out of her, shiny and hard, agitated. He asked her to stay around after the show so they could pick up where they left off. But she was nowhere to be found when he wrapped up later.

At that moment, the blonde entered, walking right up to him. "Phone call for you, J. D. The phone in the hall. Twenty minutes to showtime. And oh yeah, there's a reporter here from *Candor* magazine to talk to you about doing an interview."

The bluesman grumbled under his breath, got up, and brushed off his shiny suit. He followed the blonde out into the hall, wondering who the hell would call him right as he was about to go on. This was no time for foolishness; he'd make it short. No matter who it was.

He took the phone call. It was his daughter who was going to school down in Charleston for a degree in acting and theatre. Or drama as she called it. Margaret, his baby girl, was his heart and the spitting image of him. Of all five kids, she was his favorite and the only one who seemed to be trying to do something with her life. The only time he heard from the others was when they wanted to borrow money or needed him to get them out of some kind of scrape.

"Hey, gurl. Whassup?" he chirped, waiting for the reason for the call.

"Nothing much, Pops, I just wanted to hear your voice," his daughter said. "Are you coming to visit me next week? You know you cancelled on me the last time, broke my heart. Promise me you'll make it this time."

"I promise I'll get thar," he replied. "How's school?"

"Good, real good. I made the dean's list. And you, how are you?"

"I'm awright. My leg bothers me sometimes but other than that, I'm healthy as a hoss. Maybe working too hard but I got to do that. How's your mama?"

His daughter sighed. "She's back in divorce court. Won't tell anybody what happened. I guess this last guy started acting up. I don't know where she finds them."

He laughed. "Yessiree, your mama sure can pick 'em. Baby, I can't talk long. I got to go on stage in a minute. Is there anything else going on?"

"I need two thousand dollars by Friday," she said flatly. "Can you swing it?"

"Yeah, no problem," he said, picking at his tie. "Call my lawyer and work it out. Anything else? Whut do you need the money for, gurl?"

"A surprise," she teased. "When are you coming off tour and start to live a normal life? You just work all the time, no rest, no nothing. You need a break. Do you have a girlfriend yet?"

"I ain't got no time for that kind of mess," he said, snorting. "Womens know musicians ain't nuthin' but trouble. And the kind of womens I meet out here ain't the kind you want to bring home."

"I guess you're right," she said. "Hey, did you see your picture on the cover of *Downbeat*? Big article talking about you making a comeback, pictures and everything."

The bluesman shook his head. "Hell, comeback. I ain't been nowhar. See, that's why I don't read that foolishness. Comeback, shoot! Gurl, I got to go. Call you from Indianapolis."

"You're on, J.D." The manager came up from behind him and tapped his watch.

The first set had gone off without a hitch. They played songs from the new album, *Hot Snake Nights*, mostly at the request of the record label folks. The smart pencil pushers at the company had teamed him with a new producer who quickly paired him with a lot of the new talent on the scene for a series of duets: Joe, Eve, and Pink, along with some old faces, Stevie Wonder, Robert Cray, Bonnie Raitt, and Chaka Khan. Needless to say, the result was a hit album that had been nominated for several Grammys as it shot up the charts. Personally, he loved the old stuff best.

He almost finished off the flask, leaving a little bit for later, fluffed his conk, and ran out on stage. The band was already thumping away when he got on. He picked up the mike and launched into their new hit, "World Aflame," with the drums rolling underneath his sandpaper vocals like thunder. The audience, young white kids from local colleges and a smattering of old timers, were pumped up, really into it, singing along and shouting out the names of tunes. However, they were stunned when he switched the playbook and did songs from albums recorded nearly two decades earlier as a young man. Every tune struck home: "Baby, Please Don't Leave Me This Way," "Soft and Tight," "Clarksdale Blues," "Sleepin' Around," "I Don't Care Whut Your Daddy Say," "Darlin', You Got Too Many Mens," "She Quit Me," "Tight Cheeks," "Sho 'Nuff I Don't," "Cute and Evil," "Love On Payday," and "Let Me Ride You Tonight." All his greatest hits. The crowd was worked into a fever pitch by the time he started the lyrics to his closing song, "At Least Tonight You're Mine," a foot-stomping boogie, assisted by a local sax player who sat in with the band to add some appropriate wails in the right spots. Some of the young girls threw their panties on stage and danced in the aisles with their breasts exposed. The band, totally liquored up, loved it. They lost track of time, doing a full ninety-minute set, with two encores.

At the close of the set, the bluesman did something really dramatic. He leaned over, put his guitar down, pulled out his flask, and poured its contents on the stage. Then he tossed the flask out into the rowdy crowd, where a fight quickly broke out between guys wanting to get it for a keepsake.

He ran off stage, sweating and spent, and someone threw him a towel. The manager was still screaming about their set going on too long. Backstage, the hallway was filled with groupies, young women of all shapes, colors, and sizes. He had other things on his mind. Where was his sweetie?

"You were slamming tonight, baby, just slamming," yelled a hot young cutie, with all of her cleavage on display in a low-cut top.

"Thanks, dahling," he murmured and kept moving toward his dressing room.

"Don't go in there just yet," one of the stagehands warned him as he grabbed for the doorknob.

Inside, the guys in the band begged him to join them and get it on with one of the various groupies sitting on the chairs and sofa in the small room. He declined, putting a cigarette in his mouth, and watched the orgy with a distracted smile. Several of the girls took turns exposing their cherries to the men after pulling down their jeans. A sort of beauty pageant. This was the kind of wild stuff that went on during these road gigs. One of them played with herself as she licked on another gal while the bass player plunged into her from the rear. The drummer had one sitting on his face and still another honey, her skin beet red, bouncing on his stiff rod. The bluesman noticed he wore a silver cock ring, which glittered in the light every time the woman's ass raised into the air. In the corner, a black girl with her hair done in red corkscrews went to town on the horn player, making him tremble as if he was being electrocuted.

Although the bluesman had always thought these scenes, which were fairly typical fare on the road, were entertaining, it was all pretty boring now. Everybody was legal age. But it was old hat. He had seen enough. Where was his sweetie? His secret lover.

Outside the dressing room, he found a young woman waiting for him. She wanted an autograph and something a bit more intimate. She wore a buzz cut, a ruby stud in her nose, with a leopard-skin top that clung to her melon-sized breasts. Her skin was a ghostly alabaster. The way she stood, he couldn't help but notice her nicely proportioned ass in her tight black leather pants and silver fuck-me pumps. While she talked, she couldn't stand still, swaying and rolling her hips, as though someone had left something inside her. The girl was on simmer. Somehow she reminded him of a young Cajun girl who twisted his jelly roll a while back in Baton Rouge. Oh, what a night! It took him a month to recover from the steamy love that gal put on him.

"You kicked it out there, Mister Bluesman," she said, smiling real easy, revealing a stud in her tongue as well. She caressed one nipple and swigged from a half-empty bottle of Stoli vodka.

The bluesman looked at her cautiously and grinned. "Whut do they call you, sugah?"

"My friends call me Desire," she said, breathing sexily. "Sorta of a club name I picked up. I came with a message from a mutual friend of ours. He said to let you know that his day is coming. Your bill is soon coming due. But until then anything you want is yours. You have an unlimited credit line."

She giggled, pursed her thin lips and stroked her leather-clad legs. Purring, she took another swig of the Russian vodka, frowned from its burn, and passed the bottle to him. He gulped down a hearty portion, watching her. What was her story? Was she trying to pick him up? What mutual friend? Who the hell did she know that he might know? He stared at the small silver skull necklace around her neck, trying to figure her out while she smoked a dark cigarette with a pungent smell.

"What's in here?" Desire asked, rubbing the heel of her hand lewdly over the hump in his pants between his legs. "Damn, you're really packing!"

"Easy, sugah!" He yanked her hand and stepped back.

Giggling again, she pulled down her pants, revealing she was not wearing any underwear and didn't care if others in the hallway saw her antics. Her sex was bald, shaven. There was a silver earring jutting through its flower-shaped lips. He asked her if it was painful but she only smiled and wiggled her studded tongue at him.

* * *

Women had always been his downfall, even back in the old days. They had ruined his first marriage and his second and his third. But the only marriage that haunted him was the first one, the one to Eula, the woman who had been by his side during his salad days, the lean days. A big, heavy-set woman with an iron will, she often worked and supported them both when he couldn't land a job. Things changed after he put out two hit records, getting the attention of the club owners and fans, and the requests for his appearances picked up. She changed as a person, demanding more money, ordering him around like he was her child, becoming hell to live with. Maybe it was the change of life or something like that, since she was several years older than he was. After all, she was in her early forties while he was just in his late twenties.

Every night she nagged him about some hot young female who might have hugged him too long, kissed his cheek, or spent too much time up in his face. She watched him like a hawk, monitoring his every move. It got to the point where he hated to come home. He found excuses to stay in the streets and that was when the drinking, drugging, and womanizing started. His only regret was that they had two children together, two boys who were his heart, but she eventually turned them against him and today they hated his guts. Couldn't stand the sight of him. Thank God he had another set of kids with his second wife, including his daughter.

What would Eula have said about Miss Desire here? There would have been hell to pay, that's for sure.

Suddenly, Desire hiked her pants back up, scowled, and scurried away. He couldn't see what scared her so. What the hell? When he turned around, he saw his lover, the *Candor* magazine reporter, a pretty young black woman dressed in a casual business suit, walking toward him. Joi, his secret lover. The severe look on her face said it all. She didn't particularly like the "free love" aspect of the music scene, the everything-goes way of life, and how easy it was for temptation to be thrown in the way of the man she loved.

"Who was that?" she asked, narrowing her eyes.

"Another whacked-out groupie who wanted to give me something," he said calmly. "But I wasn't buying. How are you, Joi?"

"I was alright until I walked up here and found this white girl trying to seduce you," she replied. "Is this why you could never keep a wife?"

"Partly." His brow furrowed. "Can we get out of here and go back to my hotel?"

"Yes, sure. I think your manager is on to us. He makes a face every time he sees me. I don't think he likes me much. Did you talk to your kids about me?"

"I jus' spoke on it wit' them but they think you too young for me," he said. "They want me to get somebody more my own age. Some goldenager. But this is my life, and I do what I want wit' it. I's a grown man."

She corrected him. "No, it's our lives. I want to marry you, and our age difference has nothing to do with how I feel about you. I'm not looking for another daddy. I'm looking for someone who can love and respect me. That's what you do for me. I'm happy."

"Sometimes it's hard for your kids to see you as anything other than their father," he said. "They can't imagine I might want to have a gal of my own. The whole idea of me having sex with a woman other than their mama spooks them. To them, I's too old to be thinking 'bout love or a gal. Wait right here, baby, and I'll be back directly."

He went back to his dressing room where the party was still in progress, stepped over the naked bodies, and got his guitars. The drummer asked him to stay, a girl's head clamped to his crotch, but again the bluesman said no, waving briefly before he stepped out.

They waited in the rain for about fifteen minutes before a cab stopped for them. Cabbies were notorious for seeing every black person as a potential robber. By the time they hopped into one, they were soaked to the skin. At the hotel, they quickly shed their clothes, dried off, and settled down with hot toddies. He found her a robe to wear, a towel for her wet hair, and chose a shirt and underwear for his comfort. The hotel suite was like any other, not much in the way of luxury but practical in its furnishings and room service.

She said she had to make a call and disappeared into the bedroom where she stayed for several minutes. Finally, she called out for him to join her. The bluesman wearily rose from his seat, the fatigue from the night's show still on him, and walked to the room. A gasp left his lips as he opened the door to see her on the large king-size bed.

Joi was stark naked. Hers was perhaps the most sensational female body he had ever seen. From her lovely face, with its exotic Caribbean features, the perfect rounded shoulders, down and across to the large, round moons of her breasts, to her tapered waist, and inviting swell of her hips, she possessed a presence that would arouse the instinctual lust in any man. Her legs were long and muscled at the calves from her daily morning runs. He loved her feet, small and finely shaped. No one could say this was not one foxy black woman. His Barbadian queen!

"Like what you see?" she purred, shifting her leg to give him a better view.

"Oh yeah," he said, rubbing his hands together eagerly, tossing off his shirt.

He crawled onto the bed, which moaned slightly under his weight. She totally relaxed under his loving, tender kisses and capable hands on her warm skin. His pecker got hard as soon as he touched her. Still virile. Gone was any desire to fight with his kids over this woman, along with it her suggestion to confront them with her and demand they accept her as his lover and fiancée, despite their difference in age. He would ram it down their throats, his intention to marry this younger woman. There was no way he was giving her up. Hell, he'd even decided to stop drinking for her.

She was still in the trance that gentle loving evokes, eyes closed, letting the tingly sensations caused by his fingers and lips on her flesh bring soft, telling sounds from her mouth. With a slow swivel of her lower body, she rolled over, closer to him. Her fingers searched for his shaft, toyed with it at the root, until he groaned and shifted so his pole lay snug against her primed opening. Whatever thoughts may have been nestled in her head vanished when he whispered sensuously of his devotion against her throat, intoxicating words, which sent her murmurs of need mounting. He kissed her lips as though he was a younger suitor, torturing her with anticipation. Another choked cry came from her as she felt the weight of his erection slide up against her heaving stomach. She scooted up on him, permitting him to cup her butt cheeks, her downy soft skin filling his hands. Her juices were flowing like water from a brimming saucer, and she began to rock her hips in his grasp as he began sucking and tonguing her vortex, into her silky pubic hair. Their torsos joined; he smiled serenely, entering her, moving in small, tight circles in her sex. The unbridled fury of her passion surprised him, urging him to go at it much longer than she expected. Her muscles embraced him like a fist, when it touched places in her that released movement from her that was fierce and frantic in its tempo. She fought him for her pleasure, causing him to pin her with his arms, the grip of its molten heat taking charge at last. Then he made his rush toward the goal, ramming her with sharp, harsh plunges that sent his balls slapping against her ass, as he struck bottom. With one remaining burst of energy, he moved into her with a primal pounding that made her screech his name over and over. Her body, convulsing, milked the last drop of life from his aching dick. He shot the final spurts all over her large breasts and fell forward beside her, exhausted.

They clung to each other, their bodies molded into one form, their limbs locked in mutual contentment. He raised his head, a big grin on his face, and asked, "Did you like it?" She replied it was heavenly, sheer delight. Drained, he was quickly asleep.

The next morning, the bluesman discovered she was gone. There was no note. Nothing. That worried him. But more than that was what the white girl with the piercings at the club had said. Something about his bill soon coming due. He knew what she was talking about, his promise to the Dark Mojo Man that night so many years ago in Drew in the Delta. Him on the floor, sick from the Money Blues, too much corn liquor, and full of the heart grief after his mama died. His mama who had taken up with this young rooster following his real papa daddy's death, after her man fell up under a tractor in the fields. She stayed to herself for years after that before she took on this new man, some suitor from up in Clarksdale. Sold women's dresses out of a car. His mama was still a fairly young gal then, 'bout forty or more, still had her looks. One night, they, her and this man, were drinking corn liquor and got into a row over him messing with some skirt over in the next town. He struck her, folk say, and she hit him back with a skillet and he killed her with his hands. Beat her bad and then choked the life out of her slow. So he laid on the floor of that hotel in Drew, covered with his own puke and piss, unable to get up. Wanting to die, cursing the Lawd for letting this thing happen to his mama, who had been a faithful churchgoer before his father's passing. Where was God then? Why didn't He hear her prayers? Why did He leave her out there to face all that pain and suffering alone? No answer came to him.

He didn't have enough money to go back to Yazoo City for her funeral, not enough to even pay for it. Twenty-two years old and didn't have a pot to piss in or a window to throw it out of. Just a little above a beggar, completely hand-to-mouth. The colored folk around there scraped some coins together to plant her in a barren rocky field out near the rail yard. Like she wasn't worth nothing. And it was the Lawd's fault, playing joint after joint night after night and not a damn cent to show for it. But that night in that hotel, he made up his mind that he would never do without again. Never.

Shortly after that, this tall redbone man started turning up wherever he played. The man never said anything to him, just sat there never far from the stage, smiling and rocking his feet to the music. Not once did he ever see any women with the man, although he was the kind they liked. Slick, cold, dressed like a fella who ran women for a living. Drank his bourbon straight, one after another.

One night about four months after the bluesman's mother passed, he got into a fight with the owner of a roadhouse near Ruleville. The peckerwood called him a nigger and told him he was not paying him a damn thing. The peck didn't like his uppity-coon attitude and smart mouth.

"Git the hell out of here, darkie," the peck owner said to the young bluesman. "Be thankful I don't kill your black nigger ass. Go on and git 'fore I change my mind."

The bluesman stood tall. "I ain't going nowhere till I gets whut's rightfully mine."

When he said that, three big corn-fed white boys, some paddies Mr. Tony hired during a trip to New Orleans, came out of a back room, carrying hoe handles. They didn't say a word, just kept coming. But before they could fall upon him with their evil intentions, the door opened and there was the redbone man, casting a cold look at the men, smiling with his arms folded. He walked over, taking a place between the young bluesman and the advancing white men.

"Gentlemen, stop and think before you do something you'll regret," the redbone man said, still stone-faced. "There's no need for any trouble, none at all."

"Who the hell are you, nigger?" Mr. Tony asked, angry that the fun was being interrupted. "This is a private matter between me and this here nigger."

The redbone man touched the bluesman lightly on the cheek. "I'm his new representative, an agent of sorts. Son, you step outside. Go on over to the rooming house across the street. I'll be there in a minute. I'll join you shortly, after I straighten these gentlemen out. Don't fret. Everything'll be alright."

Whatever happened there in that roadhouse took under five minutes, for the redbone man soon joined the would-be victim in the colored rooming house. All smiles. The young bluesman sat on a lumpy couch in the building's dingy lobby, holding his guitar across his knees, watching the slick-talking stranger ease down beside him.

"Whut happened over there?" he asked his new agent.

"Nothing much," the redbone man replied, tossing a small stack of bills at him. "They agreed to my terms and saw the light. But I don't think you'll be working there anymore. You need to think about your future. Aren't you tired of working in these dives, these rat holes? Do you want the big time? The big money?"

"Who doesn't? But whut do I have to do to get it? Nobody gets something for nuthin'. I know that much."

"How about almost something for nothing? We make a small

deal, an agreement between us, between us friends. You get what you want and I get what I want. How does that sound?"

"Whut's the catch?" The bluesman knew this kind of sweet talk well.

"Nothing to sign, no contracts, no false promises. And you can be assured that I always live up to my agreements. I've never gone back on my word. I could give you a list of my clients, both living and dead, but that would be a breach of our confidentiality arrangement. It's a verbal rider on every agreement. None of my clients can ever discuss anything said between us."

"Whut do I get? I don't have to sell my soul or nothing like that?"

The redbone man grinned and adjusted his shirt collar. "Not quite. But there is a fee, a substantial one. We'll discuss that at a later date."

"You didn't tell me whut I get. I want to know that before I decide to do anything. I don't want to buy a pig in a poke. You understand that, mister?"

"Everything, everything you ever wanted or will want. None of your wishes will go unfulfilled. All you have to do is to think it and it's yours."

The redbone man motioned for the man behind the desk to come over. Once the clerk got there, he asked the man to bring over the bottle of corn liquor and two glasses from behind the counter, asking whether there was a sharp knife nearby that he could get his hands on without too much trouble. The clerk, a beat-up old guy wearing a strong cologne, brought back the bottle and knife and got a big tip from the redbone man.

"Whut is your name, mister?" the musician asked. "I need to have something to call you if we's going into business together. Whut do folk call you whar you come from?"

"Many names, most of them unflattering," he said, pouring out a glass of the corn liquor. "But if you must know, my name is Jean."

"But that's a gal's name. You ain't sweet, are you?" There was no foreign accent in the man's speech.

The redbone man rubbed his eyes wearily and continued. "I'm

French. Let's not get sidetracked. Back to our agreement, the future is my specialty. I set things right. However, you must be willing to take some risks. Still, I can assume you know that I have no dissatisfied customers, not one."

"You seem like you know whut you doing." The bluesman sat back in the chair and reached in his coat pocket for a cigarette. His hand stopped in mid-flight when he saw the redbone man shake his head.

"Yes, there is a score you want to settle with the man who killed your mother," the redbone man said quietly. "He still walks the earth free as a bird. You will do as I say. Buy a fresh cow's heart and split it open. Then you will write the name of this man on a piece of paper, place it inside the heart, and cover the entire thing in a coating of strong pipe tobacco. Carefully wrap everything in a clean cotton cloth. Tie it firmly with black cotton thread and bury it near the place where you bought the heart. You need to do nothing more. The curse will take effect within two weeks. Do you get all of that?"

"Yes." The bluesman nodded.

"Do you believe in God?" the redbone man suddenly asked. "You know, all of that garbage about original sin, shame, guilt, and repenting your sins. Judgment Day, Satan, Heaven, the Bible, and all that foolishness."

The redbone man was staring at the musician with such intensity that a tired feeling passed through his body from head to toe. It took him a few seconds to recover his powers of speech. A touch of his brow revealed he was sweating as if he had just finished a twenty-mile race, the sweat soaking his hair and running down his neck. Oddly, only his head was burning hot.

"I suppose I's whut some would call a faithless man," the bluesman said. "Somewhar along the way I lost my faith, lost my way. The road hasn't been exactly smooth for me."

"Good, I know exactly what you mean," the redbone man said. "Faith can be a very foolish commodity if applied to things not worthy of it. Like faith in family or even God. For example, the responsibility of a family is like a huge weight that wears a man down every day he carries it until it finally breaks him, ages him, and puts him into the ground. I never understood why men marry. It uses them up."

He might have been a rascal but he valued family and all that came with it. This was even before he met Eula. "I disagree with you about family and kin. Sure, nobody says you got to do it. You do it out of love but there's nothing like it. Hell, if most men didn't have families, they'd pretty much be bums."

The room became nothing but deep darkness with just a small light surrounding the two men. There was no sign of the clerk or anyone else for that matter. Warmly, the redbone man smiled. "J.D., whatever you say. So if I put you on a plan that brings you everything you want, will you agree to my terms?"

"This ain't one of those deal-with-the-Devil type of things, right?" the musician asked, laughing. "I ain't fool enough to fall for that." He was laughing that the knife was never used. It was just a prop.

"What the hell do you care what side I'm on as long as you get what you want?" the redbone man asked in a whisper that was half a shout. "Do you want me to have hooves, horns, and carry a pitchfork? So predictable and old-fashioned. No, I don't want your immortal soul. As I said before, there are no contracts to sign. Now, your good fortune won't come all at once but when it comes, it will be like nothing you've ever seen. How does that sound, Mr. Bluesman?"

They shook hands and drank the liquor. The shadows in the room lifted and the clerk reappeared. As the bluesman leaned forward to stand, the redbone man again touched him and said softly, "Now we have a deal. I will live through you and all you do. The world will be ours!" To this day, he had no idea what the redbone man meant by those words. Before the bluesman left the rooming house, his new agent gave him a small satin jewel box, telling him not to open it before he got back to his hotel room.

In the box, there was the glittering turquoise amulet that had never left his neck since that day. That was the redbone man's wish; the amulet was never to be away from the warmth of his skin for all that had been promised to be fulfilled. He never violated his benefactor's request. Yes, there had been a stretch of hard times after their meeting, Eula and all that. But then she ran off with a Puerto Rican trucker, taking the kids with her. Then his life changed overnight and it became the dream he so desperately craved. The high life indulged with every joy and thrill during a long career. His every wish was fulfilled. Strangely, he never saw the redbone man again. And his mother's killer died days after their meeting, burning to death in bed from a misplaced cigarette.

Your bill is soon coming due. With those words burning in his brain, the bluesman ordered breakfast from room service, showered, gathered his guitars and luggage and headed for the airport. As he walked from the terminal out to the tarmac for his private jet, he spotted two figures in the distance: one was his secret lover, Joi, and the other was her new friend. She later introduced herself as Jean. Both were smiling and waving, with a stack of suitcases at their feet. He dropped everything and ran to them, arms outstretched.

He remembered the original Jean, the Frenchman's sincere promise, their mysterious deal, and their conversation the last time they spoke so many years ago. It was him, Jean. The redbone man in female form. Or a messenger. Someone to do his bidding. The woman's brown eyes looked deep into his, and she murmured, "I've come to collect, sweetheart, and I promise it'll be painless."

Something came into his mind that made him laugh inside. A man he knew in Atlanta once got caught with another man's wife. He knew he was taking a chance but did it anyway. He was asked why he did it, sneaking around, going to this woman's house when he knew her old man could come home at any time. Was it for the thrill, for the danger of it? "No," the cheater replied, "it just seemed like a good idea at the time." Well, that was how this bargain had seemed, like a good idea at the time.

But deep down, he had no real regrets. It really didn't matter where his soul went after he was dead. Who cared about Old Testament justice? He didn't give a shit if Jean were Satan in human form or the voyage of his soul into the afterlife or eternal damnation. The Now was what mattered. Today. Who could save his ass anyway? Especially from this pretty Devil with tits. That was one of the joys of being a faithless man. You lived in the moment, in the Here and Now, and fuck what came after that.

Despite her transformation, he recognized her immediately for what she was, from something in her eyes, and now he was ready to fulfill his end of the bargain. She'd given him everything he wanted. Like all mortals, he understood that this time would come, the reckoning, and he would have to pick up his tab. Pay what was owed. Whatever she wanted would be given without grumbling or resistance. He really didn't mind. It had been a good life, especially the last years. Yet her arrival was bittersweet as well. Maybe he could negotiate for a few more tender years with Joi.

He was still a man, a real rooster. Doggone, he knew what she had in mind for him. Two women at once in bed. His kind of death, the stuff of legends. Totally painless. What a way to go out! As his favorite comedian, Richard Pryor, once said, speaking of his father who died of a heart attack in bed with a young girl: "He came and went."

A man who lived by the sword died by it. Or lived by his love of the flesh and died by it. All things considered, it was the happiest day of his life.

PUNISH THE YOUNG SEED OF SATAN

I did something bad, real bad. I am eleven. Now everybody is look-ing at me like that football player who killed his wife. The law is trying to make everyone think I'm this bad boy who kills just for fun. Mama tried to tell them different but they didn't listen to her. The prosecutor said the jury, all of the white folks sitting up there, should not even think about rehabilitation or me being a minor. A minor, that's being underage. My mama tried to slap him in the hallway, my aunt Thelma said, but he ducked and a court cop wres-tled my mother away. I wish she could have got him really good and left a red handprint on his wrinkly face. He yelled at her that he was going for even more time. I don't think I really knew what I was doing the whole time I did it. I am eleven. Yes, I had a gun. Yes, I used it. Yes, I did something bad but I don't know why everybody is making such a big fuss over it. People use guns every day and peo-ple get shot and die. I don't understand any of this shit.

"Punish the young seed of Satan." That's what the prosecutor said yesterday in court. The white man with his old wrinkly pink face turned as he stood in front of the jury and pointed at me and said what he said. Seed of Satan? No, seed of Jesse and Elvira. Two regular black folks who worked really hard to give me everything I ever wanted. They're cool. There was nothing I ever asked for that they didn't buy me so I don't know about this Satan stuff. Whatever I did had nothing to do with them. They are good people, both of them. So the chipmunk-looking white man pointed and said: "Give him the maximum penalty for second-degree murder. Give him twenty-five years to life." Maximum is a lot. I know that.

Hey, I know I messed up. I am eleven. That's what kids do, mess

up. Grown-ups are supposed to be there to show us things, to tell us
when we go off the path. Nobody was there that morning when I
shot Mr. Strossen. The white people on the jury were looking at me
like I was a turd in a punch bowl, as Aunt Thelma would say. Like I
was nothing. Like I didn't deserve to live. To tell the truth, I don't
understand what it means when they say "twenty-five years to life,"
because that seems like a long time. The bailiff laughed at me
when they brought me in for the sentencing, that's when they give
you the punishment, and say; "Your little black nigger ass will be an
old man before you get out."

My mama hugged me when they said I was guilty and whispered
in my ear that the white people would show me mercy because I
was so young. "You're only a child, a baby." Maybe she said that to
comfort me, to make me less scared. The court people let her stay
with me for a half hour yesterday and she spent the whole time
talking to me, saying the sweetest things. Things like how much she
missed me, how much she loved me. I felt less scared when she
talked like that and held me in her arms. But Daddy didn't come to
court. Because he's mad at me, ashamed of me, because I did this
bad thing and ruined my life. At least, that's how Mama explained
it to me. Also, I'm their only child, his only son. That's why he can't
look at me. I messed up.

As Mama tells it, they can't kill me or give me long time behind
bars because I'm underage. All she keeps saying is how I'm just a
child. Can't vote, drink, drive, marry, or join the army. So how can
they judge me as a grown man? But my lawyer, this Cuban man,
says they gave another black boy, ten years old, life in prison for
choking one of his playmates to death. Mr. Hernandez says they say
I'm a sociopath in training, a born killer, because I sat there during
the trial and didn't cry or say I'm sorry for shooting Mr. Strossen.
According to Mr. Hernandez, a sociopath is someone who kills and
likes doing it. I don't know if I liked killing Mr. Strossen. Mr.
Strossen is, or was, the principal of our school. He didn't like black
kids no way. He was on my back for the whole semester. He didn't
even say nothing one afternoon when three bullies were beating me
up outside of the cafeteria, didn't do nothing either. In fact, I could
have sworn I saw a smile on his white cracker face. The honky bas-

tard. My daddy calls them that when they shoot down innocent black guys for doing nothing. Honkies.

The prosecutor said yesterday that he told the jury to also get me for pointing a gun at Mr. Strossen, assault or something or other. My lawyer says they will give me another five years for that alone. I ain't never gon' get out. Never.

Where they held me before they took me back to jail, there was a TV in the room, and my lawyer was on there saying he thought they treated me bad. He said they treated me like some thug with a long record. He kept on saying they showed no mercy or compassion. The prosecutor was all smiles. The TV people showed him with the dead principal's family, and he talked for them because they were so sad they couldn't speak. You know something? I never thought that Mr. Strossen might have had a family and all. Folks who might cry over him if he died. Never thought about that. They seemed like nice people, especially the old white woman who walked with a cane. She was his mother. She looked at me like she felt sorry for me, like a house dog that had suddenly turned on his owner and bit him so the family had to put him to sleep. Like that.

Nobody understands that I didn't mean to kill Mr. Strossen. I just meant to scare him into making those boys leave me alone. That same day they beat me up, one of them squatted over me while the rest of them held me down and peed all over my face while everybody else laughed. Everyone laughed at me. That hurt me to no end. I went to Mr. Strossen and told him what happened, and all he said was that maybe I deserved it. Deserved it? He had a smile on his face. I was crying when I walked out of his office but I swore that I'd get them.

Mr. Hernandez says that's what the prosecutor meant by "premeditation." I planned to hurt somebody, premeditation. If that's what they call it, then they are right because I did plan it. I stole a box cutter from the grocery store down the street from where I lived and walked up on Orrin who is the leader of the bullies. Real tall and a lot of mouth. He saw me coming and laughed, asking if I wanted some more of what I got earlier. I was sick of him and how he treated me. So I stepped up to him and did a Zorro on his face with the box cutter. There was a lot of blood and he hollered and ran off down the street with his friends chasing him to take him for help.

When I went to school that same day, I took my daddy's gun. I don't know why I did it. Maybe I did it because the gun was there. Maybe I did it because I knew what was going to happen. Maybe I did it because I knew Mr. Strossen was going to mess with me.

"Young Mr. Sneed, you've really done it this time," Mr. Strossen said after ordering his secretary out of his office so he could be alone with me. "Your little nigger ass is fried this time. You won't get off so easy this go-round."

"I told you they were messing with me, and you didn't do nothing," I told him. "I asked you to make them stop. All you could say was I deserved it. I didn't deserve it."

"Shut up. You're no better than the rest of the savages around here."

I was desperate for him to let me speak. "Let me talk. I begged you to make them stop. You never liked me. You've hated me all along, and I ain't done nothing to you."

That was when he got all up on me, poking his finger in my chest. "Mr. Sneed, I hope they put you in jail and throw away the damn key. That's where your kind belong. Did I hear somewhere that your father did some time? You will be a jailbird just like your damn father."

The gun felt heavy in my coat pocket. Our school didn't have metal detectors like some of the real bad schools downtown so I walked right inside with it. I pulled it out just to make him shut up. So I could say something. The look on his face changed for a minute then he started badmouthing me again.

"What the hell are you going to do with that?" Mr. Strossen asked, holding his hand out. "Give me the damn gun before you really get in trouble. I said, give it to me, you little monkey!"

I don't really remember what happened after that too clearly. Shots went off. One right after another. And he fell right in front of me with this real scared look on his face. In court, they said I kept shooting him after he was down and that wasn't true. After the gun went off, I walked over to his desk, cleaned the gun off with my shirt, and laid it on his desk. I recall looking at his face once more. I expected him to get up and jerk me around some but he didn't. He just laid there, bleeding and dead. I was in a trance. I walked out of his office, right by his secretary and went to the study hall and waited for the police to come. I knew they would come.

Punish the young seed of Satan. I don't believe I'm evil. Mama says I'm not.

Waiting in the room for the judge to come back with my sentence, I asked the guard to bring me a soda. Mama had just left, her eyes red and swollen from crying. She said my daddy has been holed up in the bedroom for days, not going to work, just drinking. I hate what I did to them. If I could have hurt the other people without hurting them, that would have been nice. Seeing what I did to them has been the worst part of it. I feel lower than a dog. Maybe I don't deserve to live.

"Here's your soda, young Dillinger," the guard said, handing me a warm bottle of RC Cola. Who was Dillinger? Somebody bad, I guess.

I drank the soda slow, watching him watch me. I felt like crying but I couldn't. The tears wouldn't come. Maybe something was really wrong with me.

There was a knock on the door and another guard popped his head into the room. The two white men whispered and they left, closing the door behind them. I couldn't stop this low feeling I had. I poured out the rest of the soda, put the bottle on the floor and stomped it until it broke into pieces. Splinters of glass, some of it.

Punish the young seed of Satan.

I walked to the door, put my ear to it. Didn't hear nobody. I grabbed a handful of the ground glass, shoved it into my mouth, cutting my tongue and gums, then swallowed it. Maybe everything would be better if this little nigger boy wasn't around. Nobody wants little nigger boys nohow. The glass hurt going down but I was brave and strong. I went to a corner of the room, sat on the cold tiled floor behind the chairs and closed my eyes. Everything would be better when I was gone. Dead. I closed my eyes and waited for the Devil to come and take my soul.

A LIZARD'S KISS

Sometimes your body can betray you.

Sometimes your body can tell you things that your mind chooses to ignore.

Sometimes your body can lead you to discover things about yourself that others might miss in the fog of confusion. Sometimes your body takes over, transforming everything in the blink of a suspicious eye, the nod of an agreeable head or the embrace of eager arms and your life can never be the same again.

So it must have been the body, or at least Tirzah's eyes, that first connected to the advertisement for Madame Milagros, which the guy gave her on the bus. She politely read it but two weeks passed before she acted on the handbill's promises. It seemed everything in my friend's life conspired to keep her from going to this anointed vessel of God. Tirzah needed something good to happen for her. She felt like her twenty-two-year-old life was in a total shambles. Her job as a consultant for a high-tech firm ended abruptly when the company suddenly went belly-up. A poor market. Her building was going co-op and she had to move in three months. An argument with her beau had them teettering on the edge of a breakup. Her parents were talking about getting a divorce as soon as her seventeen-year-old brother, Malik, graduated from high school. It seemed that her mother wanted to start all over again and build a new life. She was bored with marriage, family, and a husband.

Tirzah worried about Malik. There was only the two of them but they weren't really close as siblings; something was missing in the heart-sense from their relationship. Nothing could make them have a civil conversation. They were always at each other's throats, yelling and screaming over the most mundane things. Things at which most people would shrug their shoulders. Maybe they were just too different. While Malik could be animated and upbeat with his friends, the very sight of her was enough to turn him into a sullen teenager seeking that next swig of wine or toke of some good herb. Malik was high most of the time.

When Tirzah asked him about the drugs, Malik would snarl at her, lips turning down in a gangster snarl, and say: "I'm not a crackhead. I'm a budhead. There's a big difference, so chill the hell out."

As Tirzah's best girlfriend, I knew most, if not all, of her business, including the really bad stuff she kept from her parents and everybody else. She could be very secretive. Although we have been friends for years, Tirzah would always say, "Lauren, promise me you won't say a word of this to anybody." That was like a ritual with her, the vow of silence and loyalty. I'd never been a blabbermouth, the gossipy type. We have the closeness you often see with black women, "sistas" as my girls always say, the kind of bond you don't often see in our men. Part of this is because Tirzah is like the sister I never had. But she worries too much, about everything, every little thing.

One of the things I liked most about Tirzah is the fact that she was a performance artist, not like the white ones, Spalding Gray or Karen Finley. She was a big fan of Finley at one time. Finley would get naked and smear chocolate syrup all over her body while she ranted against men, God, fossil fuels, girdles, and low sperm counts. On the other hand, Tirzah did little skits backed by a sax player or a violinist. Weird stuff for a black girl from Brooklyn. Her act wasn't like those chicks on *The Queens of Comedy* video but more of a mix of Chris Rock, Lenny Bruce, Moms Mabley, and Cedric the Entertainer. Skits mainly about the ongoing conflict between black women and men. And the need for a truce or ceasefire. Strange girl, always going against the grain. I met her one night at a poetry slam at the Nuyorican Poets Café down on the Lower East Side. I was there with a dancer friend who knew Tirzah and her work. My dancer buddy, with her dreadlocks and overalls, was intrigued with Tirzah's lithe body and how it moved so gracefully in her trademark skit about the mating ritual.

We talked with Tirzah after the show, and I became pals with her. We hung out constantly. With Tirzah, I was immediately drawn into a whole new world of artists, writers, photographers, and musicians. She seemed to know everybody. Nightly, we prowled the Lower East Side and the Village, going to poetry readings in lofts, coffeehouses, and computer bars. And Harlem, even the South Bronx. We listened to hard bop jazz and techno in smoky clubs, danced to hip-hop, salsa, and house in small side-street dives, and watched abstract dance numbers in various performance spaces in Chelsea. Truthfully, Tirzah opened up my mind.

Coming from a newly busted family, Tirzah loved to be around my folks because both of them were artists, both painters, and their circle of friends was quite eccentric and creative. She thought that was a kick. My parents lived in Harlem for a while before they went to the Ivory Coast for three years as a part of a cultural exchange program. My pops was in this Garvey groove and my moms went along for the ride. I stayed at home with my aunt Ida. After that, they moved to Paris for another five years before coming back to the States to renovate a farmhouse upstate. Finally, I lived with them and everything was wonderful. I didn't hold a grudge. I was just glad to be with them.

So with all of this in mind, it's not surprising that Tirzah's life changed drastically in the weeks after she met Madame Milagros. She was always open to change and adventure. Also, everything happens for a reason. Nothing is random or by chance. I truly believe that now. One reason for the change in her life was this creep, Walter Baker, a guy she met some time before going to visit the seer. He was just her type, six-three, dark-chocolate brown, finely muscled, the eternal male fashion plate. She loved them dark, the darker the better. Yellow or brown brothers, she joked, gave her a rash. Anyway, Walter looked like Tyson the model, not the pug thug, more like Djimon Honsou, that African brother from the film, *Amistad* or Taye Diggs from the Terry McMillan movie. Those kinds of guys. Get the picture? When I met Walter that first time, my body reacted to him strangely, my stomach did a full cartwheel. He didn't feel right. Something was up with him. I could feel it.

"He called me, he called me!" Tirzah squealed into the phone. "He called me last night, out of the blue, and asked me to go with him to Sizzle, the club, tonight. Can you believe it, girl?"

"You mean, the new club down on Houston Street?"

Something still felt wrong about him but I didn't say anything. That sick feeling in my stomach just wouldn't go away. Although I was just a year older than Tirzah, I sometimes felt like her big sister. The girl was so happy that I didn't want to ruin her fun, not with my intuition. Hell, I could be wrong.

"Lauren, I know what you're thinking," she said, reading my mind, at least part of it. "I'll still be a lady. No goodies on the first date."

And then the call came late in the night, frantic, desperate, frightened. Tirzah's voice alternated between a low rasp and a high-pitched yelp bordering on hysteria. "Lauren . . . Lauren . . . come get me, please. The bastard's . . . the bastard's flipped out."

Dazed, I glanced at the digital clock on the radio beside my bed and it read four-thirty. I assured her I'd be there as quick as I could. When I asked about Walter the Creep, she just ignored my question and pleaded for me to get there fast. She sounded like she was going to pass out.

"I couldn't stop them, Lauren, I couldn't," Tirzah mumbled just before she collapsed into my arms near my car. I held her tight against me and let her cry out as much of the pain and shame as possible. I cried with her.

Later, we got to my place and quickly called her folks and told them she was with me. I told them she was helping me through a personal crisis and that I needed her with me now more than ever. I let my body lie. I let my body put some weird twitch into my voice that convinced her moms that something was indeed wrong. Her mother, Judy, a real sweetheart and saint, said she understood, adding Tirzah could stay with me as long as necessary.

Good thing she said that because The Creep and his crew did a number on my girl. Her eyes, both of them, almost beaten shut, stared at me with this confused look. One whole side of her face and body was covered with raw bruises and bloody scrapes as if she had been dragged along the pavement and kicked repeatedly. She was a real mess. And I didn't see the full extent of the damage until she waddled slowly into the bathroom and began removing her ripped, soiled clothes. Only then did I see that the crotch of her panties was full of blood and long streams of red ran down both legs to the tiled floor. It took me three hours to clean her up, get her to bed, and hear the entire harrowing story of how Walter and his boys savaged her in his new BMW.

No, she wouldn't let me call the police, telling me the news of the rape would destroy her folks and cause unnecessary grief. To allay my fears for her health, she assured me that she would get an HIV test as soon as she was on her feet. About a week later, I came home to a darkened apartment and Tirzah asleep on the sofa in a robe. The ashtrays were full of cigarette butts and gum wrappers. A note on top of the CD player announced her AIDS test was negative. That was a relief. I leaned over, noticed a small golden card in one of her still hands and began reading it.

MADAME MILAGROS

HANDMAIDEN OF THE ALMIGHTY

- *Experience the joy and wonder of a true spiritual reading.*
- *Gain access to deeper levels of knowledge, well-being, and healing.*
- *Understand your personality, your life, and the many reasons for the physical, emotional, and spiritual challenges you've faced along your path.*
- *Learn what you can do to find health and wholeness.*
- *Be healed. Be transformed. Soothe your mind. Strengthen your spirit.*
- *Confidential one-hour sessions.*
- *Satisfaction guaranteed.*
- *Call for an appointment today.*

After I read the card, I slipped it back into her grasp and went to the kitchen to make a cup of peppermint tea. That was the difference between Tirzah and me. She believed all of the soothsayers, crystal-ball gazers, witches, and whatever else. I was a hard sell. Yet, I must admit something, just as I placed the card back into her hand, it became very warm, the square of laminated paper, like a skillet cooling down, and the letters on its face started to glow. Like a neon sign on those flophouse hotels. No kidding.

Something told me not to mention to Tirzah what the card had done. But I couldn't help noticing how her mood changed completely after three weeks. She was singing old Aretha and Chaka Khan tunes around the apartment, showing no aftereffects from the assault, even jogging again. In fact, she was bouncing around like a woman freshly in love. Her face was lit with this angelic glow, the skin smoother than ever, almost glistening with health and vitality. It was odd having this kind of vibe in my place.

"What's up, girl?" I asked her. "I've not seen you this happy before. You oughta see yourself. Honey, you're worrying me. This ain't you."

"I just feel good, Lauren," she said, smiling from ear to ear. "I finally know what happiness is. It's like there is this electrical current running from the top of my head to the soles of my feet."

"What's his name? Do I know him?" I was skeptical.

She plopped down on a chair near the fishbowl, tapping with one finger against the glass. "No, it's not a he, but a she."

That was understandable. Plenty of women try the lesbian thing once they face the kind of male stupidity and brutality Tirzah had experienced. I guess it's a way of healing the body and soul when some traditional methods fail. Going back to the source, to the softness and comfort of another woman. Still, I couldn't see Tirzah totally giving up men. Rape or no rape. But then what did I know about anything? Shit, I was bugging out over her sudden state of bliss. Maybe it was some sort of divine visitation.

"No, it's not what you think." She spoke slowly as if trying to educate a chimp. "It's a soul thing, an aura thing, a spirit thing. It's Madame Milagros. She's the bomb, girl."

"Madame who?" I played dumb. "Is she a voodoo goddess? Or something like that?"

"You got to check her out. I'm serious. She'll make everything cool. She sets it all straight. I mean it. There's nothing she doesn't know or see. She's like a female god or something. A deity. I can't figure it out. I've been to her place three times now and she always gets it right. Sometimes I don't even have to talk."

"I don't know about this black magic stuff," I said, getting the willies already.

It was dark, just before eleven when we arrived at the temple of Madame Milagros, a basement apartment in Spanish Harlem, converted into a temple where this priestess could practice her gift for second sight. The uncanny ability to foretell the future. The first thing I noticed was the only source of light was a million lit candles of various sizes, shapes, and colors, whose illumination set off the walls of dark velvet surrounding the seer and her large table of flawless oak. In the reflected glow of the candle fires, the impressive figure of Madame Milagros, so youthful in her startling red-and-gold robe, sat motionless before a spread deck of cards. She seemed too young for this work and unbelievably attractive with her beautiful, unlined face. Her scent, the fragrance of a blooming rose, made me dizzy with its potent aroma. She wore a gold chain around her neck with a large clear rose quartz attached to it. On nearby tables, rows of semi-precious stones were scattered in no apparent pattern, topaz, amethysts, and tourmalines. Live chickens strutted back and forth in cages tucked in the far corner of the room. They made no sound.

"I thought you said she was a middle-aged woman, Tirzah," I said, amazed at her youth. "She doesn't look a day over twenty."

"She changes her appearance every time," Tirzah whispered. "The same woman but different ages and shapes. The last time I came here, I could swear I saw a big bulge like a man's you-know-what down there underneath her robe. It's spooky as hell."

"The word is *hermaphrodite*," the seer said, offering half of a pomegranate to us but we refused. "I'm all things, both male and female, both goddess and messenger. So yes, I'm more than just a damn fortune-teller."

It creeped me out when she said that, because that was exactly what I was thinking at that very moment. This female, or whatever, was really dangerous if she could get inside people's heads like that. So easily. At will. Talk about the invasion of privacy. To switch gears and moods, I asked her about the cards on the table and their meaning.

Madame Milagros nodded at me as though she had heard that thought, too, before it ever left my lips, then she motioned for both of us to sit down. I moved to sit on a chair along the velvet wall, far away from her, but she waved for me to take a seat at the enormous wooden table facing her. For a second, the collective glow of the candles flickered with the gesture of her arm, and the light became dim and changed color, from bright white to a bluish hue. I wanted to leave real bad.

"By the way, these cards are exact replicas derived from the Egyptian Book of the Dead, written during the rule of Orisis," the seer said, then gave me the first of many commands. "Give me your hand, your right hand."

I did as I was told.

"It is all here in your hand, right here," Madame Milagros said. "You have what is called a practical hand. See the square palm and the short fingers? A heavy hand. See there, the main lines for the Heart, Life, and Head. This is the Mount of Venus. Your element is the Earth itself. Some call you shallow and fickle but there is much going on with you underneath the surface. There is a tendency to underestimate you. However, your feet are on the ground, as they say."

"Will I get a promotion on my job?" I asked, tired of the secretarial pool.

"Well, let me explain the marking first," she said patiently. "You find pleasure in the simple things. You are very careful about your decisions and guided by a knowledge of what is right. That is very important to you. Hard work, honesty, effort, and integrity are things you admire."

"All she does is work, work, work," Tirzah teased. "She doesn't know how to relax. She's going to get an ulcer one day."

I said nothing.

"All three of your main lines are deep," the seer said to me. "Both the Heart and the Life lines are much deeper and longer than your Head line. That's very significant."

"She's a Taurus, if that means anything," Tirzah interrupted.

"You do not put too much stock in things you cannot see or touch," Madame Milagros said. "You like the obvious, the plain and simple. If you marry, you should marry a man with a practical hand like yours. You may be bored sometimes but you two would be very suited for such a life. Monotony, unlike with some people, does not threaten you. In fact, you enjoy routine."

"That's for sure," Tirzah said. "Like Wade, this new guy she just met. A real boring stiff sometimes. He works hard but he's a blank in terms of personality. He can sit in front of the TV for hours and hours and not move. That would drive me nuts."

"It doesn't take much to keep me happy," I chirped.

The candles did their flickering thing again. "That's not true," the seer intoned. "All your relationships start out with such high hopes, and quickly it becomes obvious that they were not as they seemed. Illusions. Then the disappointments mount for you until you lose interest in them and wait for the next man to come along. Like this Wade. There is more there than meets the eye."

"What's wrong with Wade? He treats me good." I knew a solid man when I saw one. And that was what Wade was, solid and steady.

"But he's not for you. He has secrets. He has another woman who is now having his child. What he now presents to you is a false face and cold heart."

"What is your proof?" I yelled at her. I believed in Wade and his promises of love and commitment. A vein throbbed in my head.

"A Lizard's Kiss," the seer said solemnly. "I cannot explain it. It's an old gypsy term. You see it so rarely these days."

"What do you see, there in my hand?" Now I was curious. What was this kiss of the lizard bit? "Is it bad? What is it? Is there anything I can do to get rid of it?"

Madame Milagros blew out one of the thin, white candles. "The Lizard's Kiss means you are one of the special souls put here. You have a powerful spirit guide. There's nothing more that I can tell you now. Maybe next time. Change is coming to your life. All you must do is not resist. Surrender to it. It will come amid great challenge, disappointment, and struggle. Ah, but when it comes, it will be worth the wait. You will be filled with joy. Your heart will swell from the happiness. That is all for today."

She stood first, a signal for us to do likewise. I paid the fee and went to hug her, both in gratitude and respect, but she moved back. What was this about? She smiled, backing away, with her hands up in front of her, almost defensively. There was a look of concern mixed with affection on her face, a strange blend of caution and compassion, but still she didn't allow me to touch her person. The tainted touch of the unclean, maybe.

As I started to leave, the seer put her hand out to stop me. "Tell your mother she must go to the doctor as soon as possible. The lump in her breast cannot be ignored. It is serious. She must go now, or it'll soon be too late. She can delay no longer."

That blew my mind. I didn't know whether I should tell Moms something like that. But I would, even if she laughed at me. I couldn't think of my mother dying.

Put something else into play, another question. "Will I get married?" I asked lamely. "I don't want to be an old maid. By myself forever."

"Yes," Madame Milagros replied. "But you must wait for him."

Once in the car, we sat there completely dumbfounded, stunned, totally awed by the experience. Tirzah kept saying, "See, see, see. What did I tell you." I couldn't wait to check into the information she'd given me. This thing with Wade was a top priority. First, I went to the address of the apartment that the seer gave me, where a very pregnant Chinese girl admitted she was carrying Wade's baby. He confessed and said he'd bother me no more. Good riddance. And next, Moms, upon my insistence, went for another mammogram and further testing at a clinic uptown. Everything was caught in time. Two out of two. The woman was good, on target like Tirzah said.

I called Tirzah, gave her the rundown, and told her that I wanted her to come with me to Madame Milagro's temple so I could thank her for saving my life. On the way home from my job, I bought some red roses, a dozen, and a lovely crystal vase. It was the least I could do for the woman. She had saved my butt big time. And my mother's life.

Later, we set out for the temple but couldn't find it. We drove around for the better part of three hours and couldn't spot the building. It was as if someone just swooped down and plucked the entire structure right out of the block. The car was running low on gas so we decided to give it another twenty minutes before we'd throw in the towel and go home. Finally, Tirzah got out of the car, choosing to check the neighborhood on foot while I cruised nearby. Up and down the blocks, we searched until I suddenly heard Tirzah scream she had found it. But this was not the place I remembered, now larger and grander than the other one, although the building looked similar. It was currently situated at the rear of an alley and not on the main thoroughfare. Real strange. The sign outside was almost the same. No name. Just an invite to get your future told. Very peculiar.

I led the way, bounding down the main stairs to a basement apartment. We knocked on the door and a very ancient voice, struggling for air, said for us to enter. We went inside and immediately noticed the room was the same, right down to the candles, the crystal displays, and the pack of tarot cards spread on the large table.

"Who are you looking for, young ladies?" the old woman asked, sitting in the exact chair where the seer sat earlier.

"Madame Milagros," we said as one voice. "We saw her a few days ago."

The old woman, a collection of fleshy folds and wrinkles, pulled herself slowly from the chair, reached for a silver cane at her elbow and walked with great effort over to a line of elegantly framed photographs mounted along one velvet wall. Her dress was a bright yellow, like a miniature sun. Using her cane as a pointer, she mumbled something to herself as she wobbled past each one before coming to a shaky stop before a yellowed daguerreotype mounted in a golden frame. A photograph taken by a now-forgotten man during the early days of the camera in frontier America.

"Is this the woman you saw here?" the old woman asked, one eyebrow arched. "This one, right here?"

We walked over to the gallery of women preserved on film and nodded that yes, it was the same woman. Maybe somewhat younger. She appeared to be in her late thirties in the picture, her hair pulled back, dressed in a frilly number. But there was no doubt it was her. The same tilt of the head, the same piercing eyes, the same full mouth. The same woman, just older.

The old woman, pulling a shawl from a nearby chair, snorted and leaned back on her cane. "You're not the first to see her. That's my great-great-grandmother. Milagros. Miracles. She was stoned to death as a bride of Satan, a witch, more than one hundred years ago, for having the gift of second sight. A Queen of the Dark Loas. I doubt it was her you met here, though. She's been dead a long time, a very long time."

"Oh my God!" I heard Tirzah shout in a voice filled with horror. For some reason, she was watching the old woman while I examined the photo, never once looking away for any lengthy moment. She didn't trust this woman as she would have Madame Milagros.

Startled, I pivoted just in time to see the old woman become Madame Milagros in form and substance, a solid figure for a fleeting instant, which slowly faded first into a dull gray image like a slide projected on a living room wall, then gradually vanish from view like Lewis Carroll's tricky Cheshire Cat in *Alice in Wonderland.* Only here just the chair, not the grin, remained. Our knees were knocking from fear.

When I turned back to look at the Madame's portrait, it was no longer there but something else, even more unsettling, was in its place. It was me, the way I looked at ten, long black pigtails, all eyes and long limbs. The white cotton dress I was wearing in the photograph was one I remembered well. I stood where Madame Milagros had once stood, against the same passive background of trees from her picture, holding an enormous lizard against my flat chest. The scaly reptile appeared at ease in my embrace, with its long body, four stunted legs, and its twisting tapered tail. Although Tirzah said she couldn't see it, I could have sworn the young girl and the lizard both wore the same intense expression.

Finally, we'd seen and heard enough. Tirzah was the first out of the door. I was right on her heels. We ran, breathless, to my car, afraid to look back. I gunned the engine and peeled rubber getting out of there. To this day, we've never told anybody what happened there nor have we ever discussed it again. We may never talk about it but neither of us have ever forgotten it.

THE GARDEN OF EVIL

This was the second night in a row that the man was there in the shadows. He followed her for several blocks. Staying just feet behind her, never moving within range where she might catch a full glimpse of him. She paid no real attention to this intrusion on her privacy. Stalkers no longer frightened her since her father warned her of the male reaction to beauty such as hers. Women of her startling loveliness were known to drive men to do things they would not ordinarily do.

She slowed to let the distance between them close. The sound of his footsteps on the empty streets echoed with a strange resonance, almost bell-like, hanging in the foggy slice of sky between the buildings. When she joined a group of people gawking at a collection of exotic birds, marveling at the riot of brilliant colors on display in their plumage, the man blended into the onlookers on the fringe of the crowd.

As she stepped away to cross the street, she turned to glance back but the man was not there. A look to the left at the stragglers on the sidewalk revealed nothing. Content that her prowler had given up, she moved briskly toward the cab stand four blocks away, knowing that someone there among the cabbies would drive the fifteen-mile trek to her home out on the wooded preserve.

"Take me out to the Otica Preserve, sir," she said to the first cabbie parked in the line of yellow vehicles at the stand. "I'll make it worth your while."

"That's at least ten or fifteen miles out of town." The cabbie cast her a worried look. He was an older black man with the stale odor of cigarettes on his clothes.

"As I said, I'll make it worth your while." It was more of a command than a statement.

"Why the black outfit? Have you been to a costume ball?"

She ignored his question, looking out the back window for the stalker. He was nowhere in sight. A sigh of relief escaped her lips. Then she thought better of it and frowned.

"Are you deaf, ma'am? I asked if you had been to a masquerade party or something. With all of the black you wearing and all."

Her patience was wearing thin. "No, it's not Halloween. Can we go now?"

"Yes, if you insist." More attitude, more sarcasm.

The cab started up, coughing up dark smoke, and finally started easing up the cobbled side street toward the main road. This was a part of town frequented by musicians, artists, dopers, muggers, tourists, and fashioned tattooed youth. People looking for a night of partying, drugging, and drinking. Very rarely did you find citizens of the straight-laced variety in this now trendy district during the week. She came down here at least twice a week from her modern glass house in the sticks, seeking thrills or adventure, but seldom finding either.

"If you go looking for trouble, you will find it," her father told her just four days ago. "I've seen young ladies like you go out there looking for mischief, trying to get into whatever evil was available and getting more than their share. Be careful out there."

His words of caution only made her more hungry for something to happen to her that would make her breath short and tight, forcing her heart to pound. She wanted the hell scared out of her. Real fear. The kind of fear that put the taste of copper in your mouth. She needed to be frightened of something other than boredom. The way her life was currently going, she was going to die an old maid without ever having known a man or a real scare. At this point, she would gladly take either one.

"Anybody ever tell you that you're a real looker?" the cabbie asked, taking his eyes off the road to examine her in the rearview mirror.

"Yes, I hear it all the time. Men say all kinds of things to me. 'I know you're a heartbreaker.' 'You look just like the tall girl with that band, En Vogue.' One week, it's Dorothy Dandridge. The week before that it was a young Lena Horne. I hear it all day, every day. How pretty I am. It's a curse."

"I wouldn't complain. Pretty girls have it good, real good in this world."

Suddenly, the cabbie stopped his foolishness and adjusted the mirror. "I think somebody's following us. The car made the last turn-off with us and nobody in their right mind comes out this way."

The car's bright headlights were there, pushing their way into the absolute darkness all around them. She smiled, hoping that something sinister was finally about to happen to her. This was what her father had trained her to handle for more than ten years. Whoever was in that car was in for a surprise. A supernatural surprise. In her mind, she chanted: *please come, faster, faster, please come.* Unfortunately, the cabbie sped up, attempting to lose the rapidly approaching car around the turns and twists of the two-lane blacktop.

"Why are you driving so fast?" she asked. "Slow down before you kill us. Don't worry about that guy back there. Keep your eyes on the road. It's tricky up in here."

The cabbie was two heartbeats away from panic. "Are you crazy, woman? I'm not getting hijacked out on this deserted road. We don't know who's in that car, how many of them are there, or what their intentions are. Hell no. I'm not stopping for nothing, not one damn thing."

He gunned the engine, taking the curves of the road with the cab's tires squealing like a man stabbed. The rows of trees stood like spectral sentries along their route. Every now and then, he looked in the mirror to see if his pursuer was still there. And he was, still there, gaining ground. Nothing could save them if it was a car of young gun-toting toughs who wanted to brutalize them out in the hinterland, in the sticks, away from any possibility of rescue or escape.

"Let them catch up," she yelled, the adrenaline rush getting the best of her.

"Hell no!" His heart was now beating in his throat.

"I said let them catch us," she insisted. "Slow the fuck down."

The cabbie shook his head. "No way. My ass is on the line here."

If the thugs caught them, he concluded, there would be no chance of getting away. He imagined being forced to kneel on the asphalt in the dark with a gun placed to the back of his head, forced to empty his pockets. Robbed and then shot like a dog to be left by the side of the road. He had a family to consider, a home to be maintained, an ailing mother to be cared for. Forget this crazy girl. There was no way anything like this was going to happen.

After a few minutes of chase, they looked back and the car was gone, no headlights. No pursuit. While the cabbie was relieved, she was totally disappointed by the driver's cowardice and his refusal to play out his part of the game. Damn him! She sat quietly for the rest of the ride home, a sour expression on her face. Damn him!

Her father had built their home, a stunning tribute to the genius of architect Frank Lloyd Wright, during the heady days of the post–World War II boom. He put every penny made from his years on Wall Street into his glass modernist structure, copying each advance he could steal from the innovative Wright houses that dotted the land around the country. People came from nearby towns and cities to look upon the building from the road below. It sat on the edge of a national wooded preserve. At first, he tried to drive them away, shouting from the wrap-around terrace on the house's second floor, then setting his German shepherd attack dogs on them before the sheriff warned him that kind of behavior would not be tolerated.

The real attraction for the curious was his extensive garden, rows of rare, tropical flowers sheltered by the sloping panes of a mammoth greenhouse that covered nearly an acre of the estate. He could be seen tending to the plants every day, watering and feeding them with a special mixture of nutrients developed for him by a Belgian chemist. For years, the old man made his beautiful daughter come with him to the greenhouse, showing her how much mixture could be given to each plant. She made notes about the work in a small leather-bound notebook kept by her father.

"When I die, these flowers will be your responsibility," her father reminded her. "Yours and yours alone. They will depend on your love and care to survive, just like you have on me. These are your children. Treat them accordingly."

She stood a few inches over him, her slender hand brushing several strands of black curly hair from her face. "You have my word. I will love them as you have loved me."

He smiled warmly at her, brushing the smudges of soil from his overalls before hugging her. "Thank you, daughter."

"Crystal, Daddy. You never call me by my name. Why?"

"That was your mother's name. It hurts when I say it. Indulge me."

"Alright." She sadly turned from him and glanced at the pines bordering the estate. It was not her fault that her mother went mad from the isolation of her life out here, tried to slice her wrists and was locked away in a state institution. That had been her home for the past ten years.

Her father grabbed her hand and led her out into the fresh air, across the green carpet of lawn toward the house. There was an extra bounce in his step today. He was happy. Whistling an old Count Basie tune, he started up the long, canopied walk to the main building, his head up, moving briskly.

"Have you seen that gray car parked down at the end of the driveway?" he asked matter-of-factly. "It's been there for days. Do you know who that could be?"

She smiled, revealing a row of big, white teeth. Eyes twinkling. "No."

Inside, she knew the other night was only the beginning. The game was still on. The prey was close at hand, and it was only a matter of time before the trap would be sprung.

Before she went to bed that next night, she disconnected the security alarms and sat on her bed in her panties, smoking a cigarette and waiting for the prey to come out of hiding. It was as if she was lingering near a mouse's lair, waiting to pounce. Patient and lethal. The hours went by, slowly at first, then once midnight faded into

memory, she stood at the window, watching and waiting for the inevitable to occur. *Please come, stranger, come. Don't let me down. It's
your fate. Don't fail me.*

Waiting was never one of her favorite things. Waiting always
made her hungry. Her father listened to her as she walked down the
stairs, headed for the kitchen and the refrigerator. He knew what
was about to happen. He hoped she didn't fill herself up with junk
before dinner. A snack was alright but sometimes low blood sugar
could make you overeat. Still, the sounds coming from the pantry
were comforting, reminding him of a time when the family was together, a unit, and Mother was yet with them.

From the kitchen window, she saw the long shadow of the man
trotting with stealth across the wide expanse of the lawn, keeping
low as if that would disguise the alluring scent of his smell in her
nostrils. Her back stiffened. Smiling, she walked to the refrigerator,
pulled open the door, and removed the flask of chilled red cherry
juice. The succulent taste of the juice always prepared her palate
for other, more appealing flavors. She tilted the flask up and let the
cold stream of liquid run down into her mouth and off her chin.
The smell of him was still with her. His man smell. His food smell.

Carefully, he entered the part of the greenhouse containing row
upon row of orchids, leafy, aromatic, and colorful. Their fragrance
was almost overpowering. He crept along the flowers, carrying a
small flashlight, placing his footsteps with the purpose of a cat bur-
glar. No lights were on in the house. He knew what he had to do.
Carla, his sister, had told him about this place in one of her letters.
They had constantly stayed in touch while she was at college with
letters, phone calls, and e-mails. He was doing a stretch in jail for
breaking and entering, a series of houses along the Gold Coast, the
rich neighborhood along the city's lakefront. She knew he was getting out in a few weeks but then all contact with her stopped.
Nothing. His family notified the police of her disappearance and
they went to her apartment off campus only to find her suitcases
packed and no signs of struggle. Carla had vanished. Her purse was
there, containing money, cell phone, driver's license, and credit

cards. That made it seem strange that she would just walk away and leave everything behind. Nobody could tell him that something bad had not happened to her. And this house and these two nut-cases were the key to it all. Had to be.

Looking around the greenhouse, he was amazed at the number of plants in one area. Must have been more than six hundred in this section alone. He wasn't a big fan of flowers, any kind of flowers, especially orchids. The sound of someone walking turned him around, on his heels, but there was nobody there. Maybe it was imagination. After all, this place was somewhat spooky. All these damned plants.

When he turned back around, he saw her, a tall, shapely black girl watering the flowers with a hose, with no clothes on. She walked among the plants casually as if it was something she did every day. He looked closer. She had the face of a young girl, almost Chinese features on brown skin. Her body was slender, toned, without an ounce of fat, featuring large breasts for a girl her size and legs any model would love. Quietly, he watched her with the plants, spraying some type of golden solution on their petals and leaves. The flowers seemed to turn toward her, like they knew she was bringing them food. They seemed to have an intelligence, thinking flowers, begging for her attention, and she didn't neglect any of them.

"Surprised at how they respond, huh?" she asked, suddenly pivoting in his direction. "Orchids. They're my favorite flower. Have been since I was a kid. They grow all over the world, even in the more difficult climates. Did you know that three Australian species grow underground? For a flower, they're really quite tough and re-silient. Why are you here? Did you come to see the orchids?"

He kept the flashlight directed at her with one hand and pulled a small revolver out of his coat with the other. "I came to find out about my sister. You remember Carla, don't you? She worked for you about three months ago. One day, she just disappeared, and I think you know where she is."

"Oh yes, a small mousy girl with cornrows," she replied, continuing to pour nutrients onto the flowers. "She just called in one day and said she quit. No reason given."

"Bullshit. That's not like her. My sister was Ms. Responsibility. Stop lying."

The young woman stroked one of the orchids, and he could have sworn it leaned against her hand like a cat would do when caressed. "Orchids are considered the symbol of love and beauty around the world. It's been that way for centuries. The Greeks saw them as a symbol of virility. In the middle ages, they were used in love potions as an aphrodisiac. People have been collecting and growing them from almost the beginning of time, so much so that now it is considered illegal to do that."

He took a step toward her with the gun, and the flowers all seemed to twist in his direction. Some sprayed off a golden mist of pollen. "I didn't come here for a damn lecture on flowers," he growled. "Where the hell is my sister, bitch?"

"We must dilute their fertilizers because they're not heavy feeders like some plants," she continued, switching off the hose. "For flowers like these, you can't just use any old common fertilizer. These flowers must have just the right balance of nitrogen, phosphorus, and potassium. We've added some other goodies to their diet to make sure that they stay strong and healthy. Otherwise their roots turn black and the tips of their leaves die. Right, babies?"

He waved at her with the gun, gesturing that she come closer. "Get out of the shadows and come where I can see you. No funny stuff. Where is my sister?"

"Did you know that you must never use cold water on them?" she asked, stepping nearer to her prey. "No cold water and no fertilizer for these plants. It will kill them."

"Where is my sister?" He walked toward her. "She wrote me that all kinds of weird things were going on at this house. Horrible things."

"What kind of horrible things?" the woman asked. "Did she say?"

"No, but I intend to find out. I'll know everything before I leave here tonight."

She smiled, licking her lips with an oddly long tongue. "I'm sure you will know everything fairly soon. You seem like a pretty persistent guy. Make you a deal. I've never had a man before. I'm still a virgin. Pure. Wholesome. If you make love to me, I'll tell you every-thing you want to know. Everything. But you have to make love to me long and strong. Put everything you have into it. Think about it. How many times will you get an offer like this in your life?"

"So you're saying if I give you some bone, you'll come clean about what happened to my sister?" He was already starting to un-button his shirt.

Still grinning, she nodded, found her blouse and pants and laid them down on the concrete floor. She cupped her breasts in both hands and squirmed as if he was already inside her. Her seductive eyes never left his eager face. Without another word, she sprawled upon the clothes, held her arms out to him and parted her legs. He stared at her brown body, imagining her tightness, and finally his glance fell on her sex. It was a swollen cleft, slick and wet. There was no doubt she was very excited about what he was about to do to her.

"Everything? You'll tell me everything?" He needed some assur-ance.

She took the gun from him, laid it down next to her on the floor and leaned forward to gently kiss him on the lips. He pulled off his pants and his dick sprang out like a taut rod. Soon he was between her soft thighs, her pillow mouth covered one of his nipples, and her hands gripped him so hard that he cried out. Puzzled, he looked at her for a second, trying to figure out what she had in mind.

"I want you to do it to me like it was your very last time," she whispered in his ear. "Real hard. Like you want to hurt me down there. I want to feel all of you."

He guided himself into her, met some resistance and pushed through it. She hissed strangely for a moment, tears in her eyes, then thrust herself against him. He was amazed at how wet she was. His hips pounded into her with as much force as he could muster. Most girls would be yelling or shouting his name but she was differ-ent. She just stared into his eyes with a fury and intensity that chilled his very heart.

"Harder, harder, harder," she moaned. "I need to feel it all."

He tried to meet her passion but he was only frustrating her. Eventually she rolled him over and mounted him, easing down upon him until she sighed at the depth of his penetration of her.

She wiggled atop him, shuddering with each dip and swoop of her limber spine. Humming deep in her throat, she seized hold of his wrists and pinned him to the floor with uncommon strength. He struggled underneath her, gasping for breath but she continued her assault on his senses. His back arched as he neared his climax, throbbing inside her, and was stunned when she took hold of his head and slammed it into the concrete. He fought her yet he couldn't budge her.

"What the hell?" he screamed. "Get off me, get off me right now."

That was all he got a chance to say, for it seemed like the orchids were there on the floor, erupting, agitated, fighting to cover every available inch of his flesh with their tendrils. Growing, spreading over him in a mass of tangled vines. Their smell filled his consciousness even as she pounded his head again and again on the floor. He clawed at her face, trying to push her off him, but the plants, with their flesh that felt too much like human flesh, were filling his every orifice with their green fingers. *Oh my God, please . . . please . . . don't let me die like this . . . not like this. Save me. . . .*

She bent over and covered his mouth with hers, sealing off the last of his air, just before he felt something like a pin prick his skin at the base of his neck. Someone else was there. A man's voice. An old man. They both stood over him, watching the plants retreat, pulling back their green fingers from the man, who lay there on the floor, eyes open but motionless.

"Is he dead?" the man asked. "You didn't kill him, did you?"

"No, I didn't," she said, smiling broadly. "I learned my lesson the last time with the girl. He was so much more fun than she was. Daddy, you never said it would be like this. I still feel him inside me."

"I'm glad you had a good time," her father said warmly as he rolled a machine over to where the man was. "Help me with this. I'm not as young as I used to be."

They rolled the man over, inserted another needle into his head near his left ear, and the whirr of the machine filled the room. She stroked the clear tubing leading from the needle to the machine, watching the pink fluid rush up into the metal box. Soon the orchids would have their nighttime snack. As would the two of them. Every part of the man would be used. Nothing wasted. Just like the girl. Suddenly, the man flinched on the floor, groaned, and his legs began kicking wildly. She sat down on him, pinning him to the concrete with her knees on his arms, singing the old Count Basie melody her father loved to the erratic beat of the machine processing their prey's blood.

"Daddy, the flowers are going to be so happy," she said, winking at her father. "Don't you hear them? Don't you hear them giggling?"

THE WISDOM
OF THE
SERPENTS

"No one can find the truth in one's life for anyone else. Truth, like love and violence, is a person's own doing. No one can find truth for another."

—Krishnamurti

The skies over Pinto, Ohio, wept nonstop, the driving rain accompanied by jagged streaks of golden lightning across the agitated horizon. A cluster of people stood under umbrellas, their heads tilted upward in search of the tiny speck of silver bearing the ravaged body of the beloved old man, listening for the distant whir of the plane's engines. They had been there for more than an hour, keeping their vigil despite the bad weather. Some suggested the aircraft may have fallen, hinting this was another hoax, doubting that the flight ever took off from Bangkok, where their stricken son was discovered wandering the streets in rags. One of his saviors, who had assisted him to the small hospital where his identity was finally unraveled, said he did not know where he had been for the last few days, could not speak, nor could he communicate in any way.

A grainy photograph sent to his family and friends showed a man, frail by any standards, skeletal, looking back at the camera with empty, hollow eyes. There was a sense of serenity mixed with terror in his expression as if he had seen the unspeakable, seen something so horrible that his mind had totally shut down to avoid its lethal overload. It was hard to imagine that this thin, bearded man was only thirty-three years old, young in American terms, yet everything indicated he had been aged by some terrifying experience endured on the other side of the world. In the week since his discovery, the photo was copied, mailed, and faxed to the man's many members of the clan across the country and around the globe.

Ramsey Thomas Oates was back among the living. Ramsey's brother, David, called everyone he knew to say "The Ram" was back

in the world among the civilized and refined, back from the pagan
fringe. He was home at last!

Finally, the drone of the plane was heard and eventually the old
cargo craft wobbled as it barely cleared the rim of trees at the edge
of the landing strip. Its wings dipped dangerously before it made its
final descent. Airport personnel held back the gathering while the
aircraft taxied over to a hanger where Ramsey would be loaded onto
a stretcher and into an ambulance for the ride to a nearby hospital.
Only his father and two brothers were allowed to ride with him.
They stared at him, disturbed by the fact that he could not speak or
acknowledge them. Essentially, he was a living corpse.

"What's wrong with the boy?" Ezra, Ramsey's father, asked, laying his large brown hand on his son's clammy forehead. "Why doesn't
he say anything?" Barry, his oldest boy, the engineer, patted his father lovingly on the shoulder. "Don't worry. They say there's a
chance it's only temporary but he's been like this since they found
him. The doctors who examined him over there say there doesn't
seem to be anything physically wrong with him. No disease or injury. They think it's shock."

"Shock!" His father rubbed one of his boy's cold hands, amazed
at how old he looked, just as if the youth had been sucked right out
of him. To someone who never met Ramsey, they would think he
was his father's father, an aging man of seventy-plus.

"Damn them foreigners, those quacks," Graham, his other son,
snapped. "I want some good old American doctor to look at him.
What do those ragheads know? They're still drinking the same
water they bathe in."

His father's lined face softened for a moment before he cast his
angry son a withering look. "He looks like something the cat drug
in. What have they done to my boy?"

"What can we do for him?" his mother, a tiny woman dressed in
simple garb, asked. "Surely when Aunt Tina gets here, she will do
something. She's a nurse."

"Maybe she will," her man replied, tucking his plaid shirt into his
waistband. "The way that woman run her mouth, you think she
knows every damn thing. But if she doesn't know what to do for
him, I'm calling in Dr. Polk. He'll set the boy straight in no time."

The ring of the front doorbell interrupted all of the chatter. His wife and one of the boys went to the door and the sound of welcome filled the house, the high-pitched, irritating voice of Aunt Tina soaring above the others. When his father heard the squeal of a child's tones, he frowned and walked toward the kitchen, shaking his head.

"Lawd, I prayed she wouldn't bring that little devil with her, that little Shirley," he said, his fists balled up. "That girl is nothing but trouble. She will drive us all crazy with her foolishness."

Aunt Tina, still dressed in her nurse whites, moved through the room like an army general, a sense of purpose and mission etched firmly on her face. She held a small leather bag. Everyone but the afflicted soul's father went to the living room where they sat quietly, awaiting her verdict on Ramsey's condition.

Once in the room, his father stood back against the wall, silent and solemn. Aunt Tina walked over to the still body stretched out on the bed, took up his hand and felt for his pulse. Yes, it was there but slow and erratic. She touched his cool face, felt under his neck, and then pushed his eyelids back. His eyes were not visible, only the whites. From her bag, she pulled out a stethoscope, placed it to his bony chest, and listened for any sign of strength in his heartbeat.

"Well, what's the story?" Ramsey's father asked. "Is he alive?"

"Barely," the nurse answered, looking at the man with a concerned face. "I've never seen anything like it. What did they say is wrong with him?"

His father screwed up his face. "They say they don't really know."

"I've never seen anything like it." She repeated it like a mantra.

While she pulled the covers back over Ramsey, his father opened the window, sniffing as if he smelled something foul in the room, and motioned for them to leave. They shuffled from the room, whispering to themselves. After they were gone for several minutes, a small dark girl, neatly dressed in a brightly colored dress with her thick black hair twisted in two long braids, entered the room, and stood in a corner, watching Cutie, the family's cur pee into one of her uncle's brogans. She giggled.

"How can you lay there so stiff?" she asked the body.

There was no reply from the almost corpse there before her. The man seemed dead.

"Why don't you say something? Are you 'sleep?" She frowned at
the silence. With a tiny hand, she removed a safety pin from the
hem of her dress and eased close to the man. Her fingers slowly
moved one of the man's lifeless hands from his side. She giggled
again mischievously, watching his zombie face. Carefully, she poked
the hand with the pin, once, then twice. She put her hand on his
cheek, then started jabbing the sharp metal again into the flesh of
his hand, drawing blood. Still, the body didn't jump or twitch.

That scared her and she ran from the room, screaming as loud as
she could.

I was there in a prison of flesh, trapped in a tomb of lifeless skin,
able to hear and think. But unable to move or respond. From my
helpless state, I could hear them discuss me as if I was not even
there, talking about my future and their inability to financially
guarantee my comfort. Get rid of him. Put him in a home somewhere or a hospice. Get him out of our sight. When the life support
equipment was delivered, my entire existence became a death-
watch, a vigil, a waiting for the end.

Inside my premature burial, I was awake, alive, and more alert
than ever. I replayed my life, going through the flurry of text and
images seeking answers. Trying to understand how I'd gotten to this
point, where I'd gone so wrong for God to turn His back on me.
Now I was in the clutches of Evil, susceptible to its every whim.

When I was small, I never liked my name. Ramsey. I was named
after a friend of my father, who was one of his coworkers at the steel
mill, a guy who fell one day into a vat of burning liquid metal. His
family buried him, what was left of him, in a bronze coffin. The
spirit of the man haunted me, and often I felt his presence around
me as I was growing up. Things would often go missing from my
dresser, especially my toys or money. Sometimes I would awaken
from a night's sleep with a bloodied nose, welts on my arms, or
bruises on my face.

One morning, I got up and found my school clothes folded over
a chair near my bed and a strange smell coated everything in the

room. The odor of burned tar or maybe seared flesh. I was nine. I was trembling. I was afraid.

"I ain't afraid of you," I shouted at the ceiling. "You can't scare me."

My yelling brought my parents running to my bedroom, wondering what was wrong. I was still quivering from the experience, defiant but deeply frightened. Tears didn't come to my eyes until my mother took me in her small arms and held me against her chest. She held me there while the trembling peaked in my bones and faded.

Once I had settled down, they left the room after assuring me I was safe. I folded my puny arms and stood my ground, daring the ghost or whatever it was to come out. As I put on my pants, getting ready for school, a series of red letters appeared on the cracked mirror over my dresser, one by one. My eyes were fixed on them while they emerged in a blood-smeared sentence on the glass: *You will pay for what your daddy did to me.*

I had no idea what this spirit was talking about then. Only later would I learn that my father had been seeing Ramsey's wife behind his back, had been sleeping with her for more than four years, until she got pregnant. She went to a quack doctor and got rid of the child but it ruined her. When she could not get pregnant for her husband, he took her to another doctor, a white man who told her that she was scarred throughout her birth canal and would never give birth. The result of a botched abortion. Ramsey beat the truth out of her, hammered her with his fists until she told him the truth. Two days after that, he fell into the vat and fried to death. Nobody could explain what happened there.

You will pay for what your daddy did to me. I never thought much of what happened that day until much later in my life. It all came back to me on that horrible day in my marriage, that afternoon that changed all my tomorrows and put me on the path to rescue my soul.

Much of my teen years went past in a blur and my twenties faded swiftly into a distant echo but I grew tired of being alone and married a secretary at my job. I worked as a reporter, a position that provided me with much frustration. My marriage was nothing special, and we had few arguments and little obstacles to what I thought would be a satisfying life-long union of souls. Aleta was a wonderful woman. Whatever problems she had, she kept to herself; whatever doubts she possessed about us were never spoken.

On the night of our daughter's birth, I remember sitting at a traffic light, gripping the steering wheel hard with both hands. I fought bravely to hold back the flood of tears that I knew were inevitable. The thought of not being there for my child's entry into this world was something that tore at my heart. *I must be there. I must be at the side of my wife when it happens.*

A patrol car with two white officers inside pulled up and slowed to let them get a good look at me hunched over in the driver's seat. No doubt they thought I was up to no good. The officer closest to me motioned for me to roll down the window and I did as I was told.

"Do you need any assistance?" the officer asked with a hint of fake politeness.

"No, thank you." I offered a Hollywood smile that let the white men understand that I was harmless, just another poor civilian trying to get to be with his child-bearing wife.

The officer stared at me strangely, then whispered something to his partner, and the car drove on alongside mine in a benign creep. I could tell they were still watching me. Waiting for me to do something out of the ordinary so they could roust me. But I gave them no further cause for suspicion. Soon, the patrol car disappeared around the corner, going west, continuing its search for some wayward evildoer.

In the delivery room at St. Christopher's Hospital, I held my bluish baby daughter, Alison, in my arms and wept with joy with the full knowledge of the miracle I'd just witnessed. My wife lay weak and relieved on the bed, smiling at us. I wondered if she had any idea of the wondrous act she'd accomplished.

"Darling, see what we've done, what a marvelous thing we've done," she said, when I leaned over to kiss her. "This represents the two of us, our love. You are a part of this as much as I am."

Her words filled my heart with a glow and warmth that I'd never known. Think of fathers who never share this miracle with their women or never allow themselves to be a part of such a blessing. Both of us knew our lives would never be the same. To watch our child grow through each and every stage of maturation to young adulthood. At that moment that I became a father, I truly became a man, able to impact on the life of my child in a way my own father had never done with me. Most men resist fatherhood, I thought, because it forces them to confront their own lives. But I embraced it in the same way, with the same vigor and commitment, that I'd brought to the demands of marriage.

The happiness I felt on that blessed night didn't last. My marriage dissolved in seven years like a tablet in a glass of water, slowly, steadily, without any way to halt the process. Before I knew it, we were separated, torn apart by pettiness, and Aleta was dating another guy in no time even though I wanted to work things out. I still believed in love then.

Life is full of pivotal moments. The day that everything changed forever started out like any other day. I drove to Aleta's house to drop some off some money for the support of my daughter. It was drizzling. There was a strange car in the driveway, but I thought nothing of it. My wife hated to be alone. The house was always full of people, most of them women, folks from her job.

There was a light knock on the window on the passenger's side. It was Alison, dressed cutely in a shiny yellow slicker, carrying an umbrella with a large picture of Donald Duck and his unruly nephews on it. She grinned at me as if I meant the world to her, like her day suddenly contained the bright promise of happiness.

I reached over and let her into the car. She stepped inside, sat on the seat close to me. The smile was still on her drenched brown face. I was startled, as I always was, when she leaned over and planted a moist kiss on my cheek. In so many ways, she was the real reason why I stayed in the marriage, the unconditional love and trust she bestowed upon me, expecting so little in return.

"Have you been crying, Daddy?" The word *Daddy* was like a warm breath in my ears.

"No. My eyes are just watering a bit. I think I'm coming down with something." I hated lying to her.

"I'll tell Mommy, and she'll fix you right up with some hot tea and lemon," she said in that little girl voice of hers. "Grandma Welles always says if you take something when you feel you're getting a cold, you won't get real sick."

Grandma Welles, the matriarch of the clan, was Aleta's mother. A real hellion. Eighty-six years old. She smoked Camels, had her sip of brandy every night, cursed like a sailor and drove herself to the market every Friday. She was something else.

"Daddy, are you going to give me a birthday party this year?" my daughter asked, shaking the rain from her umbrella.

"Don't do that in the car, honey. About the party, I don't know if I can. I might have to work. Tell you what. Let's see what we can do. We got two weeks before it gets here. OK?"

A dark cloud crossed her formerly cheerful face. She frowned sadly and nodded.

"Is your mother home?"

"Yes, but she's got company."

Who?" I didn't want to ask but felt I had to.

"Dennis. He said he dropped by to see me. He brought me a gift because I got a good report card. You're not mad, are you?"

"No. Why should I be?" I was pissed. I knew about him. He didn't have a job and mooched off Aleta, but she'd hinted that there was more to their relationship. I figured that he was good in bed. Otherwise she wouldn't put up with his mess.

"We better go in or they'll be worried," my little girl said.

I nodded reluctantly, wondering what kind of trouble awaited me inside. Sullenly, I opened the door and stepped out into the rain, then scurried around to her door. She smiled up at me and handed over her cartoon character umbrella, and we trotted across the wide blue-grass lawn to the front door. For a moment I weighed the idea of a surprise entry, using my key, but I decided against it. I rang the bell five times before Aleta appeared. She was dressed in the golden kimono I'd brought back from a Tokyo trip two years before. It was obvious she was naked underneath it. She was more beautiful than ever, short and stacked was how my father had once described her.

"Hello, stranger," she slurred. I could tell she had been drinking by the acrid smell of her breath. Stale tobacco and booze. She hugged me tenderly and pulled me toward the living room.

I followed her there, where I knew her latest beau would be waiting, no doubt in a similar state of drunkenness. Dennis was sprawled across the sofa with a drink in one hand and his legs resting on the coffee table. Bald and muscular, he was dressed, as usual, in one of his sharply tailored Armani suits. A gray one. His tie was missing. Knowing that his balance had been neutralized by drink, he made no attempt to stand when I entered the room.

"Well, if it isn't Clark Kent," Dennis wisecracked. "How's it hanging, Ramsey?"

"It was hanging alright until I came here and saw you two lushes," I replied curtly.

Dennis sipped from his glass and laughed. "Alison, tell your father all of the wonderful things we've been doing together. Remember how you said it was like being in a family again? Remember? She treats me just like you, Ramsey. Like a real daddy."

Slightly irked at his betrayal, Alison watched me cautiously from across the room. Pity resided in her look. She knew what Dennis was doing and my response was already predictable. I was not one to be provoked lightly. She also saw her mother's friend was drinking and his behavior was predictable as well. I knew she was loyal to me in her heart.

"Yeah, we've had a good time," she said softly.

I had suffered through a really bad day. I didn't need his crap. "No, listen, Dennis, you're not her father. I don't like you screwing with her head. She has one natural father and that's me. I pay the mortgage here. There's nothing in this house that is yours except the cheap furniture."

Dennis started laughing, taking another drink. "It might be your house but everything else here belongs to me. Your child, your woman. You just get temporary use of the child now and then. She's on loan, so to speak."

I walked toward the sofa, ready to beat his ass, and Aleta moved in front of me. "Don't, Ramsey. Don't."

"Another remark like that and you're out of here. I fucking mean it. I won't have you filling my daughter's head with your poison." I stepped closer to the reclining figure but my wife seized my arm. Although we had been separated for years, I still considered her my wife. We had never divorced, and I still had hope that she would come to her senses one day.

Dennis' head lifted slightly, his chin jutting upward. He winked in my direction and held his glass toward me. "I'm sorry, but could you get me a refill? I'm still thirsty."

I ignored him but Aleta turned and walked over to take the glass. When she moved past me, I thought I saw something in her face that I couldn't quite place. Guilt. Remorse. Lust. Regret. I couldn't decipher the expression. Whatever it was, it worried me.

"Why don't you leave, man, and let me have a peaceful time with Aleta and my daughter?" I asked him. "I don't want any trouble."

As soon as she left the room, Dennis staggered to his feet, wobbling back and forth like a man caught in an invisible tug-of-war. "Sure, I'll go. I got what I came for. I'm trying to teach your ex some magic tricks to do with her mouth."

I wanted to kill him. "Get out!"

"You know why she really left you? She told me she needed a real man. Somebody to satisfy her needs. Not some nice guy with a worm between his legs. Some wimp!"

My hands went for his throat. I heard Aleta enter the room. "Stop!" She shouted it like she was more concerned for him, this bastard, than me. Then she turned to our daughter and told her to go to her room. She didn't need to hear any of this.

Dennis was all smiles again. "Ramsey, will you be a sweetheart and get my raincoat out of the bedroom? Please, pretty please."

Aleta pushed him from behind, her eyes narrow and hard. "Stop it, Dennis!"

"No, I'll get his damn coat, anything to get the fool out of here." I glared at him and started for the bedroom. On my way out of the living room, I tussled Aleta's hair, ignoring the look of deep worry in her eyes. I didn't want to go to the bedroom but I went anyway. Their voices could be heard, low and conspiratorial, behind me. What the hell were they talking about?

In the bedroom, Dennis' raincoat was draped across a chair facing the window to the backyard and a red tie was neatly folded on the dresser near a collection of Aleta's cosmetics. Instinctively, I stood before the bed—the bed we once slept in together—and surveyed the chaotic swirl of sheets and pillows. I knew what it meant. I sighed for a second and brought a pillow to my face, inhaling its fragrance. It smelled like sex and strictly male. There was a hint of another scent, something sprayed, something to mask the musky smell of her lover.

Damn her! In my mind, I saw Dennis on his back and Aleta lowering herself down on his erection, her mouth open in full excitement. The next slide was of her on all fours with her ass exposed to him as he entered her from behind, doggy-style. Another showed her clutching his hard manhood and bringing it to her lips, her moist tongue teasing its swollen mushroom head. And the final image captured the two of them locked at the pelvis, Dennis' rough hands holding her shapely legs apart in a V while he thrust violently into her.

Suddenly stricken with a powerful wave of nausea, I sat on the edge of the bed where they had made love not long before my arrival. I covered my burning face with my hands but there were no tears this time. After my composure returned, I stood and walked to where the raincoat was on the chair and swooped it up in a single motion. I smiled wickedly. On my way out of the room, I stopped and went back for the red tie, folding it into a ball and shoving it into my pants pocket.

During my walk to the living room, I could hear them still arguing in whispers. Who knew how many times this shit had gone on during our marriage. There was no way we could get back together. What a fool I had been to think otherwise.

I stormed into the room, tossed the coat on the sofa, and when he reached for it, I grabbed Dennis by the arm and spun him around. Aleta shrieked, thinking the worst was about to happen. It was.

"Get the hell out here before I kick your goddamn ass!" I shouted it at him, moving closer. Within range for a punch.

He gathered his coat and started for the door but stopped. "Niggers like you always finish last. Bitches can spot a chump like you coming a mile off. Hey, I'm going. I got what I came for."

I was seething. "Get out, bastard!"

I took a menacing step toward him, and he reached into one of the coat pockets and his hand came out, holding a gun. Before he could lift it to shoot, I dived on him and we wrestled on the floor, both of us punching the other. Then a single shot sounded, its echo reverberating through the room. I saw Aleta fall to the floor. We still struggled for the gun and it barked three more times as I smashed a fist to his face. Over he went. I struggled to my feet, holding my side. I looked down and there was blood on my hand. In a corner of the room, Aleta was laying facedown, and I nudged him with my foot, but he didn't move. I staggered toward the door, running from the house, with the door slamming behind me.

I didn't know how I drove back to the apartment. But I did. My head was spinning. I bled for a time, the red flow soaking my shirt despite the pressure of my hand.

It took all of my concentration to keep the car on the road. Then it struck me, the curse of my namesake: *You will pay for what your father did to me.* As soon as I entered my apartment, I blacked out, my head striking the wood floor with a solid thud.

Frightened that I had killed two people, I left that night bound for New York and the anonymity of the big city, skyscrapers and large crowds. I'd lose myself there, blending in with the throngs of people. Nobody would find me, nobody.

It was 1958. Eisenhower, the civil rights troubles, the Cold War, the possibility of an A-bomb blast, Elvis, Barbie dolls, hula hoops, and the killings of eleven innocent people by madman Charles Starkweather and his fifteen-year-old sweetie. I thought of my mother's warning that it was the last days and the world was coming to a fiery end. But I was starting anew. Something in me would not let me forget what I had done. A murderer. Two people. What had made me kill? Nothing in my childhood pointed to me becoming a taker of human life. They say violence is learned behavior but where had I picked up the knack of robbing anyone of their life? If someone struck me, it had never been my way to hit back. I was passive. I would try to talk my way out of it. Even when mad. Something was wrong with me, this much I knew.

Days went by before I went out into the night streets from my little studio walk-up apartment down in Greenwich Village, stepping around the kids of my Polish neighbors playing catch, smiling at the two Puerto Rican chicks on the stairs, and carrying paint cans up for the artist on the floor above me. The cat looked like a young James Dean, the rebel actor who died in a car smashup. He was always dressed in black.

"Daddy-O, you need some new threads," the artist said. "That jive you wearing ain't hip. You look like some hayseed. Where you from, anyway?"

I didn't volunteer any information. "The Midwest."

"Cool, baby," he said, smiling. "Why don't you hang out with me tonight? Show you the sights, hip you to the scene."

Carson was my entry into the New York beatnik scene. After setting me up in a black turtleneck, black levis, and beret, he took me out into the night. Our first stop was a small joint where two white boys beat on bongos while a thin chick in all black read nonsense poetry, something about loving the bomb. Every riff sounded suburban or stiff but the crowd snapped their fingers in approval.

"Here baby, blow your top with this," the artist, who refused to tell me his name, said, handing me a stick of reefer. "This tea will get you straight. Try it, farmer. Don't be square."

I puffed on the dope, careful to hold it in like a veteran pothead, and felt the harsh smoke take me away. Carson showed me how to take the smoke in deeper. It was uncool for me to turn him down so I did two sticks and immediately felt ill.

My face must have been green because Carson and his three sidekicks leaned over for a closer look, cackling like a bunch of rain-drenched hens. Finally, the artist poked me with his finger and asked if I was cranked up or high.

"Yeah, I guess," I mumbled, feeling an urge for two burgers and a large beer. "My head is spinning and the drumming is driving me nuts."

"Solid, Jack," Carson said. "We should go and check out the Hot Dish. By the way, do you dig bebop?"

"Be-what?" That brought a laugh from the gang.

"You know, Bird, Diz, Miles, Bud, Monk, and the crew. Hard jazz." Carson was quite intense when he spoke about music. His friends all nodded and smiled as if they were telling me a secret. Some sacred jive.

On the way to the Hot Dish, the beatniks filled me in on the merits of bebop and jazz that baffled the squares, how it could only be made by Negroes because they had soul and had suffered. I eventually fell in love with the place. According to the beats, every-thing was possible at the Hot Dish, that old-fashioned blue-collar bar at Bleeker and MacDougal, stout drinks delivered to well-worn wooden booths where the owner paid little attention to the hap-penings. Many nights I laid prone on the black-and-white tiles, pole-axed by alcohol, hipster lies, or wicked weed while Carson pointed out the stars of the bohemian world.

"Look there's that painter Jackson Pollack talking with Larry Rivers, Frank O'Hara the poet over in the corner with Judith and Julian—the Becks of the Living Theatre, Kenneth Koch, Seymour Krim, and Roy Bremser," Carson exclaimed. "Everybody's here tonight!"

"Where are the colored folks?" I asked, still dreamy from the reefer's buzz.

Carson laughed and led me over to a stout, muscular white man seated with two other hip-looking types, one chubby wearing glasses and a beard and the other thin, pale, and gaunt in a business suit. He made the introductions, going left to right, and I shook each man's hand. Allen Ginsberg the poet, William Burroughs the writer, and Jack Kerouac the writer. I recognized Kerouac from the cover of his book, *On The Road*.

"Hey, another spade. We need more spade writers," Kerouac joked. "Do you write, Jackie Robinson?"

"My name is Ramsey," I replied. "Yes, I'm a writer but not novels. Other stuff."

Kerouac nodded and smiled, then continued his chat with the other two men, completely ignoring me. When I turned around, I discovered Carson had gone, leaving me there to fend for myself. Finally, Kerouac and Ginsberg wandered away and only Burroughs remained, sitting stiffly in the booth.

"What do you know about me, Mr. Robinson?" Burroughs asked me, staring at his drink. "Did you know I was an heir to the Burroughs Adding Machine Company? Worth millions. Some call me Bill Lee. Want to hear a story?"

"My name is Ramsey," I said again. "Tell your story if you want."

"Oh, look, there's Leroi Jones. Do you know him?" Burroughs asked, downing two pills with a sip of booze. "You should know him. He's one of your tribe. Clever fellow. Anyway, my story . . . Joan, she was my wife, and I were on a drinking spree so she started egging me on with insults about how I couldn't shoot. She knew I was a good shot but she liked causing problems. I thought I would fix her so I suggested we do the William Tell act. In case you don't know, Bill Tell was the man who shot an apple off a bloke's head with an arrow, I believe. So Joan placed a water tumbler on her head and I aimed for it with my gun. I fired once. Joan didn't move at first and I thought I had missed until I saw the damn glass spinning on the floor, intact. Then I saw Joan had a neat little hole in her forehead. I killed her."

"Damn." I watched his gray face hardened and tears well in his eyes.

"I killed . . . killed her," Burroughs mumbled and gulped down another drink.

"Damn." I saw the guilt and regret on his face, understanding how the two emotions could twist and torment a soul. It was painful to watch.

A white woman, blonde with her breasts exploding out of her striped blouse, walked past, stopped and kissed Burroughs on the mouth. He laughed and stuck out his tongue. There was a red pill on the tip of it. He chuckled, winked, and swallowed it.

I experienced the sensation of being suffocated. Maybe it was the booze or the pot, but I found myself confessing to him like a parish priest in the booth. "I . . . I . . . I killed two people . . . shot

them. One was my wife and the other was . . . was . . . her lover.
Killed them dead."

At first, his face didn't register the confession but slowly I saw his
eyes widen with terror, finally staring at my hands. I didn't understand it. The terror. I looked down at my hands, held them palm up
and saw the blood on them. He grasped my wrist and pulled it to
him, wiping one hand with a tissue, but the blood kept coming.
However, there were no wounds. I bit my other hand, trying to stifle
a scream, and ran from the place.

In less than a month, I left New York and America, taking a job as
a crewman on a trawler heading for Africa. My first destination was
Egypt, Morocco, or the Sudan. That was not where I wound up. I
stood on the deck of a small riverboat going down the murky
Cubango River in Angola, my hands wrapped around my middle,
fighting a stomach virus. The dark African workers seemed to handle the heat, the dank odor of the water, and the bad food just fine.
They laughed when they saw my discomfort, teasing the American
who couldn't seem to handle the sun or the tropical vermin.

"Mr. Ram-see, do you know what they call this part of the world?"
one of the Africans, his face covered with tribal markings, asked. "It
is called the *fim do mundo*, the end of the world. The Portuguese
call it that."

I watched the sea of little green frogs that swarmed over the
deck, hopping all over one another, getting underfoot. The others
paid them no mind. However, their presence bothered me, gave me
the creeps, causing me to watch two trucks driving along the oppo-
site bank. The idea of going to Luanda, Angola's modern capital,
kept gnawing at my brain, a big city as African cities go, and plenty
of diversions. News of unrest, killing, and revolt were on every front
page in the country and scores of Portuguese colonists were leaving
on the daily flights back to the Continent.

"God, I feel so hot, drenched," I moaned, gripping the rail near
us. My legs felt unsure and weak.

The African patted me on the back and grinned. He smelled of
earth, overcooked rice, berries, and sweat. "I know a doctor who can

treat you for the fever when we get to Caiundo. He is a Kuvale herdsman who treats many people there. He is good. He can make you well."

I agreed to see the Kuvale doctor upon arriving in the town. However, I passed out and was carried below deck, where I remained for the rest of the journey. At Caiundo, the African placed me in a car and took me to a house on the outskirts of town. I barely made it. Hours later, the Kuvale doctor came, bringing a small paper bag filled with herbs, roots, and other tribal medicine. I was stretched out on a cot, delirious and feverish, not knowing in which world I now lived. A hazy netherworld.

"Why are you here, American?" the doctor asked, opening up his bag.

"I'm searching for peace, inner peace," I replied, wiping a river of moisture from my forehead. "My soul is restless, pained, and in need of something to soothe it."

The doctor, a short man with deep-set eyes, took something out of the bag, a tiny lump wrapped in large green leaves. "Where may I wash this?"

Timidly, the African pointed to the back room where the sink was located. Upon the departure of the doctor, he explained that although the man was of the Kuvales, he had been raised in Central Africa, sent there by his family who believed he was possessed by a non-human spirit. The spirit had control of his body, something that, without proper ritual treatment, would be passed from generation to generation, from father to son. He had apprenticed with a respected healer in his new village, *a midzumu*, and learned many magical skills. He knew the wisdom of the serpents, a lost way of knowing.

"American, you have become *ngozi*, a stranger from your own kind," the doctor said, delicately removing a small dried bird from the leaves. "This can mean many bad things for you. What has happened is that a spirit of a person who has been killed has risen from the grave and is now seeking revenge on you and your bloodline. Its power cannot be broken until you admit the crime and do something to pay for the wrong that you have done."

"What crime have I done?" I asked, playing dumb.

"Only you know what you have done, but it is a debt that must be paid in full," the doctor said, crushing the bird's carcass into a fine white powder in a bowl. "You must do this or you will suffer the same fate as these whites who have come here to spread their evil and disease like poison among my people. There is no escaping what you have done."

"What if I have been wrongly accused?" I was determined to keep the truth from them. However, I felt that they saw through me, without my saying a word or admitting anything. The truth was the fourth person in the room, obvious and larger than life.

You will pay for what your father did. Those prophetic words were never far away from my mind. The curse of the father passed to the son. And then my own evil deeds. Two souls erased.

The African held a single finger to his lips, blinking. "Listen to him, American."

"Yes, you lie to us but you have already admitted this deed once," the doctor said, stirring the pulverized bones into a glass of red water. "Remember our ancestors speak directly through us. They seize our bodies and free the truth. Even if we fight them, they will use our mouth to speak truth. We call this *svikro inobatwa nemidzimu*. This has already happened to you and will again. Now, drink this, American."

I raised the glass to my lips and eased the crimson fluid down my throat. Before I could set the glass down, my stomach seized up and my entire body seemed to catch afire, almost glowing. A bitter taste covered my tongue. The African wiped my face with a cloth and guided me into a chair, for fear that I would fall on the floor. They talked in English, something I should have understood, but the words, the letters appeared to leave their mouths and hang in slow motion in the humid air. As I stared at the two of them, their bodies dissolved into an outline of iridescent lines, every bone, every artery illuminated with a neon clarity.

"How do you feel, American?" the doctor asked, watching my face intently.

"Weird, like I'm plugged into a light socket," I answered, trying to still my nervous hands and feet. "It's like an electric current is going through me. Like I'm sitting in a tub of water and somebody is throwing a live radio into it. Really weird."

"Don't worry. It will pass soon." The doctor glanced at the African, and they nodded at the same time.

Everything ached on me. My head went back as if I was being lifted toward the ceiling. I could feel nothing below my waist, and that scared me. I closed my eyes, clenching my teeth, while surges of energy pulsed through me, bringing all sensation back at once throughout every cell of my body. I screamed and pitched forward on the floor, writhing and bucking violently. Soon I vanished under a big dark wave.

When I awoke two days later, the doctor was gone and the African was seated near the bed, smoking a cigarette. He got to his feet and went to the back room for a glass of water. My fever was gone as well. I felt like a young kid, full of energy, and the most re-markable thing was how clear my mind was. I could focus it like never before.

"We were worried about you, American," he said, placing the glass to my mouth. "You looked like you were dead for a while there. Your heart stopped. Your skin turned blue and the doctor thought you had passed over."

"Will I be alright?"

"Yes and no. He says you will be good for now but you must leave here or you will die. The spirit that follows you is powerful and clever. This is its ancestral home. You cannot beat it here. You must leave as soon as possible."

I finished the water, washing the last bitterness from my mouth. "When can I leave?"

"Tomorrow," the African answered. "I will set up your passage on a train leaving Huambo. You must rest up for the man will demand to see you so he can decide if he will let you on the train. Mr. da Silva is very particular. I think he will like you. You are an American and that will impress him."

That day, I did nothing. With the arrival of night, I quickly washed and dressed for my rendezvous with the man. The African drove me to a ramshackle one-story building on the far side of town, a place surrounded by late-model cars, bored chauffeurs, and armed bodyguards. No doubt there were plenty of important officials and businessmen inside. We walked to the side door, got searched, and waved past into a dark hallway.

"Mr. da Silva is upstairs, go on up," the guard carrying a rifle at the door said. "He's expecting you."

The second floor was abuzz with cheering, clapping, and wolf whistles. I walked ahead of the African, trying to see what was causing the ruckus. Most of the doors were closed, save one. In the room, I peeped inside and saw a young African woman, nude and busty, wiggling on a raised platform before a crowd of white men in suits. They tossed money, mostly coins, at her as she gyrated before them like she was having sex. Her fingers were inside herself, moving sensuously, adding to the effect. One white man jumped up and began slashing at her with his belt, across her bare buttocks, thighs, and legs. Some of the other men cheered him, pounding the tables to the beat of the leather slapping loudly against her naked dark flesh, producing a network of criss-crossed welts and blood.

I watched the scene with a mix of fascination and disgust. As the woman tumbled to the floor under the barrage of blows, she crawled between their legs, seeking refuge, baring her teeth, emitting a loud, screeching sound. The torture continued. Whenever she tried to get to her feet, someone would kick her back down. Groups of white men on her right spat on her. She groaned in pain with each well-placed kick. After their fury was spent, she rose to her feet, her face clotted with blood, and applause filled the room, and a shower of coins landed at her feet.

Other young African girls moved about the room, sitting on their customers' laps, kissing and stroking them. They reveled in their sultry roles. Like animals, like sexual playthings. If I had a gun, I would have shot the whole lot of them. The white patrons made the women submit to their wills, performing assorted acts lewdly on the colonists and each other for more coins. Nothing was taboo. Every despicable act was done. It was a disgusting sight.

The African grabbed my arm, growling. "Come on. You don't need to see that. White bastards! They will pay one day. Their hours are numbered here. We will drive them out."

"Why do these women let these white men humiliate them like this?" I asked, my rage barely controlled. "Why do they do this? And why don't you black men put a stop to it?"

"One day, we will, rest assured," the African said, his eyes full of hate. "But these women chose this life. They come to be with these whites because they want things. They want his favor, money, and clothes. They have lost their souls. One day, they will know other choices, when the whites are gone."

Reluctantly, I followed him down the hall to the man's office. He was Portuguese, scruffy, very impatient with the darker people, so he got us in and out in no time. I didn't like the way he talked to the African. And he never acknowledged my presence at all. It was like I was invisible. The only reason he took care of my problem was that he owed the African some favors, for past deeds of kindness. Something involving the black man rescuing his only son from a fire years ago. The African said he did the entire business with the train because he felt sorry for me, carrying such a spiritual debt, hounded by such a mighty curse. Anyway, we were glad to get away from there.

By three the next day, I was on a train headed east, possibly for the Orient or India. I thought about what the doctor told me, about the dark spirit dogging my trail, about the need to confess and pay the debt for the souls I'd violated. I felt the curse closing in on me. It was just a matter of time before my bill would come due.

Leaving Africa was not difficult, for everywhere I went in that part of the world, I saw the tyranny of colonialism, greed, deception, and evil. It sickened me. Eventually I made my way east to Asia, lured by the prospect of finding my elusive inner peace, working on a number of Indian ships in ports along the coast, following the seasonal tides down to Burma, Malaya, Singapore, Thailand, and on to Cambodia. The journey took up seven years of my life, years that found me no closer to the answers and solace I so desperately sought.

On the ships, the crew entertained me with talk of the large estates where the European planters grew rich from the growing of rubber and sugar, the soaring palm oil market, the beauty of the women of Bali, but nothing intrigued me as much as their detailed descriptions of the golden spires and temples of Bangkok with its great Temple of the Fig Tree and magnificent Reclining Buddha. They also spoke of the splendor of the twelfth century temple of the Anghor Wat in Cambodia. I knew that was my stop, to visit the temples, to sit among the saffron-robed Buddhist monks, to seek their wisdom. I still sought to flee the wrath of the curse that haunted me. *You will pay for what your father did to me.*

Within days, I found myself with the monks high in the hills beyond Bangkok. Behind me, the huge statue of a gleaming fourteenth century Buddha, cast in gold, sat with one hand outstretched to cast off fear. Humbled, I moved among the pilgrims making offerings with flowers and food to God, meditating on the many teachings of The Enlightened One. I kept thinking of something an old man had once told me in Rome: *There are many routes to God and salvation. Only you can choose which one suits your soul.*

I listened as an elder monk, his body silhouetted against the enormous figure of the Buddha, explained how Siddhartha, the aristocrat, who at twenty-nine years of age, began his quest for enlightenment. According to the monk, the young man embraced truth after a long search while meditating in the shade of a *bodhi* wild fig tree and became the Buddha. Maybe I could experience a rebirth, a renewal. Maybe I could find some answers there, maybe I could be freed of this thing that slowly consumed my soul.

The monk spoke of following the Noble Eightfold Path, the rules of morality, of foregoing sexual pleasure, abstaining from alcohol, and keeping a vow not to steal, lie, or kill. *Thou shalt not kill.* After the others left, I remained, following behind the old man as he walked down a rocky road toward a nearby village.

"What is it you seek, young man?" the monk asked in stiff English, turning to me with an uncommon swiftness. I wondered how he knew I was American. Being dark, I could have been from Cuba, Nigeria, Sudan, anywhere. It was uncanny.

The idea of sleeping on a straw mat, begging, reciting endless prayers in Pali, the language of Buddhism, and eating two meager meals of rice and vegetables didn't appeal to me. There was something else I needed from him. *Freedom from the guilt I carried with me. The redemption of my soul.* I sought to know the meaning of my deeds, the reason for my taking of two human lives. I wanted him to absolve me of my sins. Truth was what I desired most.

"I seek truth," I replied, walking slowly to keep pace with him. "I want to understand the why of some things I've done. Can you help me?"

The old monk stopped and tucked his robe deeper into the folds gathered about his waist. "The man who seeks truth will never find it. Truth is in what is about us. Truth is buried within ourselves. To know truth, one must know himself."

Another monk, a large, heavy-shouldered man, joined us, glancing at me, a black man walking with one of the valued elders of the brotherhood. His suspicions melted into a benevolent smile. A few Europeans and Americans climbed the steps of the temple behind us, snapping photos, and defiling the holy place with their curious mirth. It was as if they were out on a day of frolic at Disneyland, sampling the rides and attractions before closing time. No respect or reverence for anything there.

"I've killed, killed two people," I said quietly. "I cannot live with what I have done. The knowing of what I did never leaves my mind. I cannot rest. I know no peace."

The monks ceased their steps, their faces suddenly pained, and the old one took my hand. "We take a vow to kill no living thing, so what you have done is unspeakable to us," the elder said. "This violence, this thing that plagues you, you must confront it, know it totally, understand it completely before you can be free of its power. You would have never killed if you were not thinking of yourself. Only a selfish man kills. If one is selfless, there is no way he can raise his hand against another."

The big man, the silent monk, suddenly spoke up, his English not as good as his elder. "Man has always killed. Nothing is worse than the killing, and there is nothing that can remove its stain."

We stopped under a big gathering of trees, their small leaves offering very little protection from the sun and heat, and the lecture continued. I drank in every word, praying that something would lift this weight from my soul. The old monk sensed my desperation, my discomfort, and his next words offered me little solace as he recited some verses from the *Sutta Pitaka*, the earliest of the Buddhist scriptures, from something called *The Dhammapada*.

"This is like the Psalms from your Bible," he said, grasping one of my hands. "All that we are is the result of what we have thought. If a man speaks or acts with an evil thought, pain follows him as the wheel follows the foot of the ox that draws the carriage."

"Think on what he has said, my friend," the other monk added. "Oh, your nose is bleeding. Hold your head back."

My nose was indeed bleeding, dripping in a steady stream down my chin onto my shirt. I wiped at it with my sleeve. My head suddenly felt warm, and the earth danced under my feet. I leaned over, fighting off dizziness, and tears flowed from my eyes, quickly running down my cheeks as the blood kept flowing from my nose. The monks straightened me up, tilting my head back. It was then that I saw that my tears were red too.

Back at the hotel in Bangkok, I collapsed onto my bed, praying that the bleeding would stop. It did not. A doctor was called and he could not find the source of the bloodletting, concluding that it was some sort of exotic jungle illness picked up during my travels. The bleeding was followed by chills, body aches, and a high fever that threatened to burst my body into flames. I tried to escape. I walked to the streets, where I wandered for days, afraid to be alone, until I lost consciousness, my body becoming rigid and unable to respond to my commands. I could not move, I could not speak. I was a living corpse. It was that horrible condition that caused someone to notify the American Embassy and in two days, I was flown home after extreme measures were used to stem the bleeding. The information was taken from a letter from my mother found in my wallet.

You will pay for what your father did to me. The words never left my mind.

His family left the room, after hearing that there was nothing that could be done for him. None of the doctors knew what was wrong with him. It was a disease that was not included in their medical journals, a malady that ravaged his body but refused to kill him. Although he could open his eyes, there was no vision there; he could only sense the others in the room.

As the days went by, the family tired of caring for him and locked him away in a windowless room at the rear of the house. A nurse was hired to feed him. They often placed him in a wheelchair and pushed him into the center of the room. It gave the appearance that he was still more alive than dead, that he was yet a member of the clan.

One night, they forgot to take him from the wheelchair, leaving him to sit through the dark hours. He did not sleep. His eyes were open. The door opened and a man entered, dressed in a shroud. It did not seem possible, for the man wore his face. Although a feeling of terror ran through him, he could not scream or shout. Instead, he sat there staring at himself, the other one staring back at him with frightening, demonic eyes. He tried to will this other self away, to send it back to hell from whence it had come.

He tried to turn his head and this time his neck worked and his eyes fell upon a figure resting on the bed. That was him as well. In no time, he entered that self and floated above the others, looking down upon them, the man in the chair and the man at the door. When the horror became too great, he shut his eyes, blinking hard to remove the images from his mind, but those beings were replaced by a brilliant, red glow.

It engulfed the room, covering him and the chair. That glow was her, Aleta, his wife. Her presence seized him, jerking his body into the air, almost as high as his other self had been poised. He tried to rise, to run from the chair but could not. The glow cloaked him, gently embraced him, gentle as silk on bare skin, and he gave in to it, allowing it to penetrate him. Suddenly, he felt as if he was being squeezed between someone's thumb and forefinger, struggling for breath. His face burned, sizzling from the heat of her spirit, her closeness. This was not how he imagined his end would come.

"I want you to forgive me," he sobbed when the power of speech was restored to him. "I loved you. I never wanted to hurt you, only him."

Her disembodied voice came to him once more. "Your bullets

did not kill me but you left me there for him to finish what you started. He accused me of seeing you again. He was not dead when you left there. I told him it was not true. He called me a liar. He shot me, then turned the gun on himself. He completed the job that you started."

He cried, real tears this time. "Did Alison see any of this?"

"Yes, she will never be the same. You killed her just as you did me. Her mind is gone. She is locked away upstate."

"My family never mentioned that. Nobody said a word."

"Why would they? They never liked her or me anyway." The glow intensified, applying more pressure to his flesh and bones. Like a vise.

"I didn't know," he repeated over and over.

For a moment, the glow retreated and his dead wife with her ruined face and punctured body became visible to him. The damage caused by the bullets was quite apparent. His murdered wife sat before him, applying lipstick, turning toward where he sat bound by an invisible force in the chair. A ghastly gunshot wound could be seen on her neck. He shook his head, totally struck by what his rage and jealousy had wrought. The destruction of several lives in one impulsive act. The dim outline of his spectral form vanished back into the safe harbor of the ethereal glow and it flared into an angry brilliance that spoke of the vengeance to come.

"For what you have done, there is no forgiveness, no redemption, only payback," the glow said. "This is your truth. This is your salvation. Death would be too brief. You need more time to think about what you have done. Plenty of time. The grave will have to wait for you. There is more suffering for you to do. "

It started to pull at his limbs, stretching him beyond what was humanly comfortable, causing him to try again to cry out. Not a sound. He heard the voice say something about retrieving his soul, punishment for this sins, as he surrendered to her will. Was this his truth? Was this his final solace? He let go of his fear and permitted the glow to bend and twist his flesh. He'd always known she would come for him, sooner or later, but she would come. The glow dissolved into a collection of dust and molecules, spinning until it disappeared into nothingness. His silent screams continued, dying in his scorched throat.

In the morning, the nurse arrived and opened the door. Her screams brought the entire household to a room that none had visited in more than a year. He sat there in the wheelchair, his body akimbo, folded into itself. His eyes were still open, with a thick white film over the corneas as if something had seared away his sight. However, it was how he aged so, seemingly overnight, wrinkled with skin like aged parchment. To anyone who didn't know Ramsey, they would have guessed the young man to be in his late eighties, the victim of a series of major strokes. Intense insults to the brain. His family shrank from the room, fleeing to other parts of the house, vowing never to go back there again. That was not their son, their blood kin, their anything.

But Ramsey was still there in that devastated body. Alive but buried under the ravages of old age. Older than before, suspended two seconds from a death that would never come. He was trapped in a dream within a dream, barely clutching what little life remained in him. Now he didn't care much about anything. He no longer brooded over what he had done. This new world was real. He had accepted the final verdict, as the Kuvale doctor in Angola had once suggested, and paid mightily for his sins. Nothing more was needed. Nothing more was missing. All was finally right. Even as the nurse wiped the cereal from his trembling lips but forgot to change his diaper. Strangely, he felt happy, even elated.

One thing was sure. The words of the curse no longer haunted him: *You will pay for what your father did to me.* He finally knew truth, his own truth. Every action came with a price and sometimes that debt could be more than anyone should pay. Suddenly, he was without fear, in a type of blessed state. It no longer mattered what she would do to him. He welcomed it, opened his heart to her poisonous gift, and surrendered to her final, fatal caress.